"What is it?" Carol wondered. "Some kind of statue?"

"Don't know," Ron said. "But it wasn't there a moment ago."

"Wasn't there when we passed in the other direction."

"Whatever it is," Ron said with growing indignation, "I plan to sue the bastard who put it in the middle of the road. We could have been killed."

Suddenly, a hot wind swirled around them, gusting and buffeting their bodies like an invisible giant's hand pushing them closer to the object. Caught off-balance, they stumbled forward, reaching out to the stone surface to support themselves. While the wind continued to batter them, a blinding light erupted from the carved stone.

Carol tried to scream, but all the air had been forced from her lungs. With a gasp, she managed a single word. "Ron . . . !"

The intensity of the wind doubled. Carol's feet slipped out from under her, and she slid forward on the seat of her pants. Her arm flailed where Ron should be, but found nothing. She expected to slam into the stone wall. Instead, she spun into emptiness, beyond the blinding light into a vast silence within an utter darkness that swallowed her whole and snuffed out the light of her consciousness.

•

Angel™

City Of
Not Forgotten
Redemption
Close to the Ground
Shakedown
Hollywood Noir
Avatar
Soul Trade
Bruja
The Summoned
Haunted
Image
Stranger to the Sun
Vengeance
Endangered Species
The Casefiles, Volume 1—The Official Companion
The Longest Night, vol. 1
Impressions
Sanctuary
Fearless
Solitary Man
Nemesis
Monolith

Available from Simon Spotlight

The Essential Angel Posterbook

Available from Pocket Books

ANGEL™

monolith

John Passarella

An original novel based on the television series
created by Joss Whedon & David Greenwalt

New York   London   Toronto   Sydney

Historian's Note: This book takes place between the episodes entitled "Spin the Bottle" and "Apocalypse Nowish" in the fourth season of *Angel*.

This book is a work of fiction. Any references to historical events, real people, or real locales are used fictitiously. Other names, characters, places, and incidents are the product of the author's imagination, and any resemblance to actual events or locales or persons, living or dead, is entirely coincidental.

Simon Spotlight
An imprint of Simon & Schuster Children's Publishing Division
1230 Avenue of the Americas, New York, New York 10020

SIMON SPOTLIGHT and colophon are registered trademarks of Simon & Schuster.

Manufactured in the United States of America
First Edition 10 9 8 7 6 5 4 3 2 1
Library of Congress Control Number 2003114496
ISBN 0-689-87022-1

For Andrea, who took care of everyone and everything in our house so that I could lock myself in my office to finish this one.

ACKNOWLEDGMENTS

Thanks to my editor, Elizabeth Bracken. Thanks again to Lisa Clancy for bringing me into the fold, and to Tricia Boczkowski for inviting me back.

With regard to my towering pre-*Monolith* project, thanks to everyone who helped make the 1st Annual Matthew's Miles Walkathon a success. Please help us find a brain tumor cure. Visit www.matthewsmiles.org.

Thanks to Matthew, Luke, and Emma for keeping me grounded and focused on the important things.

My thanks and admiration to Greg Schauer, who continues to survive in the face of economic monoliths.

And finally, thanks once again to Joss Whedon and David Greenwalt for creating this wonderful show, and to the entire cast and crew for bringing *Angel* to life.

PROLOGUE

•

Art demands sacrifice. And with the help of the jewel-encrusted ceremonial dagger concealed in the roomy pocket of her bathrobe, Rebecca Wade was about to make her eleventh sacrifice in as many months.

He'd only been in the hotel shower a minute or two. The hiss of the spray sounded like static, a television station beyond tuning. Her hands trembled as she reached into the canvas carryall for the bottle of champagne.

Art demands sacrifice. She couldn't allow her yearlong mantra to fail her now. Nothing had changed yet, but soon everything would. The end would mark a new beginning for her. But first Steve had to go. *Yes,* she thought, *because art demands sacrifice.*

She wrapped a white hand towel around the top of the bottle to muffle the pop of the cork. Removing the sanitary paper caps from two tumblers, she filled only one with the sparkling liquid. The long neck of the bottle clinked against the rim of the glass.

"How long you plan on keeping me in suspense?"

Startled by Steve's raspy voice, Rebecca spilled a dollop of champagne across the narrow mahogany desk. She dabbed at it with the wet towel. "Not too long!" she called to the bathroom's open door.

"To be honest," he called above the rush of water, "I was surprised you had time to see me today, with the premiere and all . . ."

Three hours away from the red carpet premiere of *Zombie Island Princess* at Mann's Chinese Theatre, the twenty-seven-year-old actress was in danger of becoming a scream queen—or worse, a has-been. Plenty in the industry had already counted her out. From her debut, the Oscar-nominated supporting role in *Wisteria Way*, through a series of bad film choices leading to the current 140-minute pretentious schlock-fest about to be unleashed upon an unsuspecting public, Rebecca Wade's once-promising career had fallen from the stratosphere to near-obscurity in a dizzying five-year descent. In that time, she'd fired her first agent, been released by her second, and had little regard for her third. When she demanded perfection, the gossip rags portrayed her as being difficult. As her reputation for on-set tirades had grown, the roles she'd been offered had diminished, spiraling down from the inconsequential to the ludicrous. And it had all culminated in the title role of a film marketed via incoherent trailers and unimaginative black-and-white posters with the unfortunate shorthand title *ZIP.* She could already imagine the critics having a field day with that one.

That was the danger. Remain passive, and she would live down to the popular perception of her career arc. But Rebecca Wade had other plans. A year ago, she'd decided to be the proactive heroine in the script of her life. To turn back now would be unconscionable.

"Don't worry," she said. "I have my priorities in order."

In typical Hollywood fashion, the last sacrifice would be the most difficult. No more nameless, homeless strangers to dispatch without guilt or remorse. A small part of her continued to believe she had been merciful to end the suffering of those unfortunates. Of course, her offerings would have disagreed, but the quality of their lives had been so dreadful—they were riddled with disease and vermin—an objective eye would have admitted they were, in fact, better off dead. Their mortality rate was no doubt a crime against nature and the miracles of modern medicine they could never afford. At least she gave their deaths meaning. And really, who could find fault with that?

Steve McKay, unfortunately, was fit and healthy. Riddled with scars, maybe, but unequivocally and unrepentantly healthy. And thus she found it more difficult to rationalize his untimely exit at her hands. She took a deep breath and exhaled through her nose. *More difficult,* she thought, *is not the same as impossible.* "If you can't make the tough choices," she whispered to herself, "then *act* like someone who can."

After all, Steve had his faults. He was reckless and fearless, qualities that served him well as a Hollywood stuntman but also placed his life at risk on a regular basis. He was someone who braced himself for the possibility of death or dismemberment every day on the job. Therefore, she assumed, he must be at peace with the idea of his own mortality. More than most people, he would be aware of the inevitability of his own ending.

Lastly, wouldn't it be wrong for her to demand perfection from others before she was willing to make the ultimate commitment herself? Her art demanded no less. She reached into her carryall again and, this time, withdrew a small leather pouch containing a single precious object.

She unscrewed the black cap of a tiny glass vial containing a potent draft with a greenish hue, a viscous texture, and an exotically unpronounceable name. She liked to think of it as the essence of distilled commitment. Upending the vial, she drizzled its contents into the champagne-filled tumbler, then mixed the fizzy concoction with a plastic coffee stirrer until all traces of the green color had vanished.

"Ready or not," she said, "here I come."

A testament to Steve's penchant for scalding showers, clouds of steam billowed across the bathroom floor and rose to obscure the mirror. Rebecca almost felt as if she were stepping onto a gothic movie set. That image would prove helpful. After all, she had her part to play.

"Oh, I'm definitely ready," Steve said, grinning at her from around the shower curtain. His close-cropped blond hair was plastered to his scalp, and the diagonal scar on his cheek seemed more livid, pale against his heat-flushed face.

"I'm talking about the surprise," she said, nodding toward the glasses she held. "I have an announcement that requires a champagne toast."

Flashing an expectant smile, he said, "Let's hear it."

She was momentarily nonplussed. For someone who faced his own death on a daily basis, someone who had accepted the inevitability of his ultimate fade-out, Steve McKay seemed entirely too carefree. "The results are in," she said. "And it would appear, Mr. McKay, that I am carrying your child."

Steve's eyes went wide. "Wow," he said with a disbelieving shake of his drenched head. "Could've fooled me, young lady."

"I only just found out."

After a bark of laughter, he said, "I'll be damned!"

Quite possibly, she thought. *I'm a little fuzzy on that part of the ceremony.*

"Well, that news is definitely worthy of a toast," Steve said. He nodded toward the empty tumbler. "Looks like you've had yours already."

"I'm abstaining," Rebecca said as she handed him his filled glass. "You know what they say, 'A pregnant woman never drinks alone.'"

"Gimme," Steve said, snatching the empty glass from her hand before she could protest. He splashed a bit of his champagne into her empty glass before returning it to her. "C'mon, one sip won't hurt."

Rebecca stared at the liquid pooling in the bottom of her glass. She could almost imagine the toxic fumes wafting upward toward her flared nostrils. "Why—why take unnecessary chances?"

It probably wasn't the best argument when dealing with a stuntman, but Steve shrugged. "Suit yourself," he said. "But I choose to celebrate in style. Down the hatch!" He drank the contents of the glass in one long pull, then covered a belch.

Rebecca sighed with relief.

"Any rules against you joining me in here?" Steve asked as he handed her his empty tumbler.

With her back turned, she rinsed both glasses in the sink and said, "Give it—me—a minute."

"Fair enough," he said. "I'll even turn the heat down a notch."

He released the shower curtain and adjusted the scalding spray. Rebecca removed towels from the metal rack over the toilet tank and placed them on the counter, arranging things, then rearranging them, as the seconds ticked by.

She heard something thud against the wall behind the shower curtain. "Steve?"

"Better . . . hurry, babe," he said, slurring his words. "I'm . . . little woozy from the heat."

She took a quick peek behind the curtain and saw him standing with his back to her, leaning against the wall, arm raised with his palm braced against the tile. His head was hanging to the side, the powerful spray from the nozzle blasting against his cheek. *Perfect,* she thought.

She reached into her bathrobe pocket and gripped the ornate hilt of the ceremonial dagger. A moment later, she shrugged out of the robe, letting it fall to the floor around her feet. She stepped over the edge of the bathtub, joining Steve in his last shower. "One surprise left," she whispered. "Close your eyes."

He shook his head at the suggestion, then groaned slightly, as if that small movement had caused him discomfort. Before he could turn to face her, she pressed her naked body against his and covered his eyes with her left hand. "No peeking!"

"Okay," he said, but his raspy voice had dropped to a whisper.

He dropped his arm and, so that she could whisper in his ear, let her tilt his head back with the hand covering his eyes. "Steve . . ."

"Yes?"

"No hard feelings."

She tightened her grip on his face—

"What—?"

—and slashed the edge of the dagger across his exposed throat, left to right, cutting deep.

Crimson splashed on the tiles, turning pink and running in rivulets down, down, down to the drain, swirling into oblivion. Steve's strength abandoned him quickly, gone without a struggle. His body sagged against her—dead weight. "It's done," she whispered, stepping back, letting gravity have its way now that she was done with him. He slumped to a sitting position, supported by her legs long enough for her to rinse the blood from her outstretched arms. She was careful to leave some blood on the blade of the dagger for the rest of the ceremony.

As she scrambled out of the bathtub, Steve's body fell back with a dull double-thump, his pale forearm flopping over the edge, almost like a half-hearted wave good-bye.

She turned off the water and shoved the shower curtain aside to admire her commitment. Her gaze settled on his wide open eyes, unseeing now. But even with beads of water standing on the gray-blue irises, they seemed surprised by his fate. "Your life had meaning, Steve," she assured him solemnly. "You served a purpose."

After a moment of silence, she smiled, feeling the first stirring of excitement. She'd made the last sacrifice for her art. The hardest part was over. Time to reap her reward.

Without bothering to towel herself dry, Rebecca slipped into her robe, belted it around her narrow waist, and strode across the hotel room, pausing at the door to the adjoining room. She took a deep breath to calm herself, then threw back the bolt and opened the door. Across the narrow gap separating the rooms, the other door was already open.

A tall, cadaverous man dressed in layers of black stood before her in the doorway. Bald, he had craggy brows over sunken eyes, a hooked nose, wide bloodless lips, and a deeply cleft chin. Though his features were harsh, his gaunt face wore a pleased look. His long, spidery fingers were steepled beneath his chin, a ruminative pose at odds with the anticipatory gleam in those dark eyes. "Yes?" he said, pronouncing the sibilant with a sepulchral rumble.

"Sehjenkhai," Rebecca said, beaming with accomplishment. "It is done."

He nodded once. "Show me."

"Of course," she said. "Come in."

Sehjenkhai entered her room with unnatural grace and seemed not to make a whisper of sound as he approached her. His head turned with oiled precision as his deep-set eyes scanned the room and his narrow nostrils flared, catching the scent of blood.

"Right this way," she said, indicating the bathroom. "You were right, Sehjenkhai. This was the toughest one. But that drug you gave me worked like a charm. I had him take a shower before we— you know—not that we did, but that's what he thought was gonna happen. Of course, he never suspected—"

"You remembered the dagger?" Sehjenkhai asked, interrupting her.

Behind him prowled his two prodigious black mastiffs, chuffing and panting with growing excitement. They took protective positions on either side of Sehjenkhai, salivating with hunger but obediently awaiting his command. At one time, Rebecca had been afraid of the powerful dogs, but they too served a purpose: the disposal of incriminating evidence.

"Yes, the dagger. Not as messy as I thought it would be, thanks to the shower. Dagger, check. Slit throat, check. Everything just as we planned." She was bubbling with excitement and found it hard to stop babbling. She wanted Sehjenkhai to be pleased with her. To the outside world, she presented the gaunt man as her motivational guru cum acting coach; in actuality, he was her mentor in the dark arts. But that was their little secret. Even Sally, her personal assistant, was unaware of the true nature of their relationship.

Sehjenkhai followed Rebecca into the bathroom, the mastiffs close at his heels. She stepped aside and indicated the prone body in the bathtub with a flourish of her arm, much like a daytime game show model showing an excited contestant what prize he had won. Admittedly, Sehjenkhai appeared intent rather than excited by the pale, naked, blood-spattered corpse lying before him. But Rebecca supposed giddiness was not a quality one would value in a master of the dark arts. "Blood on the dagger?" Sehjenkhai asked.

"Another check," Rebecca said, lifting the ceremonial dagger from the countertop and flashing both sides of the blood-smeared blade for her mentor to inspect. "Hard to believe we're so close to the finish line. Can't wait to put that Kendra Wilson in her place. You know, I was a lock for that Best Supporting Actress Oscar until her studio started shamelessly plastering those 'for your consideration' ads in *Variety* and *The Hollywood Reporter.* Nobody had a clue who that bitch was until they—"

"You have done well, Rebecca."

"Oh—thank you," she said, deflated by the abrupt compliment. "Thank you, Sehjenkhai. That means a lot, coming from you."

"May I inspect the ceremonial dagger?"

"Of course." She passed the bloodstained weapon to him. While he examined the sacrificial blade, she took a deep breath and spread her fingers at her sides, imagining the excess energy flowing outward to leave an inner calm. It was a technique she employed while acting to shed her own emotional baggage before imbuing herself with the motivations of a character. "Have to admit, though, I kinda freaked out when you told me I had to kill the father of my unborn child. I mean, jeez, nothing like being preggers to sideline an acting career! Especially at my age. But you said I don't have to keep it after tonight, right?"

"Correct."

"Super," Rebecca said. "So what's left? To complete this elaborate ceremony? It's been a long time coming—"

"Longer than you can possibly imagine," Sehjenkhai rumbled softly, a poor attempt at a whisper.

"—and I'd like to wrap it up before my premiere," Rebecca finished, heedless of his words.

"You need not concern yourself with missing your premiere."

"Well, not that the premiere of *Zombie Island*

Princess is a major industry happening or anything," she said. "But I do have the title role, and if my career is about to turn around, the exposure can't hurt, right?"

"No change begins until this is finished," he reminded her. She nodded dutifully. He removed a sheet of rolled paper from an inside jacket pocket and handed it to her. "You must recite this spell three times."

"Is it in English? Because I only know a bit of French and—"

"The language"—Sehjenkhai interrupted—"predates recorded history. But I wrote the spell phonetically for you on this side of the page. Isn't that the Hollywood way?"

"Merci," she said, showing off one of the six phrases she remembered from her two years of high school French. "Before you know it, Sehjenkhai, you'll be writing scripts for me."

"I find this one sufficient," he said. "Now. Read it three times, but first . . ."

He ran his little finger through the blood on one side of the dagger like a child scooping icing out of a mixing bowl. For a moment, Rebecca expected her mentor to taste the blood. Instead, he daubed her upper and lower lips with Steve McKay's blood. She tried to repress a shudder and failed. At least he hadn't asked her to suck the blood off his finger . . . yet. "O-kay," she said uncertainly. "That's kinda gross."

"Quiet!"

Chastened, she bit her lip and instantly regretted the reflex, imagining her blood pooling with Steve's. *Not that it should matter,* she thought. They'd had unprotected sex dozens of times before she'd become pregnant. But Steve was a corpse, and in her mind, anointing her lips with his spilled blood bordered on necrophilia, or at least cannibalism. Having sex with a stuntman was one thing, but even *she* had limits.

"Now read the spell. Three times."

"All right, all right," she said, holding the curled sheet of paper open before her. Not only had he written the spell phonetically for her, he'd used capital letters for accented syllables. After a quick scan top to bottom for potential tongue-twisters, she read the spell. During the second recitation, she became unnerved as Steve's corpse began to twitch in the bottom of the tub. On her mental screening room, there were visions of zombies rising from their graves and cavorting. She convinced herself this was a test of her resolve and worthiness. Ignoring the distraction, she read the spell the third time in a bold, commanding voice, a voice worthy of everything and everyone she had sacrificed to reverse her career slide. Her art demanded sacrifice and conviction in equal mea-sures. After the third reading, Steve's corpse bled anew, droplets of red oozing from his pores and trickling down his pale, cold flesh. A moment later, his corpse seemed to deflate, as if the ancient spell had magically extracted some remaining vital essence.

Strangely, Rebecca wondered if souls lingered after death. Perspiration beaded her brow, and her hands were trembling. "I—I did that?"

"Well done," Sehjenkhai said. "Spoken as if it were your native tongue."

"I've always been a quick study."

"An apt pupil," Sehjenkhai said with a wry grin.

"Couldn't ask for a better teacher," she said, delighted. "So that's it, right? I'm done."

"Yes," he said. "You have served your purpose well. However, one small detail remains untended."

"Whatever," she said with a shrug. "What could be worse than murdering the father—?"

Sehjenkhai interrupted her with the point of the ceremonial dagger, plunging the blade hilt-deep under her ribs. He stared into her wide blue eyes, waiting for realization to dawn before he completed his task.

Rebecca's white bathrobe slowly turned red. She shook her head with incredulity as the light began to fade from her eyes. "I murdered them . . ."

"Willingly, you selfish, annoying bitch!"

"But . . . why . . . me?"

"Revolution"—the blade twisted upward—"demands sacrifice."

He squeezed her throat in a fierce grip, holding her upright while he carved her still-beating heart out of her chest cavity with the precise turns of a practiced hand. Carelessly, he dropped the dagger to the floor and focused his attention on the sticky morsel in his hand. His jaw gaped, stretching inhumanly wide—wide enough to accommodate Rebecca Wade's treacherous heart, which he swallowed whole, like a serpent ingesting a mouse. His leathery throat swelled and contracted, marking the organ's passage.

With one fluid motion, he stripped the blood-soaked robe from her lifeless body and shoved her into the tub, on top of the stuntman. He picked up the spell paper she'd dropped to the tile floor and flipped it to the side written in his native language. Rather than chance a mistake by reciting the ancient spell from his equally ancient memory, he read the words as written, three times, until Rebecca Wade's Oscar-nominated corpse seemed to sweat blood and then wither with the theft of her essence.

Sehjenkhai snapped his fingers and, with a brisk hand motion, directed the mastiffs to the warm double meal conveniently awaiting them in what amounted to a gel-coated fiberglass trough. As the mastiffs stalked forward on powerful legs, their bodies transformed, swelling with additional musculature, their teeth and claws extending as the demonic creatures abandoned any pretense of canine ancestry. Ravenous snarls accompanied the sound of crunching bones and tearing flesh.

Sehjenkhai left the gluttonous creatures to their noisy repast. When they were finished, nothing would remain of the human remains. Nothing but the result of the ceremony, which meant everything to Sehjenkhai. He found delicious irony in knowing Rebecca Wade's most significant role would go uncredited.

Now Sehjenkhai anxiously awaited some sign that the ceremony—a year in the making after intolerable centuries of waiting—had succeeded. He wasn't troubled a bit that he was waiting for that harbinger of a new world order in an average, unpretentious hotel room chosen for a clandestine tryst and a secret ceremony because of its anonymity. After so many years and so many failed attempts that the faces of the players blurred together, success counted for everything, the venue not at all. So he stood motionless, head bowed, spidery fingers intertwined at his waist, attuned to the world around him for the slightest change.

A subtle movement of air caressed his face.

A skein of darkness rippled through the ambient light, as if a fleeting storm cloud had passed overhead, marring an azure summer sky. This darkness, however, came not from above, but from within.

Then the floor trembled beneath him, and the ground for miles in all directions rumbled with the release of supernatural energy.

Sehjenkhai chuckled with uncontained satisfaction. A dreadful smile spread across his gaunt features, and his eyes gleamed with a new, unearthly light. While everyone else would assume Southern California had fallen prey to yet another natural seismic tremor, and a mild one at that, Sehjenkhai knew better. *This is the way their world ends. . . .*

The waiting was over. In complete secrecy, he'd set the endgame in motion. And nobody could stop him now.

CHAPTER ONE

Angel finally knew how to stop them. But first he had to catch them.

Leaving the GTX parked about a mile back, Angel had taken to the rooftops, his vampiric strength allowing him to leap across the gaps between buildings with relative ease. As he sprinted, his black leather duster whipped behind him, exposing the gleaming metal of the sword clutched upright in his hand. His heightened senses scanned for any telltale sign of an attack.

For several nights running, the demon-pack had been preying on solitary pedestrians, lone joggers, the homeless, and anyone else they caught outside alone after dusk. The pack would appear, strike with impunity, and vanish into the night—until the inevitable next attack, hours later and miles away. The few eyewitness accounts available were contradictory. And so far, none of the victims had survived.

Cordelia and Fred had been plotting the demon attacks on a map of Los Angeles. As the number of pushpins accumulated, so, too, did their frustration. Until yesterday, a predictable pattern to the location of the attacks—as well as the genus of this particular demon-pack—had eluded them. Finally, Fred, fresh from a mid-afternoon nap, looked at the map for the hundredth time and saw, instead of randomness, a clear pattern in the apparent chaos. Each attack cluster formed an expanding clockwise spiral. The first group of attacks was random, and the second group seemed random as well, but it was the key to how the spiral would form. If the second group was northwest of the first, the third group would be to the north, but if the second group was east of the first, then the third would be southeast. Angel's best chance of intercepting the pack was at the third point in the spiral, but pinpointing that location was an inexact science. Within a half- to three-quarter-mile radius, he had to scout likely ambush points and hope to intercept the pack before they pounced on their hapless victim and moved on.

According to the few reports, the attackers had dropped from a nearby rooftop to encircle their victim. Angel thought his best chance to stop them was to catch them *before* they pounced, so he'd taken the high ground to stalk the stalkers. Yesterday the strategy had proved successful . . . to a point. He intercepted the three pack members—lanky demons with matted black fur and yellow, ram-like horns—moments before they would have ambushed an unwary teenager cutting through a dark alley. A fierce battle ensued, but Angel thought the stacked odds were manageable—until they became worse. When he thought he'd killed the first demon, it split, hydra-like, into two reanimated demons. Three-to-one odds became four to one. Maybe he was a glutton for punishment, but he had to be sure. He killed another demon, and soon faced five of them. Instead of eliminating the demon-pack problem, he had unwittingly made it worse.

He'd had no choice but to retreat from the battle and hope the gang at Angel Investigations could find an Achilles' heel for the demonic hydra. Fortunately, the puzzle pieces had begun to fall into place. Lorne took the additional information—physical description and splitting ability—back to the demonic grapevine and returned with the name Hyconus. Wesley had researched the name all day before uncovering in a moldy tome a sparse reference to the Order of Hyconus. The entry described the demons as *marauding harbingers* without explaining what particular type of nastiness their presence presaged. The reference did, however, provide a clue as to how one might dispatch them without triggering their full-body demonic mitosis.

But first he had to catch them.

Suddenly there was a streak of movement as something predatory landed behind him.

Angel spun, wielding the sword in a two-handed grip, and braced for attack.

The old homeless man pushed his worldly belongings in a shopping cart as he walked behind the warehouse. Beneath the pile of bottles and aluminum cans, within a rolled and tattered blanket, he kept everything he possessed of any value. His meager net worth included several packages of peanut butter crackers, a twenty-four-ounce water bottle, half a pack of Marlboro cigarettes along with a disposable lighter, an AM-FM radio with a crooked antenna and missing knobs, a sock filled with loose change, a King James Bible with a frayed cover and distressed binding, and a charred wooden picture frame holding the faded image of the woman he had loved and lost thirty years ago, though lately he'd had trouble recalling her name. As usual, he kept the few bills he'd managed to panhandle that day on his person, tucked inside one of his worn sneakers. And because his trouser pockets were riddled with holes, he kept a pocketknife down in his sock.

He had no choice but to carry everything with him. When he couldn't find a bed in a local shelter, he would camp out in one of several places he favored—relatively safe places, but he never left anything behind he would regret missing if it wasn't there when he returned.

Steering the shopping cart down the alley that separated two warehouses, he paused at the first of two Dumpsters. He flipped up the lid on the side nearest him, disturbing a dozen foraging flies in the process. Too narrow for the eighteen-wheeled delivery trucks, the alley saw limited traffic, mostly employee cars during the day and trash removal service trucks at night. The old man made a point of hitting the alley before the trucks arrived to empty the Dumpsters. He tossed soda cans over his shoulder into his brimming shopping cart, but took more care with the empty juice and beer bottles he found.

It was while turning away from the Dumpster with a long-necked root beer bottle clutched between his thumb and index finger that he saw them drop eerily from the sky, landing to form a rough circle around him. Five of them. His first thought was that they were hooligans or delin- quent teenagers whose idea of an evening's enter- tainment was to torment a helpless old homeless man, which turned his mind to the knife in his sock.

But as they crept closer in the gathering dark- ness, he saw that they were not teenagers. They weren't human at all. Nor were they animals, despite animal characteristics, including fur, horns, and claws. They walked upright, these near-men, but otherwise they were creatures from nightmares . . . or hallucinations. The old man hadn't had a drink in days. Wide awake and stone-cold sober, he had no excuse and no explanation for what he was seeing.

The fleeting thought of grabbing the rusty old pocketknife to defend himself from five creatures vomited up from the bowels of hell seemed ludicrous. Terror paralyzed him. His arthritic legs trembled. His weak heart galloped dangerously. His throat was too dry to scream or even beg for mercy.

As they closed the circle around the old man, their finger-claws clicking and forked tongues flashing in wicked anticipation, the long-necked soda bottle slipped through his fingers.

Caught off-guard, Angel had assumed a defensive posture with the sword, ready to ward off the silent attacker who had landed behind him to his left.

"Gotcha," Connor said with a self-satisfied smirk.

Frowning, Angel lowered the weapon. "Did not."

"Admit it."

Angel wasn't about to admit any such thing. The last time Connor got the drop on him, the drop had been literal, Connor chaining his vampire father in a makeshift glass coffin and dumping him in the Pacific Ocean, intending to let him waste away for eternity and slowly go insane in the bargain. Connor had acted out of revenge because he'd believed—wrongly—that Angel was responsible for the death of his adoptive father, Angel's sworn enemy, Daniel Holtz.

Plenty of mitigating circumstances worked in the boy's favor. Holtz had tricked Wesley into helping him kidnap the infant Connor, whereupon Holtz had taken the boy through a portal into a hell dimension known as Quor-Toth. There, Holtz had honed Connor's extraordinary physical prowess, creating an expert tracker and a feared demon killer known as "the Destroyer" while finding time for a little brainwashing on the side.

Time passed differently in Quor-Toth. Angel was still grieving over the recent loss of his infant son when the boy returned from Quor-Toth as a teenager, filled with Holtz's venom, a pure hatred for Angel.

Making the best of a bad situation, Angel had worked to repair his damaged relationship with Connor. Angel had believed he was making headway. He had hoped his ongoing mission to "help the helpless" would convince the boy that Angel was no longer the evil Angelus whom Holtz never forgave for destroying his own family. Despite outward appearances,

Connor remained true to Holtz's quest for revenge. The final straw came when Holtz orchestrated the manner of his own death, making it appear that a vampire, namely Angel, had killed him. Connor was all too willing to believe Angel was still capable of cold-blooded murder. Holtz had raised him to believe it. And so Connor had consigned his natural father to withering death and insanity in the depths of the ocean.

Fortunately for Angel, Wesley had discovered the plot and forced Holtz's fanatical assistant, Justine, into helping him locate what was to have been Angel's final resting place. Instead of spending eternity imprisoned on the seafloor, Angel's sentence had been commuted to three months. It had only *seemed* like eternity.

With that rescue, Angel believed that Wesley had redeemed himself for the well-intentioned but misguided abduction of Angel's infant son. They were working together in an uneasy alliance, uneasy mostly because Wesley still had issues about his own gullibility in Holtz's scheme. The situation with Connor was more complicated. Angel had forgiven Connor's patricidal act of betrayal because, after three months of imprisonment, Angel knew he still loved his son. Learning to trust him again was another matter.

"I'm in the middle of something here, Connor."

"The sword was a dead giveaway," Connor said. "I might be heading that way." The impossible

human son of two vampires, Connor had superhuman strength and heightened senses. Slighter in
build than Angel, the teenager was nearly as quick
and strong. Whereas Angel had had the benefit of
a couple centuries in which to hone his fighting
skills, Connor had survived childhood in a hell
dimension. He would be a valuable ally in the
upcoming demonic melee.

"Good," Angel said. He reached inside his
duster and unsheathed a machete he'd kept hidden there as a backup weapon. "You'll need this."

"Sweet," Connor said, admiring the blade.
"What are we up against?"

"Demons."

"Naturally."

"The Order of Hyconus," Angel said. "Five of
them. Run in a pack. Attack and kill anyone they
catch outside alone after dark."

"Until we kill them." In a blur of motion, Connor swept the machete back and forth, vicious
practice strokes that made the gleaming blade
whistle in the night.

"Right."

"Edged weapons?"

"For decapitating," Angel said. "Unless we can
persuade them to kill one another."

"Why let them have all the fun?"

"One minor detail," Angel said. "We have to kill
them in order."

"What? Take turns?"

"No, it's their—"

They both heard it. A sound far enough away to be beyond the range of normal human hearing. Not a problem for either of them.

"Breaking glass?" Connor asked.

Angel nodded. "Sounds like they found a victim. Connor—wait!"

Connor had already begun to sprint across the roof. He bounded onto an air-conditioning unit and used that additional height as a makeshift springboard to launch himself to the next rooftop. "Why wait? They won't."

In a heartbeat—assuming his vampire heart had been capable of beating—Angel took off after Connor's already receding form. "Connor, it's their horns!"

"What about them?"

"Size matters," Angel shouted, but he had the distinct feeling that Connor's attention was on the upcoming fight. "The size of their horns!" Wesley had discovered that the "order" in the Order of Hyconus name referred to the demons' vulnerability. "Connor?" Angel called.

"Dead is dead," was Connor's distant reply.

Not necessarily, Angel thought wryly. Three rooftops separated father from son, and although Angel wasn't losing ground, neither was he gaining. Connor would engage the Hyconus demons first.

Connor stopped at the edge of a three-story office building, then stepped off, dropping from sight. Angel charged ahead, hoping to catch Connor before he made the same mistake Angel had the previous night.

Ahead, Angel heard the sound of metal crashing, glass breaking, and a rush and rattle of spilled aluminum cans. *Too late to stop their ambush,* Angel knew. *Maybe not too late to save their victim.*

That's when he heard a man scream in terror.

Without slowing, Angel launched himself headfirst off the office building, arcing upward until gravity overcame his considerable momentum and pulled him downward, like an inbound missile. Beneath him, Connor streaked across a warehouse roof, his legs a blur of scissoring motion. Angel tucked and rolled with the impact, startling Connor, who broke stride for a moment, even as Angel sprang to his feet and raced for the edge of the warehouse roof. "Gotcha," Angel called over his shoulder as he leaped to the alley below.

Instantly, he assessed the situation. Near a pair of Dumpsters and an overturned shopping cart, which had been filled with empty cans and bottles, five horned demons surrounded a frightened old man in threadbare clothing whose gray hair looked like an abandoned bird's nest. The alpha demon, with five-swirled horns on either side of his wedge-shaped head, held the man aloft with one clawed hand clamped around his wrist. Judging by the position of the demon's other hand, he'd been about to eviscerate the man when Angel dropped in on them.

"Demon bullies," Angel said derisively. "You guys are pathetic." He walked forward casually, his gaze flickering to the demon's nasty claws poised over the old man's abdomen. "Ganging up on a frightened old man. Where's your self-esteem?"

Connor landed with catlike grace beside Angel.

The demon shrugged and smiled, exposing a mouth lined with snarled and pointed teeth beneath flaring nostril holes and deep-set yellow eyes. "We're thinning the human herd."

The smallest demon, with a single-swirl horn, smirked and said, "What's it to you? You're not human." Nodding toward Connor, he added, "And neither is he."

Connor returned the smirk. "Shows how much you know."

"Enough!" the alpha demon bellowed. "We kill this one, then the meddlers!"

Angel sprang forward a moment before the demon's claws flashed toward the old man's exposed midsection. He swung his sword down as if it were a meat cleaver and lopped off the demon's hand at the wrist. The demon roared in pain and rage, but released his hostage, dropping the old man onto the loose pile of cans and bottles.

The homeless man rolled onto hands and knees,

scrabbled to his feet, and lumbered down the alley, moaning with fear, certain he could never escape the monstrosities, but running nonetheless.

"Don't worry," Angel said to the one-handed alpha demon, "I'm not going to kill you . . . yet."

Instead, Angel spun on his heel and swung his sword at the single-swirl-horned demon. The demon ducked, and the blade struck the nearest Dumpster in a spray of sparks. *Small, but quick,* Angel thought. *But he has to die first.*

Still enraged, the alpha demon charged with his head bowed so that his pointed horns could impale Angel. "Always wanted to see the running of the bulls," Angel said, launching a spin kick that redirected the horns toward the Dumpster.

Dazed, the demon staggered sideways.

"Relax, Dad," Connor said. "I'll take this one."

"Connor, no!"

While Angel was distracted, two of the middle-horned demons caught him under his arms and slammed him against the Dumpster. He dodged their swiping claws, jammed his left elbow into the face of one, then drove that fist into the nose-less face of the other one.

Connor's sweep kick felled the third of three middle demons, freeing him to advance on the stunned alpha demon.

Angel rushed to intercept Connor, but single-swirl-horn jumped in front of him. "You I can kill now," Angel said, but knew he would be too late.

As the alpha demon straightened, Connor wielded his machete in a two-handed grip and swung it like a baseball bat toward the demon's exposed throat.

"He's last!" Angel yelled. The alpha demon's head fell off his body a split second before Angel could decapitate single-swirl-horn. *Wrong order!*

Sensing movement behind him from the tripped demon's position, Connor pivoted on his heel and lopped off the head with an efficient but pointless stroke. "Three down," he declared.

As three demon bodies hit the ground with successive dull thuds, they began to shimmer and separate. Seconds later, three headless bodies became six headless bodies. Then fresh heads emerged from all six neck stumps. It was like watching time-lapse photography of hideous flower buds blooming.

Three down, Angel thought, then added in resignation, "And six up."

Where there had been five demons out for blood, there were now eight. The demons sprang to their feet and formed a semicircle around Angel and Connor, attempting to force them back against the Dumpsters, where they would be unable to swing their weapons effectively. When the demons weren't gnashing their pointed teeth or flicking forked tongues, they clicked their claws together in gleeful anticipation. And the accumulation of matted fur was becoming a bit ripe.

Connor shot Angel a confused look. "What just happened?"

"Would it kill you to follow directions once in a while?"

CHAPTER TWO

A little battered and bruised, but smiling despite those minor aches, Charles Gunn returned to the Hyperion Hotel in high spirits after a successful vampire sweep. Not that he would ever return from an unsuccessful sweep—at least not with his soul attached. Simply surviving out there was a success, but actually depleting the numbers of the bloodsuckers was priceless.

Before entering the old hotel—base of operations for Angel Investigations—he took a deep, life-affirming breath. The sweet scent of night-blooming jasmine seemed to welcome him back from the hostile night. *Nothin' like dusting a couple vamps to brighten a brother's day*, he thought as he walked down the steps into the spacious lobby. His custom-made hubcap ax slung over one shoulder, he twirled a wooden stake in his free hand. He maneuvered around a banquette and approached the front desk. "Vamps thought they had me outnumbered three to one," he said, grinning. "Guess they don't know when they're playin' against the favorite. . . ."

His smile wilted.

Wesley and Fred were basking in the afterglow of successful research. A knack for finding useful bits of information in centuries-old tomes was one of the many things Wesley Wyndam-Pryce and Winifred Burkle had in common. There they were, huddled over some musty old iron-bound book that weighed about half as much as Fred. Seeing Wes making Mensa moves on his girl was more than enough to sour Gunn's celebratory mood.

Well, at least Gunn hoped Fred was still his girl. Things between them hadn't been the same since Gunn murdered Professor Seidel for her. He'd wanted to spare her the guilt he feared would tear her apart if she followed through with her original plan for revenge against the man who had exiled her to another dimension, a world called Pylea, where demon masters treated humans as cattle. Rather than allow Fred to murder the professor in cold blood, Gunn had done it for her. But that hadn't been enough for him to bear all the guilt. They'd been accessories. Fred recognized that. In attempting to save Fred from herself, Gunn wondered if he'd diminished himself in her eyes. Though he would do anything for that girl, he had to face the possibility that *anything* might not be enough.

I feel like I'm losing her one agonizing piece at a time, Gunn thought, *and dear old Wes, who's carried a torch for Fred for a long time, is ready and waiting to pick up the pieces.*

Behind Fred and Wesley, Cordelia and Lorne hunched over a small color television watching some entertainment magazine program. They looked up long enough to call a greeting before returning their attention to the TV screen.

"Hi, Charles," Fred said politely. "Those vampires never had a chance."

"Just doin' my job," Gunn said. "Making the world safe for jugulars everywhere. Well, mostly greater L.A. But you gotta give me props for that, right?"

"Good show," Wes said, with a little less enthusiasm than the compliment deserved.

"Same old, same old, right?" Gunn said, deflated.

"No, it's not that, Charles," Fred said. "We've just been talking about how Wesley figured out the Hyconus problem. You'll never believe—I mean, it was right there in front of us, the mention, it was." She paused for breath, then nudged Wesley's shoulder. "Go on. You tell him."

What hurt Gunn most was seeing the old sparkle in Fred's eyes when she talked to Wes or even about him, because that same sparkle seemed extinguished whenever she'd looked at Gunn lately. "Yeah, tell me, Wes," he said.

"The key to their vulnerability was discovering they reproduce asexually and spontaneously when their immediate population is threatened." Wes brightened, recounting his daring feats of reading muddled bits of text written in dead languages. "A simple transcription error in the ancient text was to blame. In fact, the Hyconus aren't really an *Order* at all."

"The name refers to a killing sequence," Fred gushed. "To prevent all the dying and doubling."

"To defeat a Hyconus pack, one must dispatch the members in order, from smallest to largest set of horns," Wes finished.

"So glad Einstein had his eureka moment," Gunn muttered, unable to keep the disgust out of his voice—not at Wes, who was just doing his thing, but at the effect his bookish heroics had on Fred. "So that's where our fanged leader is?"

"Lining them up and knocking them down," Fred said.

"Assuming he's been able to locate the pack again," Wesley said. "It's simply a matter of beheading them in the proper order. I don't imagine it should be all that difficult for Angel."

"Surely not as difficult as deciphering all that ancient-ese without an index," Gunn said sarcastically, gesturing with the point of the wooden stake toward the demonic compendium under Wesley's elbows. "Count on those pack members to take a number and wait their turn."

"I'm not discounting the element of risk involved, Gunn," Wesley said defensively. "But Angel is quite capable."

"Never said I doubted the man," Gunn said as he walked away and stowed his weapons. *What's the world coming to,* he thought bitterly, *when an old-fashioned warrior, layin' it on the line out there every night, can't get no respect 'less he has a library card?*

Unencumbered by the old-fashioned accoutrements of wood and steel that still struck fear— thank God!—into the unbeating hearts of vampires everywhere, Gunn slipped behind the front desk to join Cordelia Chase and Lorne, the green-skinned anagogic demon and sometimes Angel Investigations telephone receptionist, in front of the television set. If nothing else, it was a distraction from the Fred-and-Wes mess.

"Grab a seat, Gunn," Cordelia said. "Have some popcorn? Lorne won't touch the stuff."

"Not a good mix with the sea breeze, cupcake," Lorne said, flourishing his red drink for emphasis. The colorful cocktail matched Lorne's red horns, eyes, and lips.

"What's up?" Gunn asked, with a nod toward the TV.

"Taped coverage of the red carpet premiere of

Zombie Island Princess," Cordelia said. "This is the glam before the gore."

"Antoine Renard's latest flick," Lorne said. "His foray into slash-with-class. He's kept it under wraps, but it's not without a little buzz. Who knows, we could be talking breakthrough, people."

"Can you believe Rebecca Wade was a no-show?" Cordelia said to Lorne. "When was her last hit? You'd think she'd be out there working it for the paparazzi."

"That girl's made a career out of sabotaging her career, sugar," Lorne said.

"Don't know how good they've got it," Cordelia said wistfully. At one time she'd dreamed of becoming an actress, but nothing had ever come of her infrequent auditions. Years passed, her priorities shifted, and now she was an integral part of Angel Investigations. Nevertheless, her dreams lingered.

Sensing Cordelia's mood shifting to melancholy, Lorne said, "Say, kitten, I ever tell you about the time I attended a Hollywood premiere?" Intrigued, Cordelia shook her head. "Oh, it was amazing! This was at El Capitan. Big-budget horror film, if you'll pardon the oxymoron. Anyhoo, they had the premiere on Halloween, so naturally everyone came in costume. Except yours truly."

Cordelia laughed, shaking her head in disbelief. "You didn't!"

Lorne shrugged. "Everyone just assumed, doll face. And who was I to set the record straight? Had a ball. Would have given Cinderella a run for her money. Chatted up the entire cast, the A- and B-list celebs, maybe even a few on the C-list. All night, I kept saying to myself, 'Lorne, you are in your element.' I mean, how many times can an anagogic demon pinch himself in one night? I even wrangled my way into an after-party and . . ."

Gunn noticed Fred refilling her mug at the coffeepot station and slipped away from the Cordy and Lorne Show before their conversation segued to red carpet fashion disasters or tabloid gossip. He grabbed a mug and waited for her to set the pot down. "Fresh brew?"

"Mm," Fred said, taking a sip. "Near enough."

"All right," Gunn said, going for jovial. "Believe I'll have some, then." Fred glanced at him briefly and frowned. "What?"

"What you said earlier." Fred nodded toward the reception desk. "Are you really worried about Angel?"

"Oh, that," Gunn said, relieved her frown wasn't in response to his barely concealed animosity over her most recent collaboration with Wesley. "No— no more than usual, that is. It's just that . . . sometimes I think we take this stuff for granted, you know? It's no walk in the park out there. Well, depending on where you grew up, maybe it *is* like a walk in the park. Look, all I'm saying is, it's never automatic."

"You think we've become complacent."

"Maybe," Gunn said. "A little bit. And no reason for it. We got Cordy's vision of the apocalypse. These Hyconus demons are supposed to be harbingers, right?" Fred nodded. "You know what I'm thinkin'?"

"What's next?"

"Exactly," Gunn said emphatically. "When's the other shoe gonna drop?"

"Around here, the question is how many shoes are going to drop." Fred flashed him a wry grin, a small hint of the wonderful smile he missed so much.

"Like that seven-legged Heptarga demon," Gunn said. "I wanted to yell, 'Dude, what's up with that seventh leg? Is that a spare or what?'"

"Those feet definitely needed shoes." Fred chuckled. "The smell! And did you see those tiny little mouths on each of the seven toes?"

"See them?" Gunn said, taking a sip of his coffee. "Hell, I think one of 'em bit me." *Now is as good a time as any,* he thought. "This is good coffee. You make it?"

Fred shook her head. "Cordelia. I made the last pot."

"Kind of quiet around here tonight," Gunn said casually. "Because, I was thinking, the diner, you know? We could step out, get a bite to eat, and—"

"Tonight? Oh—oh, Charles . . . I don't—I mean, I'm not really hungry and . . ."

"Hey, that's cool," Gunn said. "Maybe some other time."

"Some other time . . ."

Gunn had to push it. "Tomorrow?"

Before Fred could answer, the floor began to vibrate. Considering all the things Gunn had seen and experienced since joining Angel Investigations, he wouldn't have been surprised if the ground split open to form a skylight over hell. But it was only a minor tremor, and the hotel was undamaged. A hazy rain of dust descended from the chandeliers. Everyone looked up briefly, exchanging glances. Cordelia must have noted the look of alarm on Gunn's face and shrugged. "Third one this evening," she commented, unconcerned. Then she returned her attention to the procession of overdressed celebrities on TV.

Gunn looked at Fred, who cupped her coffee mug in both hands and walked back to her seat next to Wesley. The tremor had meant nothing more to her than a convenient distraction to avoid answering Gunn's question. In reality, she was avoiding a lot more than that. Not a chance he'd give up on her—on them—that easily.

Pushing those concerns aside, he couldn't help wondering if the tremor was yet another harbinger.

What if that vibration was caused by a whole mess of apocalyptic shoes dropping on our doorstep?

"We're lost."

"We are not lost."

"Well, we're going the wrong way," Carol Baker said to her husband, Ron, who was driving their blue Dodge Durango hunched over the steering wheel. "Might as well be lost."

"This is not the wrong way," Ron insisted. He rubbed his red-rimmed eyes by slipping an index finger under the rims of his thick eyeglasses. "We're on Hollywood Boulevard."

"Yes, we are," Carol said, glancing down at the street map she had unfolded on the dashboard. "Heading east. We should be heading west. According to the map, our hotel is back that way."

"East and west is relative to the cross street."

"Well, you just passed Vine, which means"—using the scale bar, she measured with her thumb—"we're about a mile too far east. How relative is that?"

"Oh, for God's sake," Ron said, finally admitting he was wrong. "I'll loop around and get back on Hollywood Boulevard."

Ron disliked night driving because of glare-induced headaches. And Carol hated checking into hotels after six o'clock, afraid that hotel management would surrender their rooms to someone who hadn't even bothered to make a reservation. The idea that they might have to sleep in the SUV or in a disreputable motel in a shady part of a strange town bothered Carol to no end. Life without a net had zero appeal for her. With the kids out on their own, Ron had been the one to suggest they take an extended driving vacation—*just the two of us, like old times*—across the country. Carol had agreed, on the condition that she would plan their route and make hotel and dining reservations. Last-minute changes to her careful plans drove her crazy.

"We'll be lucky if the Roosevelt doesn't give away our rooms." Carol had wanted to stay in the Hollywood Roosevelt Hotel after she'd read that the first Academy Awards had been held there in 1929, although they were called the Merit Awards back then. Tales of hauntings at the hotel promised to add a little intrigue to their two-day stay in the movie capital of the world.

"They won't give away our rooms."

"You never know."

"They won't give—!" Ron sighed, then shook his head in exasperation. He turned left back onto Hollywood Boulevard. "Look, if you're that worried about it, call them on the cell phone. Tell them we'll be arriving late."

"We wouldn't be late if you hadn't spent two extra hours at the slot machines in Vegas."

Ron shrugged. "I had a little run. Was I supposed to quit?"

"Right," Carol said sarcastically. "Why quit while you're ahead? Now I'm the one who has to call and apologize."

"Nobody has to apologize," Ron said. "Just tell them—look, there's Vine ahead. Let me see that map."

Carol pushed the map across the dashboard toward him and poked her finger at the intersection of Hollywood and Vine. "And the hotel is over there, past North Orange."

"Turn on the overhead—never mind, I'll get it," he said. After a moment, he nodded slowly. "You're right. You're always right. Happy?"

Carol smiled at him. Even with the overhead light, she doubted he could see the map. It was all show, him checking up on her, rather than simply admitting she'd been right all along. After twenty-seven years of marriage, they had their routines, well-worn behavioral ruts at times annoying, at other times comforting.

Unaware of her mild scrutiny, Ron pushed the map back to her side of the car and returned his attention to the road. "What the hell—!"

Carol followed his gaze through the windshield and saw something right in front of them, in the middle of the highway, something dark and big—as big as a wall—and too close!

Everything happened in an unavoidable instant.

She clutched the dashboard with white-knuckled fingers—

Ron slammed his foot on the brake pedal—

The Durango's tires screeched in protest—

—and they slammed into the wall.

She felt the solid and visceral *THUNK* of crunching steel as a white explosion momentarily blinded her—the SUV's air bags.

Dazed, they unbuckled their seat belts and stumbled out of the Durango, proceeding on trembling legs to the front of the ruined SUV. One of Ron's eyeglass lenses had fallen out when the driver's side air bag had mangled the wire frames. His scratched cheek was speckled with blood, and he blinked repeatedly as he stared at the strange object in front of them. It was fifteen feet high and blocked the entire westbound lane of Hollywood Boulevard. "It's huge," he whispered in awe. "But how . . ."

Headlights of the cars stopping behind their Durango blazed across the looming object but couldn't seem to dispel the ominous shadows inhabiting its carved surface.

"What is it?" Carol wondered. "Some kind of statue?"

"Don't know," Ron said. "But it wasn't there a moment ago."

"It wasn't there when we passed in the other direction."

"Whatever it is," Ron said with growing indignation, "I plan to sue the bastard who put it in the middle of the road. We could have been killed."

Suddenly, a hot wind swirled around them, gusting and buffeting their bodies like an invisible giant's hand pushing them closer to the object. Caught off-balance, they stumbled forward, reaching out to the stone surface to support themselves. While the wind continued to batter them, a blinding light erupted from the carved stone.

Carol tried to scream, but all the air had been forced from her lungs. With a gasp, she managed a single word. "Ron . . . !"

The intensity of the wind doubled. Carol's feet slipped out from under her, and she slid forward on the seat of her pants. Her arm flailed where Ron should be, but found nothing. She expected to slam into the stone wall. Instead, she spun into emptiness, beyond the blinding light into a vast silence within an utter darkness that swallowed her whole and snuffed out the light of her consciousness.

"None of you is the least bit worried about that baby earthquake?"

"I'd hardly call it an earthquake, Gunn," Cordelia said. "It was a tremor. L.A. usually has one minor tremor a day without any supernatural mojo involved."

"One," Gunn said. "Not three."

"True," Cordelia conceded. "But all three were minor. No harm, no foul. Why worry?"

"Well, there is one reason we should worry," Fred said. "California is overdue for another major earthquake. We could all drop into the Pacific any day now."

"Another cheery thought from science girl," Cordelia said sarcastically. "But I'm not relocating."

Wesley looked up from his jumbo tome and arched an eyebrow. "Most densely populated areas are subject to one or more climatic, seismic, or manmade hazards."

"Pick your poison," Lorne said, punctuating the comment with a sip of his sea breeze.

"Again," Cordelia said. "Not with the moving."

Gunn appreciated Fred coming, in a roundabout way, to his defense. Everyone seemed too calm. "I don't know," Gunn said, shrugging. "Maybe it's just too damn quiet around here lately."

"And let's all enjoy the quiet, gang," Lorne said. "Because it never lasts."

Cordelia nodded agreement, then she and Lorne returned their attention to the TV. When Wesley left the reception desk to refill his coffee mug, Gunn saw his opportunity. He sidled up to Fred and said, "Thanks."

Fred smiled wryly. "For what? Reminding everyone of their mortality?"

"I was feelin' a 'lone voice in the wilderness' vibe back there."

"Don't worry," she said. "Happens to all of us here."

"Right," Gunn said, smiling. "About that diner suggestion—"

"Gunn, I—"

"Don't you think we should talk about—?"

"We will," Fred said quickly. "Talk, I mean. It's just . . ."

Gunn sighed. "Fred, we had a good thing—a great thing. I don't want to lose that."

"We'll talk, Charles," Fred said, flashing a brittle grin. "I need . . . later, okay?"

"Later?"

"Later. Promise. But now . . ." She looked away from him for a moment before completing her thought. "Now's not a good time, you know?"

"Right," Gunn said, not understanding at all. They had just agreed it was a quiet time, but when *would* be a good time to talk about what had gone wrong between them—in the heat of battle? Gunn preferred to tackle a problem head-on, so it frustrated him to have to sit back and wait. Something was broken, and it was hard to accept that nothing but time could heal it. Waiting and wondering made him feel powerless. *Maybe I should go out again,* he thought. *Find me a few more vamps to dust.*

"This is not good," Cordelia said suddenly.

"Hey, gang," Lorne called to the others with a note of alarm in his voice. "Hate to spoil the good vibes of a normality malaise, but somebody just put a gigundo roadblock in the middle of Hollywood Boulevard, and I'm guessing the Los Angeles Department of Transportation won't be taking the heat for this one."

Gunn, Fred, and Wesley joined Cordelia and Lorne in front of the small television set to watch the live news report. Several police cars, roof lights flashing, flanked a dark stone statue obstructing westbound traffic. A crowd had gathered at the scene. Policemen with flashlights directed cars around the statue.

"It's gigantic," Cordelia said. "Twelve, maybe fifteen, feet high."

"Is that a face?" Fred asked, leaning close. "Carved into the stone?"

The handheld camera operator changed position, making a partial circuit around the statue, zooming in and out, trying to find a view unobstructed by the milling crowd.

"One on each side," Gunn said. "And neither face looks real happy."

Cordelia turned up the volume on the TV. An offscreen female news reporter was commenting in a live voice-over: ". . . police refuse to comment, but several witnesses stated that this amazing statue simply appeared out of nowhere, in the westbound lanes of Hollywood Boulevard.

"A sudden appearance might explain why this blue Durango crashed into the east-side face of the statue. We are attempting to locate the occupant or occupants of that damaged vehicle. At this time, we believe the police may have taken them into custody.

"Meanwhile, blocks away, at Mann's Chinese Theatre, Hollywood's best and brightest are attending the premiere of *Zombie Island Princess*. A few Hollywood insiders are speculating that this statue might be some kind of bizarre publicity stunt to promote that new movie. Obviously, if that's true, this was a marketing ploy with complete disregard for public safety and would be subject to criminal prosecution.

"Once again, the big mystery here this evening is how a person or persons unknown was able to transport this fifteen-feet-high stone statue undetected into—"

Frowning, Wesley adjusted the TV volume to a whisper. He squinted at the screen, entranced by the televised image. "A megalith here," he said in awe. "And much more elaborate than anything on Rapa Nui."

"Rapper who?" Gunn asked.

Wesley shook his head without looking away from the screen. "Easter Island. Ancient statues, maybe tens of thousands of years old."

"But this one is brand-spankin' new," Gunn said. "In the middle of Hollywood Boulevard."

"And those carved visages appear rather demonic."

"You think?" Cordelia asked sarcastically.

"Yeah, Wes," Gunn said. "Tell us something we don't know."

Ignoring their sarcasm, or at least unwilling to allow it to divert his attention, Wesley said, "Somebody should call Angel."

"Right away," Fred agreed, and hurried to the reception desk telephone.

"See, that's what I'm talkin' about," Gunn said with an emphatic nod of vindication. "Sometimes a tremor ain't just a tremor."

CHAPTER THREE

Ignoring for the moment the eight bloodthirsty Hyconian demons herding Angel and him against the pair of Dumpsters, Connor glared at Angel. "Directions? Sounded more like orders."

"Not orders. *Order!*" Angel cast a frown at his rebellious teenage son before returning his attention to the spiral-horned demons. Judging from their body language, they were about to attack—en masse. "Reverse order! Horn—!"

Eight demons roared a hideous battle cry and charged.

Surrounded, with their backs against the Dumpsters, Angel and Connor took the only avenue of escape available. They jumped onto the closed lids of the Dumpsters, then, before the demons could scramble up after them or attempt to pull them down, Angel and Connor launched themselves forward over the heads of the demons, landing in the alley behind the frenzied pack.

Connor yelled, "What—?"

"Horn spirals! Take out the one with the smallest set of horns. Work your way up to the biggest."

The demons peeled away from the Dumpsters and charged again, with two fanning out on either side in a pincers maneuver.

Angel faced the reborn alpha demon, who now had eight horns, while his erstwhile twin—*or is it the other way around?*—had seven. Both had restored hands, complete with vicious claws. Obviously the duplicated demons had been supernaturally assimilated into the new pecking order, from a single-spiral-horn demon up to the eight-spiral alpha. *Can't be age-based,* Angel realized. *Of course! It was right in front of me the whole time!* "It's a dominance thing," he called to Connor. *And if this pack gets much larger, the alpha won't be able to lift his head anymore.*

Angel leaned back to avoid the alpha's claw-swipe and resisted the urge to counterattack. Although that demon was most aggressive, he and Connor had to avoid him until the end. Unless the alpha died last, and in the right order, the pack would continue to grow.

Bad enough that the demons outnumbered them eight to two; they also had to restrain themselves from killing whichever demon came within range of their blades. That meant they had to continually sidestep attackers and attempt to position themselves to kill the least dominant demon at each stage of the battle. With the death order secret exposed, the dominant demons kept pressing the attack while shielding single-horn. Fortunately, it seemed as if single-horn couldn't flee the battle to thwart the progression. Angel imagined the pack dominance order would simply realign for a pack of seven, creating a new weakest link.

"Question, Dad," Connor said, a little breathlessly, as he ducked under sweeping claws, dodged a pouncing demon, and spun away from a third.

Angel picked up the toppled shopping cart in one hand and hurled it against the chest of the nearest demon, seven-swirl, slamming him into the far wall. The demons' battle strategy—or maybe it was simply survival instinct—was for the more dominant pack members to lead the attacks against Connor and Angel, while the less dominant members formed a matted-fur shield around single-swirl, who was the primary target. "What, son?"

Five-swirl caught Connor's machete-wielding hand and tried to pry the lethal weapon from his grasp. "You said we have to kill"—Connor slammed the heel of his free hand under the demon's gaping jaw, shattering a few gnarly teeth and stunning the demon who then released his hand—"kill them in reverse order."

"Easier said"—Angel caught four-swirl's right hand a moment before the razor-sharp claws would have ripped a gaping hole in his throat—"than done!" Angel twisted the hand back until the demon howled with pain. "What's your question?"

"Anything in the rules—says we can't—maim them out of order?"

A wicked smile spread across Angel's face. "Sounds like a plan."

Angel ducked as the shopping cart sailed his way. It smashed into the Dumpster behind him, but seven-swirl was right behind it, charging Angel, arms and claws extended. Angel spun to the side, dropped to one knee, and swung his sword in a powerful overhead arc, lopping the demon's arms off above the elbows. "Don't you just hate when that happens?"

The demon slammed into the Dumpster and whirled around enraged, spittle trailing from his chin. "I'll kill you for this!"

"Sorry," Angel said. "Already dead. Well, technically, undead. Not that it matters. You have your hands full. Oops, forgot, no hands!"

The demon's arm stumps trembled, dripping green blood, but so far, no regeneration action. *Regeneration is part of the death-and-rebirth cycle,* Angel realized. *Connor's idea just might work. Incapacitate enough of the dominant demons without actually killing them and we'll be able to work through the death progression.*

"No mortal wounds!" Angel called to Connor, who had just severed four-swirl's leg above the knee, dropping the demon in a shrieking heap. "Yet."

Armless, seven-swirl rushed Angel, perhaps hoping to provoke Angel into killing him. One slip of the sword and they would be back to square one with one extra demon to worry about. Angel grabbed the decapitated head of the old seven-swirl, the former alpha, and yelled, "Heads up!" before throwing it like a basketball at the new alpha's face.

Instinctively, the new seven-swirl reached up to catch the severed head—forgetting his hands were no longer there—and collapsed a moment after the bruising thud of horned heads colliding.

"Guess two heads aren't better than one after all."

When Connor had a clear outlet for his rage, he was a terror to behold. Angel could well imagine how he'd earned the nickname "the Destroyer" in Quor-Toth. The boy lopped off arms and legs with malevolent glee. Demons writhed on the ground in agony, opening a path to single-swirl. "Don't worry," Connor said. "You won't suffer . . . much."

Single-swirl yowled in panic and bolted, freezing in front of Angel.

"You—you're fast."

"I get that a lot."

"We—were just fooling around," the demon said with a shrug and a weak smile.

"No kidding," Angel said.

His sword was a gleaming blur.

The demon's mouth had opened to say something, but before any sound could come out his head rolled off his shoulders. When this demon fell, instead of shimmering and dividing, its body and detached head began to bubble and dissolve, leaving an acrid puddle of greenish goo. "That's encouraging," Angel said.

Connor smirked. "Messier than dusting vampires."

"Watch your step."

A demon missing hands and a lower left leg tried to hop past Connor, but the boy caught his shoulder and spun him around. "Don't think so, number two."

The demon sighed. "Worth a try."

Connor prepared to strike.

"Look out!" the demon cried.

Momentarily distracted by the exchange, Angel had failed to notice three-swirl creeping across the ground, clutching the jagged remnant of a broken wooden picture frame in his remaining hand. A split second after two-swirl yelled his warning, three-swirl lunged at Angel on two good legs, driving the pointed wooden weapon toward Angel's heart. Angel's first instinct was to eliminate the immediate threat. Catching the stake-wielding fist in his free hand, Angel rapped three-swirl on the side of the head with the hilt of the sword, rendering him unconscious. The makeshift stake clattered to the ground. Angel had come too close to killing the demon out of order.

Two-swirl shrugged. "That was worth a try too."

Angel rolled his eyes. "Connor."

"Don't have to tell me twice."

Moments later, two-swirl's remains were a bubbling green mess in the alley. Groggy, three-swirl climbed to his feet and looked around at the carnage. "Oh, this ain't good."

"It's about to get worse," Angel said, and swung his sword. The green-streaked blade cleared the demon's shoulders by half an inch.

After the fourth and fifth demons died without incident, Connor backed six-swirl against the wall with the Dumpsters as armless seven-swirl was regaining consciousness. "I got this one!" Connor called to Angel.

Angel shoved seven-swirl's head back against the Dumpster. A dull clang as the demon's skull struck the side of the Dumpster like the clapper of a bell, and the demon sagged, unconscious again. Angel sensed something was wrong. Glancing around the alley, he counted the green puddles where all the demons had died.

"Eight's missing!" he called.

The alpha demon sprang out of the open

Dumpster like a nightmarish jack-in-the-box and fell across Connor's back, the claws of his remaining hand raking downward, slicing flesh.

Connor heaved backward with his own roar of rage, dislodging the alpha demon and turning away from cowering six-swirl, raising the machete high overhead. The alpha demon snarled, but the expression seemed more like a smile, and his intact arm hung at his side.

Mistake, Angel thought, lunging forward. "Connor, no!"

Connor swung with all his strength, and would have beheaded the alpha demon if Angel hadn't rammed into him, knocking him to the ground.

"He wanted to provoke you!"

"I don't care!"

Angel looked back at the alpha demon, sprawled in the alley and glowering at him in frustration. The tip of the machete had lacerated the demon's forehead. Green blood oozed down the demon's face and speckled his matted fur. "He goaded you into making a stupid mistake." Angel then asked the demon, "What would have happened?"

"If he had killed me next?" the demon asked. "Two from me . . . and two from every one you've killed so far." He indicated the five green puddles. "The lost stay viable until the entire pack is wiped out."

Angel climbed to his feet and offered Connor his hand.

Shaking his head without making eye contact, Connor said, "I don't need your help."

"Fine," Angel said angrily, and withdrew his hand. "Don't take it."

"And I suppose you don't need mine."

"I've managed on my own."

"Fine," Connor said, tossing his machete to the ground.

Angel shrugged, shook his head, and walked over to six-swirl. "Say good night, Gracie."

"My name's not—"

Whack!

"Like I care," Angel muttered.

Before seven-swirl could wake again confused, Angel put him to sleep permanently.

Eight-swirl, the alpha demon, had climbed to his feet and was standing in the center of the alley. He glanced at Connor, who sat with his head down, projecting apathy, then back at Angel, who was approaching him from the seventh puddle of goo. "Your kid?" the demon asked. Angel nodded. "He's got issues."

"Don't we all?"

The demon glanced down at Angel's sword. "Don't suppose I could offer you anything to—"

"Get real."

"Well, then, if you don't mind, I'd rather not watch as you . . ." The demon made a slicing gesture across his throat with his remaining hand. "I'll turn around so you can—"

"So turn already."

The alpha demon started to turn his back to Angel, then paused and said, "There is one thing you should know."

"And what might that be?" Angel asked skeptically.

"You're already too late."

"What's that supposed to mean?"

"Just that, you're all about to"—the demon lunged at him—"*DIE!*"

Angel jumped and launched a snap kick at the demon's solar plexus, staggering him with a pained grunt. One last time, Angel swung his sword. Eight-swirl fell and dissolved like all the rest. Then each puddle of green goo began to smoke, wafting noxious fumes. In moments, all that remained were dark stains on the ground. *Certainly,* Angel hoped, *nothing viable.*

Connor had climbed to his feet and was walking out of the alley.

Angel called, "Need a ride?"

Connor paused, but didn't look back. "You're not going my way."

Angel waited until his son had gone, then he turned around and kicked the homeless man's battered shopping cart across the alley. He shook his head. "That went well."

Another troubling thought occurred to Angel. Hyconian demons were supposedly harbingers of great evil. Had the alpha demon's warning been real, or merely an attempt to catch Angel off-guard, one last chance to secure its own survival? If the demon had more information about what was coming, Angel should have interrogated him. *Sure, everything's always clear in hindsight.*

"*Already too late . . . you're all about to die,*" the demon had said.

Angel sighed. "That can't be good."

As he made his way back to the GTX, his cell phone rang. For about a half a minute, Angel listened to Fred's hurried explanation of what was transpiring on Hollywood Boulevard before interrupting her. He promised to stop by the hotel to pick up Wesley and Gunn.

"Oh, gee, in all the excitement about the mysterious megalith, I almost forgot to ask what happened with the Order of Hyconus," Fred said before they hung up.

"I sorted them out."

Within an hour, Angel had Wesley and Gunn in the GTX with him as he attempted to navigate the traffic snarls on the way to Hollywood and Vine. Eventually, they decided it would be quicker to park and walk the rest of the way. Whereas Angel and Wesley were dressed in black from neck to toe, Gunn played the part of a tourist in a Phillies baseball cap and a Hawaiian shirt over baggy jeans and boots. Anticipating the police presence at the site, they'd stowed their weapons in the trunk before leaving the Hyperion. Other than the disposable camera Gunn carried in his shirt pocket, they were unarmed.

Before they left, Gunn had said, "Reconnaissance mission. I'm down with that."

"Actually, Wes and I have that part covered. I need you to provide a diversion."

After his first look at the loud Hawaiian shirt, Gunn had balked. "Angel, this is not me. Besides, Wes here would make a better tourist. Man already got the perfect accent for it."

"Wes is our megalith expert. He needs to get close."

"Suppose it's better than bein' the hired muscle again."

Looking at Gunn now, Angel realized that Cordy would have made a more convincing tourist, but he doubted Gunn would want to trade the shirt for an unwieldy stack of moldy books back at the Hyperion. On second thought, book duty would have given Gunn some time alone with Fred. Lately, though, Angel had sensed the tension between those two and wondered where their relationship was heading. Maybe time alone with Fred was the last thing Gunn wanted right now.

As they turned onto Hollywood Boulevard, Angel was relieved to see that the pedestrian crowd had thinned since the early news footage. Tinsel

Town attention spans were short, and expectations had already waned. Many early gawkers must have grown tired of staring at what they came to perceive as a big but ultimately uninteresting piece of rock sculpture in the middle of the highway.

A lone traffic cop remained to direct traffic around the statue, which now had an honor guard of four wooden sawhorses with blinking yellow caution lights to keep passing cars at a safe distance. In addition to towing the Durango from the scene of the accident, the police had cleared the parking lanes in the immediate vicinity so that orange construction cones could outline a new traffic pattern designed to flow around the massive obstruction. Though fine in theory, the plan failed to account for human nature. Drivers slowed to gape at the monolith, creating delays and gridlock, the occasional shriek of brakes, and the indignant honking of horns. Striding from one side of the highway to the other, the traffic cop employed hand waves and shrill whistle blasts to keep drivers attentive and moving.

Angel spotted two television news vans, but neither crew was filming at the moment. In a city accustomed to televised high-speed car chases, the stations' news directors probably had more than enough footage of the large stationary rock. Unless the statue collapsed, caught fire, or returned to the mother-ship, its news value would continue to plummet.

"Good a time as any," Angel said. "Gunn, you ready?"

"Cop's got his hands full already, keepin' those cars moving."

"All the easier to distract him," Wes said with a mischievous smile.

Gunn shook his head doubtfully as he plucked the disposable camera out of his shirt pocket. "This plan better not land my ass in jail."

Timing the flow of traffic through the detour lane, Gunn darted between the slow-moving cars and sauntered out to the middle of the highway, on the west side of the monolith. He raised the camera and took a picture of the statue, then dropped to one knee, turned the camera ninety degrees, and took another one. No reaction from the police officer, who must have seen more than his share of photo-taking pedestrians all evening. Gunn walked several yards closer to the statue, closing on the west side sawhorse. Finally, the cop took notice and intercepted Gunn en route.

"That's our cue," Angel whispered to Wesley.

Clad in black, they crossed the street at a casual but brisk pace and had their first close look at the fifteen-foot-high demonic monolith.

CHAPTER FOUR

"Just takin' some pictures, Officer," Gunn said to the ruddy-faced policeman who looked as if the last ounce of his sense of humor had been wrung out of him hours ago. "Something to show the folks back home in Philly."

"You got your pictures. Now move along."

"Okay, sure . . . but, uh, what do you call this thing, anyway?" Gunn asked as he glanced down to read the narrow name badge on the policeman's uniform. "Don't recall readin' about it in my tour guide, Officer Jarrett."

"It's a new arrival," the cop said sardonically. "Doesn't have a name."

"Does it spin? Or light up or what?"

"No. It sits there quietly and makes my life hell."

"Bet you need all kinds of permits for something like that. I mean, c'mon, a tourist attraction in the middle of the street? That's just askin' for trouble."

The policeman waved his hand and blew the whistle at a driver who had come to a standstill in the eastbound lane. "Keep moving!" Exasperated, he turned back to Gunn. "Look, buddy, don't you watch the news?"

"I'm on vacation," Gunn said, as if the very idea of keeping abreast of current events while on vacation was preposterous.

"Listen, I'm busy here and—"

"That's all right. I'll let you get back to business. See you got your hands full with these rubber-neckin' fools."

"Thank you." Another whistle blast.

"But, um, could I ask one small favor? I was wonderin' if you wouldn't mind posin' in front of—"

"As a matter of fact, I do mind. Now move—"

"Then could you take *my* picture in front of—what's this thing called again?"

"For the last time, buddy, it doesn't have a name, it doesn't do anything, and the only way I'll be taking your picture is with a matching set of fingerprints. Understood?"

As Angel and Wesley neared the monolith, Angel turned his attention away from his surroundings and focused on the statue itself. Twelve feet wide by nine feet deep, the dark gray stone slab tapered as it rose to its fifteen-foot height, like an obelisk whose pyramid cap had been lopped off.

The two faces, each twice as tall as a man, were carved into the broad sides, one facing east, the other west. The western face, the side where Gunn was distracting the police officer, appeared human, but with a contorted expression of intolerable pain, eyes squeezed shut, mouth stretched wide open, as if the model for the sculpture had been screaming in agony. The east face, behind which Angel and Wesley were crouched in concealment, was clearly demonic, with brow ridges, a flattened, furrowed snout, and a fanged mouth, also open wide, but with an expression of rage, not torment.

Considering the faces, Angel wondered if he might have the obelisk analogy backward. What if the faces were the tip of a full-body sculpture? If that were true, the full statue would be over one hundred feet high.

Aside from the subject matter depicted in the carved faces, Angel noticed something else disturbing about the monolith. "You feel that?" he whispered to Wesley.

"What?"

Angel tried to express his emotional and physical response to the statue's presence. "Bad vibes," he said at last. "This not only looks bad, it feels bad. Wrong, somehow. It shouldn't be here. Feels like supernatural radiation poisoning."

Wesley nodded. "Have you noticed the base?

How it seems fused to the highway? There's more to this than can be accounted for by the violent artistic aesthetic of the subject matter." Wesley looked at the ground, at the glittering pieces of plastic, glass, and metal littering the highway, then back at the surface of the statue again. "The Durango struck the monolith on this side, yet there isn't a single scratch here to mark the point of impact." He reached out to touch the stone, his palm almost caressing the surface as he moved his hand side to side in a gentle arc. "I thought so."

"What?"

"There's a slight discrepancy between the visual and tactile surfaces of the megalith."

"Meaning?"

"It registers out of sync to our senses. The surface isn't quite where our eyes tell us it should be. I believe the megalith is slightly out of phase with our dimension."

Angel touched the surface, tracing the curved line of a stone fang, which was slightly farther away than it appeared, an unaccountable refraction of light on the surface of the statue. "And it's vibrating," Angel said. "That can't be good."

Wesley touched the stone again, pausing in utter concentration before finally shaking his head in defeat. "Imperceptible to humans, perhaps. But vibration would certainly confirm my theory."

"Good, you have a theory," Angel said. "Let's hear it."

"What's it gonna be, pal?" Officer Jarrett said as he dramatically patted the handcuffs attached to his service belt.

Gunn hesitated at the implied threat. If he pushed his luck any further, he would definitely be spending some time in lockup. He shuddered at a fleeting vision of becoming lost in the system, his paperwork misfiled, victim of an improper and unrecorded transfer to a maximum-security facility where his protests of innocence would fall on deaf ears, assigned to a chain gang where he'd spend years making little rocks out of big rocks until, one day, in the prison laundry, some lifer decided the best way to settle a petty grudge would be to plant a shiv between Gunn's ribs and leave him for dead.

Enough with the irrational, he thought. *Focus on the situation.*

Gunn glanced over the cop's shoulder at the monolith. He'd seen Angel and Wesley duck behind it to perform their examination, but he hadn't seen them slip away yet. Could be they needed more time. But the last thing he wanted to do was give the cop an excuse to lock him up and lose the key. *That's it,* he thought. *The last thing!*

"Officer Jarrett, please, allow me to tell you how sorry I am," Gunn said, hoping he reeked of sincerity. "In all the excitement of seein' this tower out here, I must have lost what common sense the good Lord gave me. I can't believe I was standing here asking an officer of the law to pose for a picture. I mean, that's whack, you know? I promise I will never, ever—"

Jarrett shook his head. "You don't need—"

"No, no, no, please allow me to apologize. I am completely at fault here and—"

"That's enough."

"But I—"

"Enough!"

Game over, boys, Gunn thought. *This is where me and Officer Angry part company.* "Right! So I'll be leavin' now. . . ." Gunn smiled as he backed away, raising his voice to call out, "Thank you, Officer Jarrett!"

The policeman jabbed a finger toward Gunn's baseball cap. "Count yourself lucky I grew up in Philly."

Gunn sighed. *Hope that was enough time, guys.*

"Running out of time, Wes," Angel said. "Spill it."

"If I'm not mistaken," Wesley said, "the megalith is gradually coming into phase with our dimension."

"Probably not a good thing."

Wesley was about to reply when they heard Gunn yell, "Thank you, Officer Jarrett!"

"Let's move," Angel said. "We'll have to return here, and I'd rather not be too conspicuous yet."

Using the monolith for cover, they stepped outside the perimeter of the sawhorses before walking across the street. After a few steps, a voice called out. "Hey! You two!"

They stopped. Angel tapped his chest innocently.

"Yes, you," Officer Jarrett said, walking toward them.

"Yes, Officer?"

"Next time," he said, pointing toward the intersection, "cross at the light."

"Oh, absolutely," Wesley said.

As they neared the curb, Angel said, "Let's find Gunn and get out of here before we make the next news update."

Cordelia dropped a weighty tome on the already unwieldy stack of books piled on the reception desk. A cloud of dust billowed up around her and Fred, causing them to sneeze in unison. "Ironic, isn't it?" Cordelia said.

"What?"

"Some of these books about monoliths are big enough to *be* monoliths."

Fred pulled the latest volume in front of her, flipped it open, then waved a hand in front of her face to dispel a fresh cloud of dust, but not soon enough to forestall another sneeze. "I'm more worried about death by dust mites."

"They're a lot smaller than the dust bunnies."

"Well, yeah, smaller, but dust mites are alive," Fred said. "They're on your skin, your clothes, your pillowcases, in the air. And now I have about eight billion of them creeping around in my lungs."

"Yuck," Cordelia said with a grimace, but then she smiled. "Look on the bright side . . ."

"What bright side?"

"When you sneezed, you probably gave five billion of them whiplash."

Fred laughed. "Think they'll hit me with a class-action lawsuit?"

"Sshh," Cordelia said, finger pressed to her lips. "Don't give Wolfram and Hart any ideas."

Fred turned a few pages, skimming the text. "Maybe it's part of your vision," Fred said. "The megalith, I mean."

"What are you thinking?"

"Well, first the Order of Hyconus appears, and they're considered harbinger demons," Fred said. "Then this megalith shows up right around the time Angel stomps out the Hyconus. So maybe the megalith is another harbinger, and it's all pointing toward your apocalyptic vision, the arrival of the major big bad."

Cordelia shook her head. "I don't know, Fred. What I saw was horrible—end-of-the-world horrible.

But . . . the Hyconus, and this megalith, not really ringing any vision bells. I think I would know if they were connected. I think I would feel it. This . . . Tinsel Town Tower seems . . . unrelated. Does that make sense?"

"Sure . . . I mean, I guess," Fred said. "As much as this craziness can make sense, it makes sense. There's even a kind of inherent logic to it."

"Right," Cordelia said. She tapped a pen against a legal pad filled with sparse notes and pursed her lips. "Well, I can't say I'm one hundred percent positive they're unrelated."

"Oh . . . ," Fred said, frowning. "You're not?"

"There might be a small chance they're related," Cordelia said. "Not more than two, three percent. Tops."

"Three percent?"

"Definitely not more than five."

When Gunn finally left Officer Jarrett's side, he made a hasty retreat, fading into the crowd of onlookers on the sidewalk without showing any more interest in the monolith. He worried that if he stared at the demonic monument, the police officer would follow his gaze at the precise moment Angel and Wesley decided to come out of hiding behind it. So he blended into the crowd of onlookers who were rapidly losing interest in the massive hunk of rock. Except for one old man in a grease-stained, hooded sweatshirt and threadbare jeans, who was attempting to hold a bottle-shaped brown paper bag inconspicuously under his arm as he stared at the monolith with glazed, almost unblinking eyes. Took Gunn a minute to recognize the look in those red-rimmed eyes. Fear. "Spooky, ain't it," Gunn said, hoping he'd come across as a kindred spirit, even if only one of them was sober.

"Pop."

"Excuse me?"

"It popped," the man said, nodding toward the statue. "Right before that car crashed. Heard it myself."

"That big hunk of rock? It popped?"

"Not the rock," the man said. "The air. Felt it in my ears. Pop"—the man snapped his fingers—"then smash!"

"Did you see how the statue . . . where it came from?"

"Nope," the man said. "Wasn't lookin' that way. I heard the pop, then the crash. One—two! Like that. Turned around and saw the car—one of them big gas guzzlers—had smashed right into it. Car's gone now. Towed away."

"Damn," Gunn said, shaking his head. If the old man had looked a second earlier, he might have witnessed the appearance of the monolith.

After a moment, the man said, "They popped too."

"Who?"

"Folks was in the car."

Gunn grabbed the man's shoulders. "Did you see them? What happened to them?"

"Nobody could see nothing," the man said nervously. "On account of the light that come right out of that thing. They was standing there lookin' all confused, and the wind grabbed 'em. Then the light come out in a flash and they was gone, like the blink of an eye." The man cast a nervous glance at the monolith, as if worried that speaking about it might trigger a recurrence of the phenomenon and this time he would be a victim instead of a witness. "But that ain't the strangest part. . . ."

"It's not?" Gunn dropped his hands from the man's shoulders.

The man shook his head slowly. "What happened next . . . don't know how to describe it except to say *dark* light . . . flashed out the other side, as dark as the white light was blinding, if you know what I mean."

"Dark light?"

"Right . . . and two dark . . . figures appeared on the other side."

"Dark how? Brothers?"

"No, not like that. Like armored . . . storm troopers, you know," the man explained. "And there was something . . . weird about the way they moved."

"L.A. weird?" Gunn asked, imagining the bobbing

and swaying forms of Venice Beach Rollerbladers, but knowing the man's response would point to something far more insidious than a little roller-boogie.

The man shook his head. "Not L.A. weird. Martian weird. Whatever they were, it wasn't human." He shuddered, then pointed to the south side of the intersection of Hollywood and Ivar, his extended arm trembling. "They ran that way," he said. "Like bats outta hell."

"Gunn!"

Wesley's voice.

Gunn glanced back along the sidewalk and saw Angel and Wesley approaching. He waved them over. "Listen, you mind tellin' my friends what—"

"This is a setup, ain't it?"

"What?"

"It's a trick! You set me up!"

"No, man, it's cool," Gunn said hurriedly. "Honest."

"Why do I have the feeling you're about to tell me this problem can't be solved with a precise application of high explosives?" Angel said softly as they walked among the spectators on the crowded sidewalk. "Not that we have high explosives . . . but I know a guy."

"I believe the megalith is impervious to damage in its prephase state," Wesley said. "The impact of the Durango failed to scratch it."

"So let's wait till it's in phase," Angel said. "Then—*boom!*"

"We would need to know the precise moment it came into phase," Wesley said, shaking his head. "And its purpose."

"I'm willing to chance—"

"Really, Angel, I would hesitate to—"

"This thing has piqued your curiosity, hasn't it, Wes?"

"Not at all," Wesley said, stopping to make his case. "I'm certain it will serve no good purpose, but neither will an ill-timed explosion. Suppose for a moment that this megalith is designed to open a portal to another dimension—a reasonable hypothesis given the face symbolism. Then is it not also reasonable to assume that an explosion might create an even larger portal? Or create a permanent rift instead of a temporary opening? Explosive energy might provide just the fuel to make a bad situation catastrophic. Would you really want to chance *that?*"

"One of these days, Wes," Angel said. "High explosives will be the perfect solution to one of our not-so-little problems. For now, let's find—"

"Gunn! There he is," Wesley said, pointing. "Next to that suspicious-looking man."

Angel cast a sidelong glance at Wesley. "Wes, that's a wino. The only thing he's suspicious of is being homeless."

"Regardless of his social status," Wesley said defensively, "the man looks ready to flee."

"Can't say I blame him," Angel muttered.

"Gunn!" Wesley called.

Gunn looked toward them, indicated they should hurry over, then returned his attention to the man, who seemed more agitated than he had been a moment ago.

As they drew near, Gunn told the man, "It's all right, man. These guys are cool."

Angel asked, "Who is this?"

The man eyed him suspiciously. "Who are you?"

"Interested parties."

"I know who you are," the man said, his red-rimmed eyes wild with paranoia. "You're with one of them secret government agencies."

"Hardly," Wesley said. "We're private—"

"I heard how you make people disappear," the man said, verging on panic. "Well, you're not taking me."

"We have no intention of—"

Gunn interrupted. "Tell them what you saw."

The man shook his head. "Didn't see nothing," he said, starting to back away. "Just mindin' my own business, is all." He looked past them. "I knew it! Here comes another one!"

"What—?" Angel followed his gaze and saw Connor striding purposely toward them. "Connor?"

"Wait!" Wesley shouted.

Angel turned and saw the man running down the street in the opposite direction. Gunn caught Wesley's arm before he could give chase. "Let him go, Wes," Gunn said. "He won't talk to y'all now. Besides, I got his story."

"What's up?" Connor asked as he joined the group. "Other than stone face over there?"

"Thought you weren't going my way," Angel said.

Connor shrugged. "Small world." He glanced at the monolith, then back at Angel. "You get a good look at that thing?"

"Yes," Angel said. "Why?"

"I don't know," Connor said with a smirk. "Two-faced demon with fangs. Reminds me of you."

Gunn chuckled. "Nothin' personal, Angel, but the fang-face side does bear a slight resemblance to—"

"Setting aside petty jibes and insults for the moment, let's concentrate on the matter at hand," Wesley said in an attempt to steer the group away from the ever percolating animosity Connor employed in his interactions with Angel. "I believe this megalith is coming into phase with our dimension and there's little chance its purpose is benign. We need to find a way to stop the process before it's too late."

"'Too late' came and went, Wes," Gunn said. "Way I hear it, the tower of terror is already spitting out the nasties."

CHAPTER FIVE

Connor had edged close to the monolith until he picked up the scent of something other than human, something demonic. Knowing the two escaped demons had fled south on Ivar Avenue, Connor took that path on faith. He'd offered to follow the hours' old trail because he was the most qualified, and because it afforded the quickest path to unleashing some unbridled rage.

Angel confused him—a vampire with a soul who was also, incredibly, Connor's long-estranged father—but most demons were easy outlets for a bit of self-righteous fury. Not easy because they were weak—far from it—but because they lacked ambiguity. Connor's sense of right and wrong had been forged in a hell dimension, where everything was black and white. No shades of gray. Ambiguity caused indecision, and in Quor-Toth, indecision could get you killed.

Angelus was evil, but Angel was good. Yet the

potential for Angelus remained inside Angel, caged beneath the surface. Angel was skin deep, with Angelus one mistake away from taking over the body they shared. How could Connor trust something like that? And yet, the more Connor learned about his father, the more confused and conflicted he became. He couldn't kill Angel, but he wasn't prepared to ignore or forgive the part of his father that was Angelus. In comparison, most demons were easy to understand, if not always easy to kill. Connor would never say he was homesick for Quor-Toth, but he had to admit he was most comfortable in Angel's world when he had some convenient demons to hack and smash.

After sprinting for almost a mile, Connor stopped, nostrils flaring at the coppery scent of human blood. A lot of blood. In the dark, his eyes tracked the gruesome remains scattered across a well-manicured lawn, glistening in the reflected light of a streetlamp.

Shredded, Connor thought. Dismembered limbs; flesh ripped from gleaming white bone; a trail of organs and intestines; a man's mashed and serrated face, with a fringe of gray hair, clinging to a crushed skull. Blood tacky and cool to the touch.

The first victim, Connor thought, *but this one won't be the last.*

Miles away, in front of a second-story window of a condemned office building, Sehjenkhai stood with his hands clasped behind his back. Had his eyes been open, it would have appeared as though he were looking out into the night. Instead of staring out, he turned his mind inward, tapping into his other sense, and reaching out to the otherworldly presence he'd detected a short time ago, after the third and final tremor. *It is out there now, closer than it has ever been, and yet far away. It is a bridge, a passage, a gate, a door, and a key. All of those things and none of them, and so much more. Already it has delivered on its dark promise. Two beings. A mere sample of what is soon to come, of what cannot be stopped, a leak in a dam about to crumble and change the landscape forever.*

In the deeper shadows behind him, his demon mastiffs sat on their haunches, panting. In the dark, their yellow eyes burned like unearthly jewels. They waited in silence upon the will of their master.

Sehjenkhai extended his mind, reaching out to the new arrivals. As he sensed them, they sensed him. In a heated rush of emotion, he knew what they were and what they had done. That they had flaunted their supremacy over humans, unleashed their rage upon any who had the misfortune to cross their paths. That they risked discovery and worse.

He called to their minds, becoming a beacon in this strange new world so that he might guide them to him, offer them sanctuary and secrecy until the crossing was at hand. *When the gate swings wide, my long centuries of caution will be over,* he thought. For a few days more, the new arrivals and Sehjenkhai would have to abide the world of men.

He spoke to their minds: *"Their rage has given you lease upon this land, but you must control yourselves now. Run not wild, but make haste to me. We will wait. And soon, we will be legion."*

When Angel and Wesley returned to the Hyperion, Cordelia and Fred looked up from behind twin mounds of books, splayed around two legal pads upon which the women had written several pages of scrawled notes. Littering the reception desk were crumpled balls of paper, several of which had spilled over onto the lobby floor.

Cordelia looked up at them with a hopeful smile, but Fred wore a concerned expression. "Where's Charles?"

"Stayed behind to keep an eye on the monolith," Angel said.

"What was it like?" Cordelia asked. "More exciting than the made-for-TV version, I hope."

Fred was more animated. "Any secret engravings or mysterious runes for us to decipher?"

"Nothing so linear, unfortunately," Wesley said. He explained his theory that the megalith was coming into phase with their dimension and, while out of phase, was impervious to harm.

Angel told them what Gunn had learned from the eyewitness, including his description of two escaped demons. "Connor is attempting to track their scent," he finished.

"Those two must be part of some sort of vanguard action," Wesley said. "Most likely reconnaissance for whomever or whatever is behind the appearance of the megalith."

"Wait!" Cordelia said, alarmed. "How do we know there aren't more than two escapees?"

"Unlikely," Wesley said. "Since its appearance, the megalith has been under constant observation."

"Those two were able to sneak away in the initial confusion," Angel said. "If anything else tries to crawl out of there, it will be on all the news stations. Plus, Gunn will call us the moment anything unusual happens."

Wesley gestured toward the mounds of books. "Any luck on the research end?"

"We've looked through every volume concerning megaliths, monoliths, whatever," Cordelia said. "And no joy."

"Up to our ears in dolmens and menhirs," Fred quipped. Her smile faltered a bit when her joke didn't go over as well as she had expected. "That is, um, most megaliths are simply massive upright slabs of stone. We found no picture, drawing, or description of anything as elaborate as the double-face design. Even the faces on the Easter Island statues are crude in comparison. They've all been around for thousands of years. We also checked the Net, looking for recent appearances of mega-liths anywhere else in the world—"

"And, again, no joy," Cordelia said.

For the moment, they seemed at a loss. Angel recalled something Wes had said at the site. "Wes, you mentioned something about face symbolism."

Wesley nodded. "Janus was the two-faced Roman god of change and transitions, for whom the month of January was named. Originally his two faces represented the sun and the moon. One was bearded, the other clean-shaven, and they were usually depicted with a key. Janus embodied various progressions in nature, day into night, past into future, planting into harvesting. He was also seen as the balance between barbarity and civilization."

"Or, maybe," Angel suggested, "civilization into barbarity?"

"That's a big assumption," Cordelia said. "L.A. being civilized."

"I don't see why not," Wesley said, answering Angel's question. "Other than the flow of time, those progressions are circular."

"Ah," Cordelia said, nodding. "The circle of life."

"Includes a whole lot of death," Angel added.

"Whoa, Angel-cakes," Lorne said as he stepped into the lobby and joined them at the reception desk. "Let's not take morbid liberties with a classic Disney soundtrack."

"Any word from your sources, Lorne?" Wesley asked.

"Everyone I talked to in the demon underground was as surprised as we were by the megalith-in-the-box."

Angel told him about the two escapee demons. "Assuming Connor loses their trail, they'll probably go into hiding."

"Gotcha, chief," Lorne said. "I'll stay tangled in the demon grapevine. Any new players hit town, we'll be the first to know about it."

Wesley's face lit up. "Perhaps we're wrong to take the direct approach—with regard to research, that is. I have several volumes of lore on transdimensional relics. We should cross-reference megaliths in those."

"Ugh, more books," Cordelia moaned as Wesley left to retrieve the volumes. She massaged her temples and tried to look contrite. "Sorry, guys. Of course, I meant to say, hooray, more books!"

Angel shrugged sympathetically. "I'm open to suggestions."

"I prefer the TV theory," Cordelia said. "The news stations are convinced this is an elaborate stunt orchestrated by Antoine Renard, the director of *Zombie Island Princess*. You know what the KTLA reporter said? 'The movie premiered hours before the statue premiered.' And she doesn't think that's a coincidence."

Recalling the bad vibes he had sensed coming from the monolith, Angel shook his head, discounting the broadcast news theory. "Whatever that thing is," he said, "it's not a movie prop or some publicity stunt."

"Plus, how would that explain the escapee demons?" Fred asked Cordelia.

"Maybe they just happened to be nearby when mega-rock appeared, and it scared the bejeebers out of them."

"But how could the megalith appear out of nowhere?" Fred countered.

Cordelia shrugged. "Ask David Copperfield," she said. "He made the Statue of Liberty disappear. A fifteen-foot rock tower would be a piece of cake."

Behind them, the television was on with the volume muted. Angel saw an image of the smashed Durango. He walked behind the reception desk and said, "What's this?"

"Oh, well, the rock doesn't exactly scream 'action news,' so they've been replaying tape from earlier this evening," Cordelia said. "That's one of the high energy shots with actual movement, when they towed away the wrecked car."

•

The camera zoomed in on the back of the car as the tow truck driver finished the hookup, then held the shot as the SUV was towed from the scene of the accident. "Delaware plates," Angel said. "And that's a national car rental agency bumper sticker." He looked over to Cordelia. "Have they released the names of the occupants?"

"No," Cordelia said, catching his idea. "But you're wondering if maybe I could hack into the rental agency's computer and find out the name of the last renter."

"At least it's not another book," Angel said.

"Say no more," Cordelia said. "I'm on it."

Fred turned to Angel. "Are you thinking the people in the car were somehow responsible for . . . conjuring the megalith?"

"Probably wrong place, wrong time," Angel said. "But there's a small chance they were involved and it blew up in their face. We need to examine every possibility."

"On that note, Angel-buns," Lorne said. "Maybe you shouldn't be so fast to give Antoine Renard a get-out-of-jail-free card."

"I touched it, Lorne," Angel said. "It's not some Hollywood special effect. It's the real deal."

"Hey, I'm not pooh-poohing the major bad mojo vibe, chief," Lorne said. "But if somebody conjured that insta-wall, ask yourself who had more to gain, a couple of Dela-renters or—"

"A movie director with a multimillion-dollar movie to promote."

"Exactamundo."

"Okay," Angel said. "Renard's worth a look."

After Lorne left to let his contacts know he'd be interested in hearing about any new players in town, Angel decided to leave the others to their research and computer hacking and look for Connor. The boy could handle himself better than any human—with the possible exception of a Slayer—but there were at least two escapees out there, if not more. If they split up, Connor would have to choose one to track, which left one free and clear. And if they stayed together, Connor might need backup.

The hours had seemed like days.

Uneventful, unenlightening, and utterly uninteresting.

Gunn must have slipped into a boredom-induced stupor at some point before calling it a night. Leaning against a traffic light with just a little bit of drool on his chin. Okay, maybe he had imagined that last part. But at some point he must have passed boredom on his way to walking catatonia. He had imagined the excitement of watching grass grow, lounging in a hammock with a beer in hand, or the thrill of watching paint dry, on the off-chance the fumes might produce some interesting hallucinations. He'd pictured himself on the edge of his seat, waiting for a phone to ring, and welcoming a call from a carpet-cleaner telemarketer. The rock—or The Rock, as he'd come to think of it—had them all beat in the boredom department. Hands down. No contest.

He'd tried to pass the time talking to the gradually dispersing spectators, hoping to find another witness, but every one of them had come after seeing The Rock on TV. Nobody could tell him anything he didn't already know or suspect. When Officer Jarrett was relieved, Gunn decided he'd had enough as well.

An hour before dawn, he made his way back to the Hyperion to tell them he had nothing to report. As he entered the lobby, he succumbed to a jaw-cracking yawn, and gazed longingly at the round banquette.

Fred was sleeping at the reception desk, using an opened book as a pillow. In Angel's office, Wesley had fallen asleep in the chair, chin against his chest, a pile of opened books on the desk before him. *Those two warm and cozy,* he thought. *And lucky me gets to spend all night starin' at a butt-ugly jumbo statue.* He took a deep breath and thought, *At least they're not sleeping together. Not beside each other, knocking heads.*

Angel returned to the hotel a moment later, wearing a grim, haunted expression that almost made Gunn thankful for his uneventful night. Cordelia joined them and started a fresh pot of coffee. "Anything happen at the statue?" Angel asked Gunn.

"Nope."

"What about all the excitement this morning?" Cordelia said.

"Excitement?" Gunn said. "Waited all night at that statue and, other than three fender benders, there was no excitement. Period. Unless you're talkin' about the mangy dog and the fire hydrant."

"No, Gunn, fortunately, I missed the dog," Cordelia said. "I was talking about the construction crane they brought in to move mega-rock. Five-hundred-ton lifting capacity. About a half hour ago. All the local news affiliates carried it live."

"Damn," Gunn said. "Waited all night for nothing and soon as I leave . . ."

"They couldn't move it," Angel said. It wasn't a question.

Cordelia gave him a questioning look. "How . . . ?"

"It's not here yet," Angel said.

Wesley joined them, running a hand through his hair. Either the talk or the smell of fresh coffee had roused him. "It can't be damaged or moved until it's in phase with our world."

"Well, you're both right," Cordelia said. "They couldn't budge it an inch. Some spectators are calling it a miracle. They're talking about holding a candlelight vigil. And there's lots of talk on the Internet chat rooms and newsgroups. Some people have already formed a doomsday cult based on the statue's mysterious appearance, calling it a sign of the impending apocalypse."

"Ought to be a law," Gunn said. "One apocalypse at a time."

Wesley looked at Angel. "Were you able to find Connor last night?" he asked. "Any luck tracking the escaped demons?"

"Found Connor," Angel said. "We followed a trail of . . . well, entrails, for a while."

Cordelia grimaced. "Whose, um, entrails?"

"Apparently anyone who got in their way," Angel said. "Innocent bystanders. Teenager on a skateboard. Old woman out walking her miniature schnauzer. Some of the . . . pieces . . ." He shook his head, reliving some of the gruesome images. "Like butcher's scraps, tossed aside."

Cordelia dropped into a chair and whispered, "Oh, God."

"We lost them in Inglewood," Angel continued. "It was odd, as if they'd suddenly realized they were leaving a trail of gore for us to follow."

"More likely someone warned them to cover their tracks," Wesley said. "Or to stop making tracks."

"Our monolith conjuror," Angel guessed.

Wesley nodded. "Precisely," he said. "Late last night, Fred—"

Fred's sleepy mumbling interrupted him. Her hand, sprawled across an open book, twitched. "'Persecution by the Book,' for five hundred, Alex . . . what is the Malleus . . ." Fred sat up, blinking her eyes groggily. ". . . Maleficarum?" She looked at all of them, confused, then embarrassed. "Oh, this isn't, I mean, I was dreaming."

They continued to stare.

"Oh—I was on *Occult Jeopardy*," she said, shrugging. "And . . . I think Alex Trebek was a golem. He's not, right? A golem, I mean."

"Last time I checked," Gunn said, with an amused smile. *Considering the alternative,* he thought, with a suspicious glance at Wesley, *I'll take a* weird *Fred dream every time.*

"Right. Because that was just part of the—okay, I'm done now."

"As I was saying," Wesley continued. "Last night Fred pointed out the potentially unique nature of this type of dimensional portal. Most portals are rather instantaneous and represent temporary rifts between dimensions. As such, the threats posed by them are transitory. The appearance of the megalith so far in advance of the actual portal opening suggests that this dimensional rift might have a protracted nature, representing a long-term, possibly permanent threat from some unknown quarter."

"Other than the Janus face symbolism, why use a monolith at all?" Angel asked.

"Right," Gunn said. "Why give us the heads up? And don't none of y'all say 'two heads are better than one.'"

"Not always true, by the way," Angel commented mysteriously.

"Anyway, I can only speculate," Wesley continued. "Earth's ancient megalithic sites are oriented toward solstice points on the horizon. They mark sunrise or sunset at summer and winter solstice. Others mark lunar events. But this megalith may have a far more nefarious purpose. Its appearance could signal the approach of optimal conditions for a major dimensional gateway."

Fred was nodding, practically beaming at Wesley.

Gunn noticed and frowned. Despite himself, he couldn't help thinking about Wesley and Fred getting cozy together all night with the books. *The farther I am from Fred,* he thought, *the closer she seems to Wesley.* "You're talking about a demonic equinox."

Wesley nodded toward Gunn, but addressed everyone. "The mere occurrence of a 'demonic equinox' is not, in itself, sufficient to open the portal. Taking Fred's idea of a protracted portal, I finally found information relevant to the current situation."

Angel's interest was piqued. "How so?"

"If the portal is the door, the Summoner is the key. Or the means by which the key is formed. An elaborate ritual of sacrifices must be performed—

and apparently has been performed—in the year prior to the equinox."

"Any idea who this Summoner is?" Angel asked.

Wesley shook his head. "No, unfortunately. The entry was incomplete. Nothing to indicate what qualifications are necessary for one to become a Summoner. And no further information about the nature of the sacrifices required to leverage the equinox. However, now that I know what I'm looking for, I have other sources of information that might prove valuable."

"Good," Angel said. "Find out what you can about the Summoner, Wes. Odds are, if we find the person responsible, we'll know how much time we have left to stop this."

"This makes no sense," Gunn said. "Of all the places for this mega-rock monolith to appear, why Hollywood?"

Cordelia chuckled. "Hollywood is the perfect place!"

"Say what?"

"Think about it. All those people out there on the street. Candlelight vigils. Don't you get it? Idol worship in Tinsel Town! Oh, forget big, goony two-face and think little golden man." Cordelia struck a stiff, upright pose, legs together, hands against her abdomen, one over the other, as if she gripped the hilt of a sword. Everyone stared at her, clueless. "Hello? Anyone?" Then, in a serious voice, she said, "And the Oscar for Best Apocalypse goes to . . ."

CHAPTER SIX

Angel sat behind his office desk, sipping from the tall glass of pig's blood he'd warmed in the microwave as he flipped through the accumulation of notes. They'd made some progress, but not nearly enough. Until they learned the identity of the Summoner or captured one of the escaped demons, they were just killing time until the arrival of the demonic equinox.

Wesley and Fred continued to look for information that might help them expose the identity of the Summoner, anything to narrow the search in a city of 10 million. In the meantime, they had a few mundane leads to track down, including the possibility that Antoine Renard, the director of *Zombie Island Princess*, might be involved.

Angel was about to take another absentminded sip of pig's blood when he heard Cordelia entering the office. He pushed the glass aside, feeling a bit awkward. Everyone at Angel Investigations knew he was a vampire. At the same time, he suspected none of them were comfortable watching him drink blood, even the porcine variety. "Yes?"

Cordelia held several sheets of paper, which she waved dramatically as she approached the desk. "Fruits of my hacking," she said. "Searched the rental car agency's database for records associated with the license number of the damaged Durango. Rented ten days ago from the Wilmington, Delaware, office. Two drivers listed, also from Wilmington: Ronald and Carol Baker."

"We know anything about them?"

"Like, are they the Summoner type?" Cordelia asked. "I Googled them and found something. Apparently they were on an extended vacation. Carol was keeping a blog—that is, a Web log, kind of an online journal—on the family Web page. They were—*are*—a couple of empty nesters in their fifties, driving cross-country. Carol posted digital photos of their stops along the way. Last one was Vegas, posted yesterday morning, before they checked out of their hotel."

"Tourists."

"Or one hell of a cover story," Cordelia said. "Dead end, huh?"

Angel nodded. "Any word from Lorne?"

"No, but he's due to check in soon."

"Anything else?"

"Just so happens I had a little chat with an actress friend of mine—I still have a few—and she knows somebody who happens to know where a certain up-and-coming film director always likes to have lunch whenever he's in town." Cordelia handed Angel one of her sheets of paper, which had the name of a restaurant on it. "Voilà!"

"Thanks, Cordy. Good work," Angel said. "One more thing. I need you to track down everyone who worked on that film. Find out if they noticed anything unusual before, during, or after production."

"One impossibly tall order coming right up," Cordelia said, finding it difficult to maintain her good-natured smile.

It was hard for Angel to look at Cordelia and not think about what could have been—what almost had been. He'd known Cordelia since her high school days in Sunnydale and he, more than anyone, had witnessed her complete transformation from materialistic teen queen to compassionate young woman. When her family had suffered financial collapse, she moved to L.A. and pursued her dream of becoming an actress. That dream never materialized, but working with Angel, which had started out as a part-time job to help pay the rent, had become her passion and her purpose. After losing everything she thought was important to her, she had found what truly mattered.

Throughout it all, her courage had been a constant. Years had passed and Angel accepted that what he had left behind in Sunnydale was truly gone, that it was time to move on. When he finally allowed himself to feel again, he shouldn't have been surprised by the mutual attraction he and Cordelia shared.

She had known Angel's nature for years and accepted him for what he was, and she had dedicated herself to the work that had given his life new meaning. He appreciated the woman she had become, and he had begun to depend on her in his life. They had been working toward a real connection, something they were finally prepared to admit to each other, when fate had sent them on a wild detour. While Cordelia was tagged to become a higher being and exist on another plane, Angel's confused and vengeful son was consigning him to eternity at the bottom of the ocean.

After several months, Angel had resurfaced, and eventually Cordelia had reappeared, but they couldn't simply pick up the pieces. For one thing, Cordelia returned with amnesia, unable to remember her prior life or her existence as a higher being. Worse, she had no idea that Angel was no longer a card-carrying human. Lorne had found a way to restore Cordelia's memory but, in addition to her human memories, she regained access to everything she had learned on the higher plane, including complete and intimate knowledge of all Angel's atrocities during the century and a half when his demonic side, Angelus, had reigned as the terror of Europe.

Angel had spent a hundred years coming to terms with his numerous crimes against humanity. How could he expect Cordelia to accept it in a few days or weeks—or in a human lifetime?

He had been content to stand back and give her as much time as she needed. But Connor had stepped into that gap. He'd developed feelings for Cordelia, and, for her part, in all the confusion of her return, Cordelia had responded to his caring and protectiveness enough to give the boy hope that she might reciprocate his feelings. Naturally, Connor's animosity toward Angel was compounded by his belief that Angel was keeping him from the woman he loved. The whole situation was like a knot that became tighter the more its ends were tugged.

"Look, Cordy," Angel said, "I know it seems like an impossible task now. But somehow we manage to pull off the impossible around here . . . what, at least once a week?"

Cordelia quirked a genuine smile. "No," she said. "Improbable is every week. Impossible is alternate Wednesdays."

"My mistake," Angel said, his own mood buoyed by her resiliency.

"I'll get right on it," she said as she left his office, calling back over her shoulder, "Oh, and you might want to wipe that spot of blood off your chin before you see any paying clients."

He checked, but of course there was no spot of blood on his chin. She was acknowledging that she'd seen him drinking the blood and letting him know it wasn't something that disturbed her. Even in sarcasm, she gave him hope. Was it any wonder he'd fallen for her?

After checking the time, he glanced at the restaurant address, a destination in daylight he'd have to reach via sewer tunnels. He'd hoped to get an update from Lorne before leaving, but decided he'd better not wait any longer. Grabbing the half-filled glass of pig's blood, he raised it to his lips and drank deeply.

Unannounced, Connor walked through his office doorway. "Tried again, but wherever they are, they're lying low—" Connor froze, a look of disgust on his face. He shook his head in disbelief and revulsion. "Sometimes I almost forget what you really are."

Angel set the glass down deliberately. "And what would that be?"

"Holtz was right," Connor said. "You're one of them. You look human. Usually. You pretend you're human. But you're not. You're one of them. Another disgusting demon. The enemy."

Not this again, Angel thought. But he refused to back down, not without defending himself. "Yes, Connor, I'm a vampire. Never denied it. But I hope my actions are more important than what I have for breakfast. And I'm sorry this world isn't as simple as Quor-Toth. It's a little more complicated here than human good, demon bad. Besides, Holtz was no sai—"

Connor stepped forward aggressively and pointed at Angel's face. "Maybe you should wipe the blood off your mouth before you talk about Holtz."

Angel touched the rim of the glass. "It's pig's blood."

"Like that's so much better!"

Though Angel blamed himself for Holtz's violent obsession, the man had crossed a line when he'd corrupted an innocent life in his quest for revenge. Holtz had kidnapped Connor as an infant, brainwashed him in Quor-Toth to hate Angel, and had staged his own death to appear as though Angel had murdered him. If Holtz had kidnapped Connor to raise him as a surrogate son, to replace the family Angelus had destroyed, then Angel might have forgiven the man, in time. But Holtz had not raised a son—he'd forged a weapon. The perfect patricidal weapon to fulfill his own desire for revenge. Holtz had denied Connor a normal childhood filled with wonder and possibilities and love.

Instead, he'd taught the boy how to hunt and kill, how to hate and exact revenge.

In one fateful moment—Holtz's leap into Quor-Toth with the infant bundled in his arms—so many of Connor's opportunities had been forever lost. None of which mattered to Connor at the moment, because where Holtz was concerned, Connor was irrational. He remained steadfastly loyal to Holtz's memory and would not allow anyone, especially Angel, to question Holtz's place on his posthumous pedestal. Never mind that Holtz had died a false martyr. Wherever Angel was concerned, Connor's old patterns of hate and loathing kicked in, a conditioned response Angel could never trump with something as simple and direct as logic.

Before Angel said anything he might regret, Lorne stepped into the office and tried to defuse the situation. "Neutral corners, kiddies. What's all this fuss about pig's blood? A serving of steak tartare or a plate of sushi and you're more than halfway there, if you ask me."

Connor gave Lorne a deliberate appraisal, as if seeing him for the first time and finding him lacking. "Of course you'd take his side."

"*Moi?*"

Connor glared at Angel and had one last parting gibe before storming out of the office. "Don't know what she sees in you."

That's it, Angel realized. *Cordy walked out of here smiling just before Connor came in. Figures he's losing her. Not that he ever had her in the first place, but . . . he was looking for an excuse—any excuse—to start a fight.*

"Honk if I'm out of line here, boss, but a few dozen anger-management classes would not be wasted on Junior Jump-down-your-throat."

"He'll cool off," Angel said, then frowned. "Eventually. Got anything?"

"Nothing on the two newbies. They're lying lower than low," Lorne said. "Otherwise, general rumblings in the demon community, but nothing specific. There's definitely a surprise party in the offing, but nobody's received an invitation. About half of them say this town might be getting too crowded real soon."

"Demon invasion," Angel said grimly.

"Took the apocalypse right out of my mouth."

Lorne had turned to leave when Angel asked, "What about the other half? What do they say?"

"That if they wait around long enough, the demon underground won't have to bother with the whole *under* thing so much."

Unless one counted the stack of newspapers and trade papers next to his plate, dapper Antoine Renard was eating alone. And if the size of the pastrami on rye indicated a healthy appetite, then the number of papers folded open to reviews, gossip, or celebrity columns showed an equally hungry ego.

Green's Quake Deli on Sunset Boulevard resembled a long, spotless tunnel lined with white tile, chrome rails, and a twin procession of small Formica tables. Fortunately for Angel, the entrance and the row of small windows faced an overshadowed alley.

At randomly spaced intervals, the walls and the ceiling were decorated with faux cracks, a theme chosen to illustrate the general equanimity of Californians, perhaps, or to bestow upon the deli diners a state of grace under pressure. *Either that,* Angel thought, *or a not-so-subtle attempt to discourage diners from lingering at their tables during lunch hour.*

Renard sat at the back corner table, as far from the commotion of the deli ordering counter as possible, his back to the wall. Aside from a slight paunch, every detail about the director's appearance was impeccable. From his expensive, tailored gray suit to his gleaming black Italian loafers, from his close-cropped red hair with its dramatic widow's peak to his precisely sculpted goatee. Even the three diamond stud earrings in each earlobe seemed to form equilateral triangles.

A perfectionist, Angel thought. *Not the type to suffer fools gladly or interruptions lightly. A self-important stickler for detail with zero tolerance for impropriety. But is he also the type to employ—or condone—supernatural assistance to boost his box office receipts? Time to ruffle some feathers.*

As Angel approached the table, Renard spoke without looking at him. "Where is it?"

"What?"

"Your screenplay, of course," Renard said, glaring at Angel as if he were brain-damaged. "You just happened to have brought it with you to lunch today, and by freakish chance—will miracles never cease—you've stumbled upon renowned director Antoine Renard. At last, your big break has arrived. Your talent will be discovered, and your masterpiece will revolutionize filmmaking as we know it. How am I doing so far?"

"Wait—you're renowned?" Angel asked as he slipped into the seat facing Renard. "I had no idea who you were before yesterday."

"Yes, well, I'm sure my films would tax your meager intellect."

"Yeah, I hear *Zombie Island Princess* is real deep."

Renard jabbed his right index finger at one of the longer movie reviews. "Yes, well, this one says the film is 'a cleverly veiled metaphor for the mindless conformity wrought on the masses by a media-saturated society.'"

Angel tapped a paragraph in another review, "This one says 'naked native girls with buckets of blood and guts.' But, hey, gotta break a few eggs to make an omelette, right?"

"Obviously you're not here to dazzle me with your rapier wit."

"Nor to enjoy your mixed metaphors," Angel said, fingering the extra place setting. "This is a nice place. Cloth napkin. Stainless-steel flatware. One would expect plastic utensils and paper napkins in a deli, but no. This is a high-class establishment."

"If you're thinking of dining here," Renard said, "you should know I plan on having management toss you out on your presumptuous ass."

"Fortunately, I've already eaten," Angel said, holding the fork up as if he were checking for dishwasher spots.

"You were about to explain your purpose here," Renard prompted impatiently. It clearly bothered the director that he'd been forced to leave the rest of his sandwich on his plate uneaten. He desperately wanted his lunch to proceed as planned.

"I have a question."

"Ah, you're with some local gossip rag, looking for an exclusive interview," Renard said with a knowing nod. "Forget it. Run along."

"Not an interview," Angel said, leaning forward menacingly. "A question."

"Then ask your stupid question and leave, you annoying cretin."

"The Hollywood Boulevard statue," Angel said. "How did you manage that?"

"Oh, this nonsense again," Renard said, rolling his eyes. "I've already spoken ad nauseam to the police about this. I certainly have nothing to say to you." Renard snatched up the napkin in his lap. "Now, if you'll excuse me, I must tell Sal to toss you out on the street and ban you permanently from the premises."

As Renard started to rise, Angel slammed the fork tines down through the cuff of his suit sleeve and into the Formica tabletop. Angel's expression was taut. "What makes you think I would let you do that, Antoine?"

Renard was aghast. He stared at the tines pinning his suit to the table and spoke in a voice almost breathless with incredulity. "This is a three-thousand-dollar suit!"

"Past tense."

"Who are you?" Renard hissed, glancing down the length of the deli.

Angel couldn't tell if the man was more concerned about his safety or about causing a scene in a public place. Either way, the situation worked in Angel's favor. "Answer the question."

"I can't answer your infernal question," Renard said. "Because I had nothing to do with the appearance of that stone monstrosity. There are a couple hundred witnesses who will testify that I was inside Mann's Chinese Theatre watching the premiere of my film when that blasted statue was discovered."

"Lots of people work for you, for the studio," Angel said. "Lots of people looking to impress the 'renowned director.'"

"I assure you that nobody in my employ or under instructions from me had anything to do with that statue. As to the rest, I can't answer for the actions of fools hoping to impress me. Good enough?"

"What about the studio?"

"The damn thing is in the middle of a busy highway," Renard said. "The liability issues would give them nightmares. What do you think?"

"I'm thinking that you, as a big fan of 'buckets of blood and guts' filmmaking, probably know a few creative uses for a fork."

"What?" Renard said softly. His fear had turned inward.

"I'm sure you see what I mean," Angel said. "For now, anyway."

Renard blinked rapidly. "I swear it's the truth! I had nothing to do with it. Pure coincidence. That's all. Am I grateful for the publicity? Yes! Who wouldn't be? Listen"—Renard's voice dropped to a desperate whisper—"I—I haven't had a hit in years. If that damn rock helps sell tickets, I'll throw it on a flatbed and take it on a cross-country tour. Now, please . . . please go."

Angel lifted the fork out of the fractured table-top and out of the suit, examining its mangled tines briefly before tossing it aside. "A tour, huh? Guess you haven't heard," Angel said as he stood. "They can't budge the thing."

CHAPTER SEVEN

It was hard for Fred to spend so much time researching transdimensional portals without thinking about the five years of her life she'd spent exiled in Pylea, where demon masters treated humans—Fred included—like livestock. She'd escaped, eventually, and hid in a cave, slowly losing her grip on her own humanity. Until Angel had saved her, after coming to Pylea to rescue Cordelia. *A two-for-one special,* Fred thought with a light chuckle.

Of course, thinking about Pylea reminded her of Professor Seidel, the man responsible for conjuring the portal that had sent her there in the first place. But that was information she'd discovered only after Seidel, a man she had considered her mentor, tried to send her through another portal so that he could continue to take credit for her theoretical physics work. Discovering that first betrayal in the wake of the second had caused something to snap inside Fred's mind. Though she'd plotted her revenge against Seidel with Wesley, she'd exacted that revenge with Charles . . . unintentionally. She hadn't meant for Charles to know about it. But he'd stepped right into the middle of it and, in some chivalrous but misguided attempt to save her from herself, he'd helped her rid this world of Seidel. Seeing Charles shove Seidel into the portal— or seeing her own cold-blooded anger reflected in Charles's eyes, or maybe all of it—had caused something to die within her. She couldn't say exactly what she'd lost, but she knew something was missing. *Innocence, maybe,* she thought. *I know now I'm capable of terrible things.* She no longer felt worthy of Charles's love. Especially knowing what he'd done for her because of it.

She pushed the book away with frustration and disgust.

Odd that Lorne—formally Krevlornswath of the Deathwok Clan—a native of Pylea, never really made her think about those awful, lost years, scrabbling for survival, clinging to her fragmenting identity. *Well, maybe not so unusual,* she thought. Though he had the same physical characteristics as other Pylean demons, the resemblance was skin deep. Lorne had been born a fish out of water in his own world. Fred couldn't imagine Lorne, former host and owner of Caritas, the defunct karaoke bar and demon sanctuary, in a world without music. He was an anagogic demon, with the ability to read people and demons while they sang. *Pretty much a wasted ability on Pylea,* Fred thought. *He belonged there about as much as I did!*

At the same time, she had to put aside her own misgivings about researching portals night and day simply because the work might bring back unpleasant memories. Angel Investigations was a team, and she wasn't about to let the team down. Besides, the lives of many people were at stake if they failed to avert the demonic equinox.

With a weary sigh, she grabbed the next book in the stack dealing with transdimensional portal artifacts and whispered, "One for all, and—"

"Everyone is a mercenary," Cordelia exclaimed as she came through the lobby entrance, shaking her head and tossing her hands up in the air.

"Not quite what I was about to say."

"What?"

"Never mind," Fred said, grateful for the interruption. "What happened with the movie people?"

Cordelia looked around. "Where's Wesley?"

"He remembered he had a few more volumes on transdimensional portal artifacts that he never unpacked."

"Who knew there were so many?"

"I think he's cornered the market," Fred said,

chuckling. "So, nobody in Hollywood wants to take credit for the megalith?"

"Nobody will admit any involvement, naturally," Cordelia said. "But they're all hoping the news coverage surrounding it boosts ticket sales. All I kept hearing all day was 'there's no such thing as bad publicity.'"

"Those darn mercenaries," Fred said, trying to share in Cordelia's indignation.

"You'd think they might be a teeny bit worried about the fate of humankind, but no . . ."

"Well, in all fairness, Cordy, I kind of doubt they share our dimension-spanning perspective on this one."

"Right," Cordelia said, and heaved an almost wistful sigh. "Ignorance is bliss."

"So, nothing at all?"

Cordelia plopped down on the banquette, kicked off her one-inch heels, and wiggled her toes. "Ever hear the phrase 'scattered to the four winds'?"

"Sure, but—"

"I know what it means now," Cordelia said. "These people aren't exactly gathered at a convention for convenient interrogation. We're lucky most of them were in town for the premiere last night. I've been running and driving around chasing them down, and phoning anyone even remotely connected to the film, and that was after running and driving around, and phoning anyone I could think of who might know someone who worked on the set. Are you following this? At this point, I could be speaking in tongues and not realize it."

Fred walked out from behind the reception desk and sat next to her. "Only one tongue so far," Fred said. "So, you're good."

"Speaking of tongues," Cordelia said. "The set dresser had two."

"Two tongues?"

"One tongue, split down the middle, like a serpent," Cordelia explained. "He kept flipping the points over each other. Very distracting."

"I can imagine," Fred said, grimacing. "Was he the type to conjure a megalith?"

"There's a type for that?"

"There must be."

"Well, my gut said no . . . when it wasn't getting a little queasy. Anyhoo, nobody admitted knowing anything about mega-rock before last night's grand entrance. Generally, they were curious, intrigued, and excited. A few even mentioned that the zombie island shooting location and sets had statues."

"Maybe we should see this movie," Fred said. "And we could pay for popcorn and Jujubes out of petty cash."

"No, they showed me some pictures, and these statues were more like totem poles . . . with these

117

sharp spikes, which became meat hooks for the cannibal zombies."

"Okay, not craving the Jujubes so much anymore."

"Speaking of food," Cordelia said. "I did manage to pick up one interesting piece of gossip from a craft services worker. Seems she saw the lead actress getting cozy with a stuntman outside her trailer during the filming of the movie."

Fred arched an eyebrow. "How cozy?"

"Cozy enough to take said stuntman into her trailer."

"Ooh," Fred said, intrigued. "Wait, does that mean anything?"

"Might," Cordelia said. "If you remember that Rebecca Wade was a no-show at last night's premiere."

"Why would I remember that?"

"Oh, that's right, you weren't exactly watching," Cordelia recalled. "Rebecca Wade played the princess in *Zombie Island Princess*."

"Ah, the leading lady."

"Correct," Cordelia said. "Missing last night. And missing today. But here's the weird coincidence. Steve McKay, the cozy stuntman, is also missing."

"So . . . they're missing together," Fred said. "Maybe they eloped."

"In Hollywood, anything is possible," Cordelia

said. "Even leading ladies eloping with stuntmen."

"We could start calling chapels in Vegas."

"That could take forever, but . . ."

"What?"

"The Bakers had just come from Vegas."

"The Bakers were the ones in the Durango who went poof," Fred said. "You think there's a connection?"

Cordelia frowned. "It's a stretch," she said after a moment. "Besides, we don't know if Rebecca Wade and the stuntman actually went to Vegas."

"Then all we have is some gossip-column fodder."

"I left a bunch of Angel Investigations cards all over the place," Cordelia said. "Most have probably been round-filed by now. Let's face it, my whole exhausting day was basically a big waste of time."

"Is this . . . Angel Investigations?"

Startled, Cordelia looked up at the lobby entrance, where a slender young woman with long brown hair stood, glancing down at a business card as she confirmed the business name. She wore a denim vest over a shapeless yellow flower-print dress that flowed to her ankles. In her other hand she held a black three-ring binder.

"Yes, this is Angel Investigations," Cordelia said, abruptly slipping her heels back on. "And how may we help you? I'm Cordelia Chase, and this is Winifred Burkle."

"Oh, but everyone calls me Fred."

"Hi, Fred," the woman said before turning her attention to Cordelia. "I believe it was you, Cordelia, who left this business card and a note about the Hollywood Boulevard statue in my office mail slot while I was out." She had a pale complexion, untouched by makeup, and wore narrow, black-rimmed eyeglasses. "Oh, don't worry, you wouldn't recognize me. I'm Sally Ainsworth. Rebecca Wade's personal assistant."

Professional and attractive in a plain, unpretentious way, Sally marked a—perhaps intentional—contrast to Rebecca Wade, who exuded glamour and eccentricity at every personal appearance. From what Cordelia had read about the young actress, she wouldn't want anyone in her company to steal the spotlight, on or off the soundstage.

"Hi, Sally," Cordelia said jovially. "Glad you could stop by. Do you know anything about mega—I mean, the monolith?"

Sally seemed hesitant. "You really are investigating it, then?"

"Doing what we can," Fred chimed in.

"Yes," Cordelia said. "But, please, feel free to help!"

"I—I'm sorry, I don't know anything about the mono—the statue."

"Oh," Cordelia said softly, disheartened. "Then why did . . . ?"

Sally clutched the black binder against her chest and worried her lower lip before responding. "I thought . . . I was concerned," she began. "Thought they might be related somehow."

"What might be related?"

"This card . . . it says Angel Investigations." When Cordelia nodded, Sally continued. "So you're, what, private investigators?"

"Basically," Cordelia said.

"More or less," Fred said.

"Somebody hired you to investigate the statue?"

"Well, if someone had," Cordelia said, "that information would be confidential. But . . . it's kind of something we're investigating on our own."

"Oh . . ."

"Were you interested in hiring us to investigate the megalith?" Fred asked.

"No, not at all," Sally said. "I mean, not specifically, but . . . it really is private, then? If somebody hired you."

"Believe me," Cordelia said with a broad smile, "we know how to keep secrets around here."

"Good," Sally said. "That's good. Because I wouldn't want this information to get out there. It's pure speculation on my part. I mean, it may be nothing, right?"

"Possibly," Cordelia said, unsure what she was

agreeing to but convinced she needed to keep Ms. Ainsworth talking. "Is this about Rebecca Wade?"

Sally dropped her chin, and it seemed as if she were consulting the black binder for permission to speak. "She—she missed the premiere last night."

"I know. Everyone noticed," Cordelia said, then caught Fred's frown out of the corner of her eye. "Almost everyone. That is, those of us who follow these kinds of things noticed."

"That's what's so strange," Sally said. "Rebecca—Ms. Wade—she would never miss something like that. She had the lead in that movie—a starring role! Not that she loved the film—hated it, actually. And the director. Called him Antwerp behind his back. But she was good in *Zombie Island Princess*. Renard brought out her best work in that film. She was proud of her performance. Obviously, she won't get Oscar notice for a part in a zombie movie, but . . . she was convinced *ZIP* was the start of a big comeback for her. 'Back to the big time, Sally,' she said. 'You wait and see.'"

"Doesn't sound like something she'd want to miss."

"No . . . but she did. She missed it. And"—Sally took a deep breath to steady her nerves—"I haven't heard from her since late yesterday afternoon."

"That's not so long," Cordelia said, hoping to ease her concern.

"But after missing the premiere . . ."

"Have you talked to the police?" Fred asked. "Filed a missing person report?"

"It's—no, it's too soon for that."

"In California, there's no waiting period to file—"

"It's not that," Sally interrupted. "She's been missing before. She takes off sometimes, without telling me. You know, gone for the night. But she usually calls me the next morning."

"Maybe she hasn't had a chance to call," Fred offered.

But Sally shook her head. "First the premiere . . . and now this."

"Are you here to hire us to find her?" Cordelia asked. "Because I have a theory."

"What? You know something?"

"I know that she was having an affair."

Sally looked away demurely. "I suspected . . ."

"A stuntman named Steve McKay."

"Really? That's . . . surprising."

"Why?" Fred asked, as if realizing a missing puzzle piece had been placed back on the table.

"She . . . Rebecca was outwardly pleasant to everyone, but . . . well, she definitely had a pecking order about . . ."

"About whom she should be seen with?" Cordelia guessed. Sally gave a discomfited nod. "Maybe that's why she was keeping it a secret."

"Maybe."

"Know anything about McKay?"

"Not much," Sally said with a noncommittal shrug. "Met him once or twice. Pleasant, brawny, a little loud after he's had a few."

"Think he could be, you know, violent?" Fred asked.

"No, no, it's not that," Sally said. "Although, how well do we ever really know someone? He was practically a stranger to me, so maybe . . . I don't know. I'm sorry."

"Could they have eloped?" Cordelia asked.

Sally shook her head violently. "Oh, no! Never! Rebecca would never do that. Not with—well, not with McKay. Her image. No, I'm sure of that."

"A little confused here, Sally," Cordelia said with a patient smile. "Do you want to hire us? To find Rebecca?"

"Not necessarily," Sally said, clutching the binder a little tighter against her chest. "I thought if somebody had hired you, about the statue, I mean, that maybe they . . . might know something about it. About Rebecca."

"What about Rebecca?"

"You won't tell the police? Because, I could be wrong. Completely wrong! It's why I can't go to the police. If I'm wrong and this gets out . . . I—I don't know what to do."

"Start by telling us what's in that binder," Cordelia said. At her own mention of the word *police,* Rebecca had clutched the binder in a telling, white-knuckled grip.

Sally took another deep breath. "I found this binder in her bedroom when I was looking for some sort of note to explain where she'd gone."

"What's in it?"

"I don't know what it is. I thought it was a script—it *looks* like a script, but . . ." She shuddered as she handed the binder to Cordelia. "But when I started reading it . . ."

"What?" Cordelia said as she opened the cover and flipped through the pages.

"I'm not sure," Sally said with a worried frown, "but I think Rebecca may have killed some people."

CHAPTER EIGHT

"It looks like a movie script," Angel said, flipping through the pages of Rebecca Wade's binder. "You've read the whole thing?"

"Yes," Cordelia said, then nodded to Fred. "We both have."

The three of them had gathered in Angel's office. Cordy and Fred had been uncomfortable with the idea of talking about the binder's contents out in the lobby.

After his lunch meeting, which had seemed to eliminate Renard as the suspected Summoner, Angel had visited the monolith briefly, edging close enough to lay his palm on its surface. Unless his imagination had been playing tricks on him, the vibration was faster and more pronounced. Had Wesley been able to compare the difference in the vibration, he might have described the changes in terms of amplitude and frequency. Angel didn't need to attach scientific gadgets to the statue to know it was that much closer to phasing into their dimension.

Although Gunn was watching the monolith again, detecting changes in the phase shift would be beyond his human senses. *By the time humans can notice a change*, Angel realized, *it will be too late to stop the portal.* Gunn was acting as security, waiting on the chance something else might escape from the statue.

Angel returned his focus to the binder, skimming a page that described the midnight murder of a homeless man who'd been sleeping on a bench in Central Park. "What's your impression of this . . . story?"

"Creepy," Fred said. "Reads like the journal of a serial killer written in screenplay format. Almost like she wanted to have a record of these killings, so she decided to disguise them as a movie script in progress."

Angel glanced at the name of one of the characters, listed in capital letters on the first page of text. "Regina Wells?"

"An alias for Rebecca Wade," Cordelia suggested. "The character is an actress whose once promising career has taken a nosedive. The actress's assistant in the script is Sherry Arrington, a name similar to Sally Ainsworth. Regina is filming a horror movie called *Voodoo Island Priestess*, and the director is Arthur Redstone, compared to real-life director Antoine Renard. And the title of the script is *Phoenix,* and the Regina character talks about how her movie career will rise from the ashes—something that Rebecca had been telling Sally."

"What proof do we have that she wasn't taking creative license with her life?" Angel said. "Maybe she really was an aspiring screenwriter and she was simply writing about what she knew."

"Serial slaying?" Fred asked pointedly.

"Well, that would be the creative license part."

"First of all," Cordelia said. "The movie locations listed in this script—each one a place where the character Regina committed one of her murders—match Rebecca's actual movie location schedule over the past year. Toronto, Vancouver, Amsterdam, New York City, Philadelphia, L.A., yadda, yadda, yadda."

"Again, maybe she used familiar locations to keep it real."

"Shouldn't the vampire be playing devil's advocate here?" Cordelia asked.

"Hey, I'm only trying to see if your theory is bulletproof," Angel said. "Have you checked the police records in those cities to see if murders similar to those in the script occurred during Rebecca's stay?"

"Haven't had time," Cordelia said. "Besides,

most of the early murders are of homeless people and there are . . . extenuating circumstances. But I have a good—well, a bad—feeling about this. I think Rebecca was involved in something that triggered mega-rock's appearance. And I think you'll agree with us when we tell you the rest."

"I agree it's suspicious," Angel said. "Does she implicate anyone else?"

"None of the film's cast or crew," Fred said. "She makes a point of treating their characters like ignorant buffoons. But this is the weird part. Regina plans to rise above the mediocrity with the help of her mentor-slash-acting coach."

"Who is that?"

"A character named"—Fred flipped through the script—"Mr. Serpentipity."

"Serpentipity? As in serpent? Seriously?"

"Not only that," Cordelia said. "This creepy guy has demonic watchdogs who remove all evidence of the crimes."

"Remove how?"

"By eating it—them—the corpses," Fred said, an expression of extreme disgust on her face. "Bones and all."

"Want more similarities?" Cordelia asked. "Rebecca has had an acting coach guru-type with her the past year. His name is Sehjenkhai, and he has two jumbo dogs. In the script, Mr. Serpentipity tells Regina that in order to reverse her career slide, she must complete a yearlong series of ceremonial offerings to prove she is worthy of renewed success and acclaim."

"And these offerings would be . . . ?" Angel already suspected the answer.

"A euphemism for sacrifices," Fred said. "Human sacrifices."

"Where is Sehjenkhai now?" Angel said. "Wait, let me guess. He's missing."

"Rebecca was the only one who had his contact information," Cordelia said. "She never gave that information to Sally, who thought that was odd all along. Takes all types in Hollywood, is what she figured. Anyway, Sally said this Sehjenkhai gave her major creeps, so she was glad she never had to contact him."

"Where's Sally?" Angel asked. "Why isn't she here?"

"She must be really freaked out by this Mr. Sehjenkhai," Cordelia said. "Because she gave us the binder for safekeeping and said she was heading to the East Coast to visit an aunt—indefinitely."

Angel flipped through the last third of the script. "She calls these offerings—the sacrifices—part of some grand ritual."

"Yes," Fred said. "I don't think Regina—I mean, Rebecca—realized it, but reading between the lines, I have the feeling that Serpentipity—that is, Sehjenkhai—was manipulating her, making her perform the sacrifices of the ritual for his own reasons while leading her to believe it would benefit her."

"But if he's the Summoner, why wouldn't he perform the sacrifices himself?"

"Because," Wesley said, striding into the office with two weighty tomes and an expression of recent accomplishment, "that would violate the requirements of the ritual."

"Wes?" Angel said, feeling hopeful. "You found something?"

"At long last," Wesley said, as if asking forgiveness for taking so long to unearth ancient secrets. "I believe we are finally on the right track." He placed the books on the corner of the desk, then opened the top one to a page he'd bookmarked with a thin red ribbon. "Here it is," Wesley said, indicating the start of a passage with the tip of his index finger. "This is where I see mentions of the Summoners, the bringers of demons."

"Plural?"

"There were two of them," Wesley said. "Identical twin brothers. Their names were Rehjenkhai and—"

"Sehjenkhai," Angel finished.

"How did you—?"

"Apparently Sehjenkhai is masquerading as an acting coach these days," Cordelia said.

"But this story is three thousand years old," Wesley said. "I assumed these were proper names, although it's possible they've been handed down. Of course, they could just as well be titles or functions. Unless . . ."

"Unless what?" Fred asked.

"If this acting coach named Sehjenkhai is the same Sehjenkhai in this story, then he would be over three thousand years old. I had my doubts that the brothers were human, but that would make them—Sehjenkhai, at least—virtually immortal."

"Or maybe he's the granddaddy of all vampires," Fred suggested.

Cordelia shook her head. "No, Sally mentioned seeing him waiting outside Rebecca's trailer once, and that was in broad daylight."

"Right," Fred said. "So he's a very slow-aging demon?"

"Definitely not human."

"Why not let Wes tell us what happened to the brothers grim three thousand years ago?" Angel said.

"Oh—right! Go ahead, Wesley," Fred said.

"Thank you," Wesley said with an indulgent smile. Then he cleared his throat and assumed a more businesslike—or Watcher-like, considering his past—demeanor. "According to this account, the twin brothers attempted to bring forth 'the hordes of evil' through an elaborate ritual involving monthly sacrifices over the course of an entire year."

"We have the Hollywood treatment right here," Cordelia said, tapping the screenplay journal. "Oops—sorry!"

"No, not at all," Wesley said. He started to flip through the pages of the binder, nodding at— Angel suspected—the similarities he saw. "A thinly veiled account of ritual murders."

"That's what we were thinking," Angel said, but he caught the reproachful look from Cordelia and amended his statement. "*They* were thinking."

Wes continued: "For the ritual to succeed, the sacrifices had to be performed by a woman of childbearing age, participating of her own free will. Any form of coercion, during any point of that year, would nullify the ritual."

"But lying or deception wouldn't be considered coercion," Angel reasoned.

Wes thought about his response for a moment. "Not unless the lie or deception had a coercive nature. For example, suppose the Summoner told the woman he was holding her father captive and would kill her father unless she cooperated, when in reality the Summoner was not holding the father and had no intention of harming him."

"That type of lie would nullify the ritual?"

"Definitely."

"What about false promises of fame or fortune?"

"Permissible," Wesley said. "Possibly even key to the ritual's success. Within the context of the ritual, the woman acts as a representative of humanity. By succumbing to greed or ego gratification at the expense of human lives and human welfare, she gives power to the darkness, a cooperative kindling for the demonic fire. Aside from demonstrating human gullibility, her actions simultaneously debase and betray our species."

"Talk about a lousy role model," Cordelia said.

"Quite," Wes said. "Although the woman of childbearing age performed the sacrifices, the Summoner presided over the blood rites. The first eleven could be strangers, not so the twelfth. Her last sacrifice must be the father of her unborn child."

"And that's the end of the ritual?" Angel asked, suspecting otherwise.

"Not quite," Wesley said. "There must be one last sacrifice, this one performed by the Summoner."

"Let me guess," Angel said. "Miss Gullibility."

"Precisely," Wesley said. "In this account, Rehjenkhai gave away his plan. He proclaimed to the villagers that they would know the faces of their enemies that night. By 'faces' he may have been referring to the two-faced megalith that would appear."

"So what happened?" Cordelia asked, intrigued. "Rebecca's script stops before that point, obviously."

"The villagers located Rehjenkhai that evening, surprising him before he could kill the woman. The ritual was halted. Enraged, they dismembered Rehjenkhai and burned the pieces in a funeral pyre. Sehjenkhai, his twin, who had kept a much lower profile, fled and was never seen again by the villagers."

Raising one eyebrow, Fred asked, "Do we even want to know what happened to Miss Gullibility?"

"The villagers faced an interesting dilemma," Wesley said. "Considering the severe nature of her crimes, which Rehjenkhai had also exposed in his bold but ill-advised proclamation, she would have been executed. But realizing that her sacrifice was the final element in Rehjenkhai's demonic plan, they were fearful that her execution would bring about the prophesied death and destruction. So, they *merely* removed her eyes and tongue, and banished her from the village. Whether she died of exposure, starvation, sickness, or was the victim of predatory animals, there is no record of the megalith appearing, so her eventual death did not satisfy the last requirement of the ritual. In fact, that is the reason we've had so much trouble locating this particular entry. Since a megalith never appeared, and the exact nature of the suspected portal was unknown, the account has no specific mention of a megalith. I found this only because of the 'faces' comment. And, of course, I had already exhausted every source of information I have concerning transdimensional artifacts before I stumbled upon this."

"No need to be modest, Wes," Angel said. "This was a great find."

"Uh-oh," Fred said.

"What?"

"When the ritual's finished," Cordelia said, "old mega-rock appears?"

"Yes, why?"

Cordelia said, "Rebecca had been having a secret affair with a stuntman. And before Sally Ainsworth—Rebecca's assistant—left for parts unknown, she said she'd found something in Rebecca's bathroom trashcan. The ripped-up box of an early pregnancy test kit. And now Rebecca and the stuntman are both missing."

"Since the megalith has appeared," Wesley said, "we must assume the ritual has been completed successfully this time. Ms. Wade and her paramour are in all likelihood both dead, along with the unborn child, whose death represents the lost hope for humanity."

"So old Sehj has been waiting to finish what his twin brother started three thousand years ago?"

"Wow, those demonic equinoxes are a long

time coming," Cordelia said. "Not that I'm complaining!"

"What about Sehjenkhai? Kind of a second fiddle in that story," Angel said. "In all those years he never tried to make a name for himself?"

"Rehjenkhai was the elder brother, by a few minutes," Wesley explained. "He was in charge, if more foolish than his brother." Wesley flipped open the second book. "There is only one other mention of Sehjenkhai, assuming it is the same . . . being, and that is a thousand years after the failed ritual. He was said to travel with two guardians, called 'khaipuhr,' but alternately referred to as 'bear-dogs,' lesser demons, indentured demons. Some thought they were demons inhabiting the flesh of dead dogs reanimated by a necromancer. Again, assuming this is the same Sehjenkhai, he must have acquired the khaipuhr guardians after his brother was executed."

"After his brother was chopped and grilled," Fred said. "Can't say I blame him for wanting guard dog demons."

"Sally mentioned that Mr. Sehjenkhai had two black mastiffs," Cordelia said.

"As bulletproof theories go," Angel said to Cordelia and Fred, "yours is beginning to look like Kevlar."

"It fits," Wesley said, nodding. "And there's one other thing you should know. Both Summoners were said to possess a third eye, turned far away to look upon evil and see when it is near. I assume this describes a paranormal ability and not a physical third eye."

"Would sort of make him stand out in a crowd," Angel said. "We can also assume he's gone into hiding while he waits for the monolith to phase into our dimension. Do we have a physical description of Sehjenkhai?"

"Sally described him as a tall, gaunt, bald man with bushy gray eyebrows and dark eyes, who always wears black or black suits," Fred said.

"Accompanied by two demon dogs that eat human beings whole," Cordelia said, shuddering. "Let's not forget that part."

CHAPTER NINE

On the second floor of the condemned office building in Inglewood, Sehjenkhai sat in a frayed lawn chair salvaged from an alley Dumpster. He stared through the cracked and missing windowpanes at the setting sun, marking the passage of another day. On either side of him, the khaipuhr slept, growling contentedly as he scratched behind their heads. Lesser demons that were bound to him, they were controllable through the force of his will. He wished that were true of the two early arrivals . . . and yet he knew they would be incapable of overthrowing the human hegemony of this world if they were as weak-minded and malleable as the demon mastiffs. To achieve final victory, the demon warriors would need every ounce of their wild and fearsome nature.

Nevertheless, since the final sacrifice and the herald of the three tremors, Sehjenkhai had not dared to sleep. As part of their unconquerable nature, the early arrivals were supremely impatient. Waiting, for anything, was a foreign concept to them. He had to stay alert simply to remind them of the stakes involved, a new world order. Sehjenkhai worried, too, about the possibility of more early arrivals, roaming the city, wreaking havoc prematurely. And it could happen, with the proper human provocation of the megalith. Actually, he was surprised it hadn't happened . . . again.

What concerned him most was the possibility that the early arrivals would lead the humans to his doorstep. While it was too late for the humans to stop the crossing, they could stop him from taking part in the final victory. He was not a true immortal. He had stared in disbelief as humans hacked his brother to pieces, and watched numbly as they burned him to ashes—a memory he would never forget, regardless of how long he lived. To come all this way, through thousands of years of waiting, and after several agonizing, failed attempts at completing the ritual, it was almost inconceivable to him that he could die before the final glory swept over the human scum. *Almost.*

"When you first arrived on this world," he spoke softly, but loud enough for the early arrivals to hear him where they stood in the back of the room, "I sent the khaipuhr to clean up the evidence of your . . . excesses."

If not for the khaipuhr, the several gruesome murders leading from Hollywood to Inglewood would have been the lead story of every newscast in the city for days. Granted, humans had limited attention spans. With lives that lasted mere decades, they flitted from one area of interest to another, never lingering over anything. They were born, weaned, bred, and died, quickly making way for the next generation. Already the megalith had begun to bore them, which suited Sehjenkhai fine. They would become complacent. However, news of the eviscerated remains of several of their kind would have captured and held their interest much too long, perhaps triggering investigations, law enforcement sweeps, and possibly searches of abandoned and condemned buildings, leading to his exposure. Humans were weak, tiresome, and puny, but they outnumbered him, in this city alone, 10 million to one.

Sehjenkhai continued his admonishment. "This was a strange new world for you, full of . . . opportunities to indulge. Easily forgiven. Yet I warned you of the consequences. . . ."

Until the crossing, he would hide from humans as he had always hidden, lurking in the shadows, waiting hundreds of years for each rare opportunity to seize their world from them, to seek from within their ranks a willing acolyte who would betray them. After thousands of years of caution, he required the patience of one more night to enjoy his reward. *One night,* he thought, *such a very small price to pay indeed.* But the two early arrivals had already jeopardized his position.

They listened to him without interrupting, but without turning to glare at them, he could tell they were tossing their trophy back and forth, a bit of forbidden fruit. The wet, fleshy sound of the impacts assailed his ears and offended his ingrained sense of caution. But with his inner eye, he could *see* them as well, revealed as ghostly shadows. His second sight was attuned to them and their world, which was soon to be aligned with the human world.

"You are fierce but not invulnerable," he warned them. "Across the world, they number in the billions. In this very city, they are ten million strong. Until your brothers arrive, they will remain the dominant species here."

Two quick barks of laughter from them.

He knew then that nothing he said or did would restrain them from their dark impulses. *Two options remain,* he thought, *continue to minimize their damage . . . or risk the khaipuhr against them.* If the khaipuhr caught them by surprise, the demon dogs might prevail. But Sehjenkhai was loath to risk his personal guardians when a little more patience might suffice. His own inattention had been at fault this evening.

The two early arrivals had slipped away from the office, drifted out on the street, scouted several blocks, until they encountered a middle-aged woman loading grocery bags into the back of her minivan in the far corner of a parking lot. They had gleefully ripped her to shreds, savoring some of the remains before returning to Sehjenkhai with her blood smeared all over them. Sehjenkhai had sent the khaipuhr to clean up their mess before the body was discovered. But the early arrivals had refused to surrender their trophy to the dogs.

Instead, they stood behind him and played with it, to mock his restraint, a quality they neither possessed nor understood. They had called his name before one of them ripped out and ate the tongue, and again before the other plucked out and swallowed both eyeballs. By ignoring their taunts, Sehjenkhai hoped they would grow bored and eventually toss the woman's severed head to the khaipuhr.

The sun winked out on the horizon, a metaphorical precursor to the snuffing out of human lives and hope. Sehjenkhai stood and turned to face the two demon warriors. They wore gleaming black helmets and armored breastplates. At the end of their long, muscular arms, their savage claws twitched, visible signs of their inbred impatience. "All I ask is that you be patient, as I have been patient, though your test is exceedingly brief. Soon your brothers will come to us by the thousands and tens of thousands." Sehjenkhai clenched his fists with excitement. "This ripe world is wasted on humans and their petty schemes and foolish ideals. We will show them the meaning of power, of fear and destruction, the utter devastation of global conquest and species subjugation."

Sehjenkhai would be rewarded in the new world—the remade world—in the aftermath of the furious hordes that would sweep across the land like a hellish breath of foul air. When the demon overlords ruled, Sehjenkhai would have an honored place at their side. "True glory of combat awaits you! Would you risk your lives for so little when you could share in the ultimate victory over humankind?" he asked the warriors.

After long moments of silence, the demon holding the woman's severed head let it fall to the floor with a wet thud. Then both demon warriors removed their helmets, revealing red-and-black-mottled faces, ridged foreheads, deep-set smoldering red eyes, mashed noses, sharp gnashing teeth, and scores of wormlike shapes writhing under their skin. By removing their helmets, they showed vulnerability, which was a sign of agreement, a proof of trust.

His tension evaporated, and Sehjenkhai smiled. "Before this night is over," he assured them, "we shall ring in the new world order."

The warrior demons nodded and laughed, a harsh sound not unlike rocks scraping together, but pleasing to Sehjenkhai's ears all the same.

Angel gathered everyone at the Hyperion to discuss the latest developments in the case. Before discussing a plan of attack, he thought it best to get the latest reports. "Gunn," he said. "Anything unusual at the monolith?"

"Couple teenagers tried to climb it," Gunn said. "Cop chased them off. Most people are taking pictures, but keeping their distance. Two clusters of fanatics hangin' around, though, and no love lost between them. The candlelighters waiting for salvation and the doomsayers waiting for the sky to fall or the ground to open up. I mean, what's up with that? If you believe the ground's about to open up, why wouldn't you hop in the old Ford F-150 and get the hell outta Dodge?"

"You don't know how many times I've asked myself that," Cordelia said. "Well, except for the F-150 part."

"People are treating that block of Hollywood Boulevard like a shrine," Lorne said.

"Let's hope it doesn't become a sacrificial altar," Angel said, putting their fears in perspective.

"I gotta say, no way you're gettin' either camp to budge," Gunn said. "And when that monolith opens up, they'll be like chum in the water."

"We all know the stakes are high, Gunn," Wesley said. "This is why it's imperative we stop the megalith from opening the portal."

Cordelia asked Angel, "Don't you think it's strange that nobody has connected the violent murders you and Connor discovered with megarock?"

"Police could be keeping the details from the press to avoid a panic," Angel suggested.

Connor shook his head, pleased to contradict his father. "The bodies are gone." Angel noticed Connor had taken a position next to Cordelia and, subconsciously or not, he had placed himself between Cordelia and his rival for her affections.

"But the police and the medical examiner would—"

"Not a trace of blood, flesh, or bone is left," Connor said. "I revisited each of those sites a couple of times, but the first time I went back, I caught a weird scent . . . reminded me of dog."

"The demon mastiffs," Cordelia said. "The kippers!"

"Khaipuhr," Wesley corrected. "Sehjenkhai's demon guardians."

"If he sent the dogs out to clean up after the escapees," Angel said, "then he must have made contact with them."

"And warned them they were being careless," Wesley said, nodding. "I imagine if we find Sehjenkhai, we'll also find the khaipuhr and the two megalith demons."

"A demon jackpot," Fred said with a nervous chuckle.

"How could this Sehjen-dude know they were here?" Gunn asked.

"His third eye," Wesley said.

"If the kip—khaipuhr—wiped the murder sites clean, that would explain the lack of news coverage, and the minimal police presence at megarock," Cordelia said. "Although there *have* been news reports speculating that the city might try dynamite. That would put a real damper on the apocalypse, right? Solve all our problems?"

"Doesn't matter," Angel said. "Until that thing finishes phasing into our world, it's indestructible. Of course, the city doesn't realize that little fact. . . ."

"It's never gonna happen, anyway, kiddies," Lorne said to Cordelia. "They'd never try it. Too high on the risk-o-meter. All those huddling masses yearning for salvation—or, well, destruction—the booming businesses and souvenir shops, the potential for collateral damage, not to mention lost profits."

"Is it true Hollywood Souvenirs is already selling monolith key rings and postcards?" Cordelia asked Gunn.

"Got that right," he confirmed. "Nice to know somebody's makin' a profit on the apocalypse."

"Unless anyone has something new to add . . . ?" Angel waited. "Good. Now, as far as we know, the Summoner's ritual is complete. Nothing we can do to stop it. That's a dead end. The monolith is on its way here. We can see it and feel it, but it hasn't aligned with our dimension yet. We have some time before the portal opens. And two objectives. Find Sehjenkhai. Make him cancel the alignment." Angel frowned. "Otherwise . . ."

"We're in for the mother of all border crossings," Gunn said.

"In a nutshell," Angel said.

"And if Sehjenkhai refuses to put the genie back in the bottle?" Cordelia asked.

"I'll persuade him," Angel said. "I can be very persuasive." But another, unspoken, possibility bothered Angel. *What if it's too late to stop the crossing? The seven of us against a demon army?* Even if they somehow convinced the mayor to evacuate L.A., or persuaded the governor to call in the National Guard, the invasion would not stop at the city limits.

Angel looked at each one of them and drew strength from their belief, however fragile at the moment, that they would find a way to prevail against this latest threat. The answer was simple: Stop the invasion before it started. Otherwise, the monolith would be their last stand. *There has to be a way to stop it!* Angel thought.

"Cordy," Angel said, "I need you on the phones with your movie contacts. Fred, get on the computer. Find any leads you can on Mr. Sehjenkhai. Maybe he's left a trace of himself somewhere, an address, an acquaintance, someone who knows where we might be staying, or his favorite haunts, restaurants, bagel or doughnut shops, anything. Assuming he doesn't have the ability to drop off the face of the earth, he's out there somewhere. Lorne, keep checking with your sources. We don't know when the new blood might make contact with L.A.'s resident demon populace. And ask if anyone has seen unusually large dogs prowling around. Sehjenkhai and the escapees are lying low, but the khaipuhr might be out there somewhere and could lead us to them."

"Will do, chief," Lorne said.

"Wesley and Gunn, stake out the monolith," Angel continued. "There may be more escapees, who could also lead us to the Summoner. Or . . ."

"The portal could begin to open," Wesley finished the grim thought.

"First sign of anything unusual," Angel said. "Call me."

Wesley nodded.

"Connor and I will return to Inglewood, where we lost the trail," Angel said. "It's likely that Sehjenkhai is hiding somewhere in that vicinity. If he steps outside for a breath of fresh air, I want to be there when he inhales."

"No," Connor said, savoring the one word of defiance a little longer than necessary. "I should stay with Gunn at the monolith."

"Why?" Angel asked, annoyed. *Other than for the sheer pleasure of disagreeing with me in front of everyone?* He resisted the urge to send Connor packing rather than become argumentative with him. But Connor surprised him.

"Our best chance of finding the Summoner is to track one of those monsters right to his doorstep. If you position Wesley and Gunn there and one of those things pops out, neither of them has the speed to keep up with it or the heightened senses to track it. I can."

"Then you and I should stay at the monolith," Angel reasoned.

Connor shook his head. "You follow the cold trail, and I'll wait to follow a hot one. It makes more sense for us to split up."

Angel suspected Connor merely wanted distance from his father, but he couldn't argue with the boy's logic. *I'm all about giving him his own space,* Angel thought. *Especially if it increases our chances for success.* After taking a moment to examine his own motives, Angel had to admit that he'd wanted to arrange the team so that he could spend some time with his son. Since they were usually at each other's throats, Angel and Connor rarely had a chance for father-son bonding. If

Angel tried too hard to reach out, Connor withdrew, resentful, the ingrained hatred resurfacing. Only in battle, while facing a common foe, was their connection effortless and promising. In the life-and-death struggle, Connor had no time to carry around all the emotional baggage that kept them apart. If Connor was guilty sometimes of fueling the fire between them, then Angel was just as complicit in trying to force a truce. *Give it time,* Angel thought. *And here, it actually makes sense.* "Okay, then," he said. "Connor's with Gunn. Wes, you're with me."

"Sounds like a plan," Gunn said.

"Any questions?" Angel asked to a round of head shakes. "Good. Let's go stop an apocalypse."

CHAPTER TEN

Angel and Wesley dropped off Gunn and Connor near Hollywood and Vine, then, after wishing them luck, Angel swung the black '67 Plymouth Belvedere GTX around and drove south toward Inglewood. Gunn turned a wistful gaze at the departing convertible, shaking his head until Connor nudged him.

"What?"

"Ain't no thing," Gunn said.

"Something's bothering you."

If it's that obvious, Gunn thought, *better fess up.* "Just getting tired of the night-watchman routine, is all."

They walked toward the intersection. "Don't worry," Connor said. "If we're lucky, we'll be at ground zero when all hell breaks loose."

Gunn stared at him. "One hell dimension wasn't enough for you, kid?"

"I'm not a kid," Connor said.

"My mistake," Gunn said, cutting the boy some slack. Then, after a moment, he added, "But you are strange."

Connor smiled, taking it as the intended compliment. He shrugged. "I bore easily."

"Know that feelin'," Gunn said. "And yet I don't think I'll ever be bored enough to crave a little hell on earth."

"Give it time."

"Not gonna happen," Gunn said. After a moment, he looked sidelong at the boy. "You know, Connor, sometimes I think you have a death wish."

"You're wrong," Connor said dispassionately. "I don't want all the monsters to kill me. I want to kill *all* the monsters."

"What about your father? And Lorne? Are they monsters?"

"There's an expression I heard recently . . ."

"What's that?"

"'If it walks like a duck . . .'"

Kid's got major issues. "Connor, you gotta know, man, just 'cause we're not wearin' uniforms don't mean we're not on the same team."

"That must confuse Angel," Connor said. "I hear he changes teams."

"Then you better pay real close attention."

"Thing about Quor-Toth," Connor said. "You learn to never let your guard down."

They turned west at the intersection and saw the monolith looming ahead in the far lane. The police had added more sawhorses to their makeshift barrier and had moved them farther out, to discourage the milling crowds and passersby from approaching. Although the faces of the statue were too sheer to climb, that hadn't stopped adventurous teens from making an attempt. The widened ring of sawhorses would give the police more time to respond to any random acts of mischief or vandalism.

A lone news van remained at the scene, its microwave mast extended to its forty-two-foot height in preparation for a live spot. A photogenic blond KTLA reporter, wearing a tailored, cornflower blue business suit and a white silk blouse, talked to her cameraman, using her wireless microphone like a pointer as she gestured to the crowds and the monolith itself. The cameraman shrugged. Neither one of them seemed particularly enthused about their ongoing assignment.

Two policemen were on monolith detail. One kept the vehicular traffic moving, while the other monitored the pedestrians and bystanders, ready to intervene at the first sign of trouble. A boring, thankless job. Gunn could sympathize.

The steady stream of passersby repeated a similar monolith ritual. Invariably, each person would stop and take a few minutes to gawk at the rock tower rising from the middle of Hollywood Boulevard. Those with cameras would take snapshots or have someone take their picture with the monolith in the background. They'd strike up conversations with strangers, wait around for something to happen, and finally decide nothing was going to happen and move on.

Obstructing and annoying this continual flow of foot traffic were two distinct groups, one on each side of Hollywood Boulevard. The doomsayers gathered on the south side, carrying signs that promised imminent doom and gloom, chanting "the end is near." This group was comprised of old men—most of the sign bearers—and disaffected male teenagers, although a sizable goth contingent, some looking like grim-reapers-in-training, had members from both genders. Over on the north side of the street, those expecting salvation—or maybe just a miracle—held candles cupped in their hands, or clutched prayer beads with reverent devotion, some talking peaceably while others prayed in hushed tones. This group had a wider demographic, old men and women, along with some middle-aged mothers clutching young children, a few young men, but teenagers of either gender were scarce.

Connor shook his head in disbelief. "How can they look at those faces and think something wonderful is about to happen?"

"Don't know."

"What do those faces say to you?"

"Run or die screaming." Gunn smiled at his own gallows humor.

"Then why are you still here?"

"Right," Gunn said. "I should definitely know better."

Connor stared at the salvation crowd. "I don't get it."

Gunn considered the praying contingent again and wondered too. "Maybe they think it's a test of their faith."

Connor scoffed, "Then they *will* die screaming."

"Happens like that," Gunn said. "Sometimes."

"What's the point?"

"That *is* the point, Connor."

Connor thought for a moment, then shook his head. "Still not getting it."

"Faith," Gunn said, "is like that."

Assuming another escapee demon would also flee toward Inglewood, Gunn and Connor decided the best position to intercept such a demon would be on the south side of Hollywood Boulevard. To assure themselves mobility, they stayed clear of the doomsayer bunch. For the first half hour, Connor remained poised for battle. Near the end of the second half hour, he leaned against a street sign. Finally, he sat down on the curb next to Gunn. "Does it do . . . anything?" Connor asked.

"Hell, no," Gunn said, shaking his head with a smile. "It's a big hunk of rock."

"Hmm."

"If it's any consolation, Angel says he can feel it vibrating."

"Why would that be any consolation?"

Gunn shrugged. "Just saying."

Connor looked irritated. "What?"

"Maybe you could feel it too."

"Why bother?"

"You're right," Gunn said, spreading his arms. "I mean, take a look around. You got these ten-, twenty-story buildings on both sides of the street. Hell, if you line it up right, you could take a picture of mono-rock with the Capital Records tower in the background, and yet a fifteen-foot-tall hunk of rock has these people bent outta shape."

"Well, it *is* an ugly rock," Connor said, grinning.

"Damn ugly!" Gunn exclaimed. "Of course, if I were Wesley, I would say it's fascinating. Would have brought my stethoscope and a chisel, a sample kit or something to take a chunk back to the hotel for analysis."

"Instead of being the night watchman?"

It was a simple question, asked in a lighthearted manner, no slight intended, but it hit home with Gunn. Reminded him of Wesley scoring points with Fred, having research mini-dates with her, spending uninterrupted hours with her, while Gunn sat on the curb, a stone's throw away from a much bigger stone, surrounded by a bunch of people with too much free time and not enough common sense as they mugged for the cameras.

Gunn stood up.

"Gunn? Something wrong?"

"Tired of watching this damn thing," Gunn said. "Sick of waiting. That's what's wrong."

"What do you want to do?"

"Jumpstart the apocalypse."

"Now you sound like me."

Gunn scoffed. "Yeah, how nuts is that?" He rubbed his hands together and nodded. "Actually, I was thinkin' I might do some investigating of my own."

"Really?"

"Why the hell not?"

"Go for it," Connor said. "Anything I can do to help?"

"Now that you mention it . . ."

Gunn positioned himself on the opposite side of a photo opportunity group, temporarily hidden from the two policemen, while Connor drifted into the assemblage of doomsayers. Angel and Wesley had relied on Gunn to provide a diversion when they inspected the monolith, so it seemed appropriate that Gunn should have someone to provide the same service for him as he prepared to examine the interdimensional doorstop. Gunn didn't have to wait long.

"You're all crazy!" Connor yelled from within the gathered doom-and-gloomers. "Get out of here!"

Instantly, the crowd began to churn upon itself, all eyes seeking the malcontent. Signs dipped as old men spun around asking, "Who?" over and over again. The teenagers and the goth contingent looked indignant, ready to fight to defend their right to despair.

"Go home, you bunch of freaks!"

Connor broke free of the group and backed away to the north side of Hollywood Boulevard, slipping into the salvation group, as if for sanctuary. The doomsayers started across the street.

Car horns began beeping. The policemen shifted into alert mode, pinpointing the source of the commotion, which wasn't too difficult considering the source was screaming and waving his arms over his head.

Connor started yelling taunts at the salvation crowd: "Blow out your candles! No miracles today! Salvation is cancelled!"

As all the activity and interest focused on Connor, Gunn strode deliberately across the street, dodging a taxicab and ducking under a sawhorse along the way. After those few seconds of exposure, he slipped behind the monolith, hidden from the two cops who were closing in on Connor. Realizing his time was limited, Gunn immediately placed his palms against the carved surface of the statue, running his fingers down the cold lines of the demonic face, the slight depression that was the wide-open mouth. Wesley had talked about a discrepancy between the actual and the perceived surface of the stone. Gunn noticed the difference, but it was ever so slight. If he hadn't been looking for it, he would have missed it. *Means it's closer,* he surmised. Of bigger concern was the vibration Angel mentioned that only he, and possibly Connor, could detect; that was no longer true. *I feel it,* Gunn thought. On the chance he was falling victim to an overactive imagination, he raised his hands from the surface, took a deep breath, and lowered them again. *Nope. It's definitely humming.*

"What's wrong with you?" Connor yelled at the onlookers. "Get these kids home! It's past their bedtime."

"That's enough," shouted an authoritative voice.

If Gunn had brought scientific instruments with him, he wouldn't have known what to do with them. He'd joked about Wesley analyzing samples, but that was more Fred's area of expertise. Fred was the self-proclaimed science nerd. Wesley was the mystical and supernatural lore hound. Gunn was a soldier in the ongoing war against evil, and a damn good one at that. *But how do I fight a rock?* he wondered. *'Cause I'm feelin' a little useless here.*

Connor was buying Gunn time, but Gunn hadn't thought his plan through. He was running out of ideas—fast. And his frustration was worse now than it had been when he was on the curb. His investigative foray was proving how ineffective he was in this type of situation. *Miss a few classes in Aramaic and nobody lets you forget it!* he thought.

"What's the point?" he whispered to himself as he shoved futilely at the statue. "Nobody home yet."

Connor yelled, "Wake up, people! It's a hunk of rock!"

"You need to cool off, son!"

"Get away from me!"

Gunn shook his head. *Connor's about to spend the night in jail, and for what?* Gunn pounded the side of his fists against the smooth rock. "Knock-knock!" he bellowed, forgetting stealth in his frustration. No change in the vibration, no response from within, nothing. A big waste of time. "Hello! Any rock-heads in there?"

A flashlight beam played across his face. One of the cops had heard him and come running. "Step away from the rock!"

"Why?" Gunn asked irritably. "Not like I can hurt it. You can't hurt it. Go ahead, shoot it. It's indestructible. It's just a big wedge between me and my—"

"Step away from the rock." The policeman's

voice had gone dangerously calm. Gunn noticed the policeman's free hand had dropped to his waist to unsnap the flap over his handgun. "Hands in the air!"

"Right," Gunn said. "No problem." Gunn raised both hands high in the air, demonstrating he was no threat to the police officer. "Just a big, stupid— rock!" With the last word, he swung the toe of his booted foot against the base of the monolith, as if to prove his point about its impervious nature.

"Look, pal, you want to spend the night in lockup?"

Gunn started to shake his head. "You feel that? Like a storm comin'."

A series of wind gusts buffeted them. Gunn staggered toward the vertical face of the monolith, reaching out to catch his balance. The policeman turned in a quick circle, as if looking for the source of the wind. A moment later, the street began to tremble.

The indignant yelling on the opposite side of the monolith transformed into startled cries and screams. Gunn saw one pedestrian drop his disposable camera, turn tail, and sprint down Hollywood Boulevard in the opposite direction. The milling crowd began to scatter.

"What's happening?" the cop asked softly.

Gunn had no answer.

The wind gusted again, worse than before,

sending extinguished candles and abandoned doomsday signs swirling around the street. A moment later, Connor lumbered around the statue, his forearm in front of his face to shield him from the blast of wind and grit. Trailing behind Connor, the other policeman staggered against the force of the wind.

"Gunn?" Connor called. "You didn't . . . ?"

Jumpstart the apocalypse? Gunn shook his head, confused. He half expected the tail of a twister to drop down and snatch him into the sky. "Maybe this thing is booby-trapped, Indiana Jones–style."

"What?"

"Movie reference," Gunn said. "Never mi—"

A flash of white light blinded him, accompanied by the strongest gust of wind yet, driving Gunn against the stone demon face and effectively erasing existence. With that thought, the ground dropped away from him. Gunn's arms thrashed about, finding nothing. . . .

Connor's ears had popped, as from a sudden change in air pressure.

A moment after the bright light faded, Connor blinked his eyes rapidly, attempting through sheer force of will to dispel the blotchy white afterimages dancing across his retinas. He recovered enough to see the monolith, the two policemen bumbling around blindly, but not Gunn.

Connor backed away from the statue to increase his field of vision. At most, a few seconds had passed. No more than that. Not enough time for Gunn to run away or hide. He would have been blinded by the light as well, momentarily helpless.

The wind had stopped, but the air seemed charged with something like electricity, something that made his skin itch in anticipation. The mass of people had scattered. Most were blocks away. They hadn't been standing in front of the demon side of the statue. On the other side, they would have been shielded from the blinding light, by the statue itself. The other side . . .

Connor circled around the statue to the side showing the agonized, screaming face frozen in the slab of stone. Nobody waited there.

Connor shook his head in disbelief.

Gunn was gone.

CHAPTER ELEVEN

Confused by Gunn's sudden disappearance, Connor was about to turn away from the opposite side of the monolith when the ambient light winked out as an eerie conical ray of utter darkness erupted from the agonized stone face. It blotted out Connor's view of the north side of Hollywood Boulevard, as if that side of the street had been ripped out of existence.

With the wave of darkness came a rush of cold, foul air.

And again his ears popped.

As abruptly as the inky darkness had flashed from the agonized face, it faded, and the world across the street emerged from that disturbing memory of blackness—revealing something unexpected.

The stone face expelled a black and gleaming shape, like a rippling shadow of a hurtling inhuman form that became substantial as it hit the ground—running.

Though the sudden manifestation startled him, Connor recovered with uncanny reflexes and amazing speed to give chase. The unanswered questions didn't interfere with his hunter's instincts. With no guarantee that he would find Gunn by staying at the monolith, Connor's priorities shifted. He formed a two-step plan. Catch the demon; make it talk.

Surprisingly, he wondered what Angel would do. Would his vampire father blame him for abandoning Gunn at the monolith to pursue the demon, or would he agree with Connor's choice? Holtz wouldn't have questioned the decision. Angel was a warrior, but one who would sometimes place his friends' lives above victory in battle. Gunn was missing and might be lost forever, but the demon was right in front of Connor, the only link to what had just happened. If Connor had to make the decision again, he'd make the same decision. *If Angel has a problem with that*, he thought, *too bad*.

On powerful legs, the demon sprinted across the street, heading south, as Connor had expected, darting between moving cars. Connor dashed after him, a second behind. Too late to shoot the gap between the cars, he leaped into the air. His right foot landed on the rounded hood of a silver PT

Cruiser, which he used as a springboard to launch himself out of traffic and to the sidewalk.

The demon wore a black helmet, a gleaming black breastplate, and coarse trousers tucked into heavy leather boots. His pumping arms revealed broad hands, with thick-clawed fingers ending in hooked points. Despite the added weight of the armor and boots, the demon was surprisingly fast. Connor ran at top speed to keep pace with him.

Because of the police presence at the monolith, Gunn and Connor had carried no weapons to the stakeout. Connor had mixed feelings about that intentional oversight. Although the burden of a portable arsenal would have slowed him down, one well-placed crossbow bolt could have ended the chase within a block.

As if avoiding some hidden obstruction, the demon veered across Ivar Avenue. *Not away from something,* Connor realized. *Toward something— someone. Two people!*

A young couple, a man and a woman, walking side by side, both drinking from disposable coffee cups. The woman wore a light, sleeveless sweater and a short black skirt. The man sported a short-sleeved shirt over dark jeans. Casual night out. The rush of footfalls alerted them, but their reaction time was all too humanly slow. They pivoted curiously, looking back over their shoulders, completely oblivious to the cold certainty that they were a handful of seconds away from a gruesome death. Their eyes went wide, jaws dropping.

From deep down, Connor found an extra burst of speed. But he watched in horrible frustration as the demon's claws rose high, then swept down in a vicious stroke calculated to tear out the man's throat. He had no time to stop the attack, so Connor tried to avert it. He drove his left shoulder into the demon's back and swatted the powerful arm down, hoping to alter its deadly trajectory. Connor's desperate attack knocked all four of them to the ground. Coffee geysered from squashed cups. A whipping line of blood sprayed up from the injured man.

Connor and the demon tumbled straight ahead, driving a wedge between the couple. The woman screamed while the man writhed, moaning, on the ground. But a quick glance revealed that the man's arm—not his throat—had been sliced open. "Compression!" Connor yelled at the woman. "Stop the bleeding—call for help!"

While Connor was distracted, the demon roared and slammed into him before he had climbed to his feet, knocking him flat, stunned. The sole of a worn leather boot rushed toward Connor's face. He caught the boot in both hands and twisted viciously. Unbalanced, the demon staggered sideways and fell against the passenger door of a parked green Honda Accord. Connor plowed into the demon again, ramming him against the car.

Claws swept toward Connor's face, almost shredding his nose as he jerked back out of reach. The demon sidestepped a snap kick aimed at his midsection, and Connor's foot shattered the car's side window.

The demon thought about returning to the couple to finish what he'd started, but after taking one glance at Connor, he decided to resume his southbound course. Although Connor had thwarted the demon's homicidal intentions, he hadn't injured or slowed him. The demon's head and torso were protected by the black armor. The helmet covered his head with a T-shaped opening in the front. The horizontal gap revealed deep-set, smoldering red eyes, but the vertical slit exposed only a hint of nostrils and a toothy maw.

Behind Connor, the woman talked frantically on a cell phone, while her male acquaintance moaned softly. Connor had done all he could for them. If he hadn't interrupted the demon, they would both be dead by now, their corpses a scattered, unrecognizable mess of viscera and bone.

Ignoring the tenderness of his ribs, Connor chased the demon down North Cahuenga. In all the battles he'd fought in Quor-Toth, he'd never broken a bone, and he didn't expect to start now. He had the confidence of youth bolstered by endless years of battlefield experience. His biggest problem now was getting close enough to lay his hands on the fleet demon. *Stay close*, he thought, *and I'll get another chance*.

Connor's opportunity came sooner than expected when, once again, the demon altered his course to attack an unwary human. The intended victim was a pudgy, gray-haired man who had just stepped out of a corner tavern and paused to light a cigar.

As the demon stopped to swing his claws, Connor dove at a low angle and struck the demon behind the knees. They rolled apart on the ground and sprang to their feet. The demon lunged, his claws tearing through Connor's shirt and biting into flesh. Connor roared, gripping the demon in a bear hug and driving him into the side of a parked conversion van. The impact damaged the side panel and set off a wailing car alarm, which startled the demon. With a roar of his own, the demon shoved Connor back.

After jumping backward to put some space between them, Connor tried to sweep the demon's feet out from under him. Missing, he rolled over, planted both palms on the ground, and snapped a kick at the demon's kneecap. In the process of leaping back to avoid the attack, the demon slammed himself against the side of the van, which continued to hoot and screech.

Connor sprang to his feet and used the distraction of the alarm to back the confused demon into the street. Cars swerved around the pair, and outraged drivers laid on their horns in a concerted show of disapproval. Enraged by the attack and the wall of sound, the demon plucked a tall man with thinning blond hair out of the driver's seat of a blue Mustang convertible as it shot past. He hurled the blond man at Connor like a weapon. Reacting on instinct, Connor ducked low to the right, and the man sailed over his left shoulder, clipping Connor's arm with a tasseled loafer.

A moment later, the derelict Mustang slammed into the back of a taxicab with the weighty bass crunch of crushed metal. Meanwhile, the Mustang's owner crawled, then staggered, to his feet, one hand pressed to his scraped, bloody forehead as he wandered, dazed, toward the sidewalk, and out of immediate harm.

When the demon reached the far side of the street, he grabbed a man off a bicycle and tossed him against the brick wall of a law office. The man slumped to the ground, unconscious, and Connor half-expected the demon to eviscerate him. Instead, he hoisted the bicycle in one powerful hand and flung it at Connor. Its wheels spinning lazily, the lime-colored bike whizzed toward Connor's head. He dropped forward, into and out of a somersault, letting the bike sail harmlessly overhead and crash into the highway behind him with a screech of mangled metal.

The demon paused, head cocked to the side as if listening to a faint sound. Connor guessed that the sound was actually inside the demon's head. The Summoner was calling him! And hadn't the original plan been to follow an escapee back to the Summoner's hideout?

Connor had two options. If he failed to capture the demon, he might be able to revert to Plan A, letting the demon lead him to the Summoner. But only if there was no other way. Connor couldn't risk losing sight of the demon on purpose. He'd already lost its scent once. There was no guarantee that a second attempt would end differently. Connor would much rather catch the demon and, should it be necessary, force him to lead the way to the Summoner's lair.

While the demon was taking silent instruction from the Summoner, Connor closed the gap. He grabbed a street sign in both hands and pushed off with a double kick aimed at the demon's head, hoping to dislodge the helmet.

Distracted, the demon noticed Connor's attack a moment too late and staggered backward under the powerful impact, colliding with the wall. But the helmet remained secure. Though the demon didn't seem to suffer any harm from the kick, Connor had no choice but to press his advantage, until the demon crouched beside the unconscious bicyclist and gripped the man's exposed throat in a handful of nasty claws. He looked up at Connor and shook his head. The message was clear: Connor held the bicyclist's fate in the demon's hands. One threatening move and the demon would tear out the man's throat.

"Let him go," Connor said tightly.

The demon shook his head again and squeezed a little harder. Droplets of blood trickled down the man's exposed neck. Connor wondered if the demon had any intention of sparing the man, regardless of Connor's next move. Would the man be a casualty of the demon war either way?

Across the street and around the accident scene, people were shouting hysterically, urging bystanders to call the police. No one took a step closer to Connor and the demon.

"You and me," Connor said. "Leave him out of it!"

The demon cocked his head again, as if he were considering the merits of the honorable challenge . . . or listening again. Then he shrugged and squeezed once, a fierce convulsion of claws, slicing deep into the man's throat.

Connor roared, "Son of a—!"

As Connor surged forward, the demon heaved the bicyclist into his path. Connor caught the man. He didn't know if the man could survive the wound, but he feared he was already dead, and laid him gently on the ground. When Connor looked up, he saw the demon scaling the brick wall, his claws gouging into the surface as he propelled himself upward.

Connor sprang toward a downspout on the wall, clambering up the rickety metal pipe even as the supports groaned and began to pop free of the brick; up and over, as the rain gutter collapsed under his scrambling feet and hands. Across a slanted roof he ran, targeting the fleeing demon, who then dropped off the far side without hesitation. Connor was seconds behind him, leaping down to the sidewalk, then sprinting across the street.

Over the course of the next several blocks, the demon tossed two trash cans, a newspaper vending machine, and a parked Harley-Davidson motorcycle at Connor, missing by inches each time. Police sirens began to fill the night. Connor imagined they were getting closer, following the trail of destruction, screeching car brakes, and screaming pedestrians.

Though the demon continued to run southward, it seemed he was trying to lose his pursuer before joining the Summoner. But Connor was relentless, following the demon onto rooftops, down alleys, and across multiple lanes of speeding traffic. In desperation, perhaps, the demon crossed a supermarket parking lot and slipped inside the store's automatic doors. Connor was right behind him. In seconds, the screams began. Panicked cashiers and evening shoppers ran for the exits, abandoning filled shopping carts in the aisles and checkout lanes.

Connor followed the demon down one aisle after another. Whenever Connor came too close, the demon tried to slow him down by tipping over end displays of snacks and two-liter soda bottles, or by flinging toys, hardware supplies, lightbulbs, books, and economy bags of pet food in his path.

Connor thought about returning to the front of the store to wait for the demon to escape by the automatic doors, but what if he slipped out the back, exiting the store via an employee entrance or the rear loading bays? He had no choice but to keep the demon in sight.

Every time he stumbled or tripped over an obstacle hurled at him and let the demon put too much distance between them, he thought about how Angel would react to his failure. If he lost the demon, Angel would blame him for Gunn's disappearance, insisting that Connor should have stayed at the monolith and called for help. Anticipating Angel's second-guessing reaction, Connor let his rage fuel him, channeling that burst of adrenaline into his dogged pursuit of the demon. He would *not* fail!

The demon turned down the canned-food aisle and stopped midway. He swept an armful of cans off a shelf and began using them as missiles, firing at Connor's head and torso. Connor ducked behind an overburdened shopping cart and waited as cans pelted the metal bars of the cart with loud clunks and clangs, dislodging boxes of laundry detergent and sugar-coated cereal from the top of the prepackaged food mound.

He thought about grabbing some cylindrical missiles of his own, but he would have to expose himself to have a chance at an accurate throw. He couldn't risk taking a shot to the head. A few dazed seconds on his part and the demon would be long gone. Instead of reaching for cans, Connor gripped the back of the shopping cart on both sides and rushed forward, using the cart as a battering ram.

Direct hit!

The demon, the shopping cart, and Connor went down in a pile of groceries. Connor hurled a large bag of flour at the demon, but its claws slashed through the bag, and a cloud of flour dust billowed up around them.

Coughing, Connor climbed to his feet in time to see the demon turn the corner at the end of the aisle. Without hesitation, Connor clambered up and over the emptied shelves. From there, he leaped from top shelf to top shelf, clearing each wide aisle in a single bound. He caught fleeting glimpses of the figure in black armor making a beeline for the front doors.

At the frozen food aisle, Connor leaped on top

of the nearest freezer, turned right, and raced along freezer tops toward the front of the store. He saw the demon pause, then dart through the automatic doors into the night. Connor had to move fast if he hoped to make up lost ground.

He jumped from the edge of the last freezer across the gap to the twelve-items-or-less express lane, landing on the conveyor belt but taking out a rack filled with impulse purchase items in a piñata-like eruption of tabloids, batteries, chewing gum, breath mints, and chocolate bars.

Dropping to the floor, he hoisted a shopping cart in both arms and hurled it at the wide plate-glass window bearing signs announcing double coupons. As the window shattered, Connor dove through the gap, following the shopping cart's trajectory as he shielded his face from pelting shards of glass. He hit the ground rolling, then hurdled the sliding cart in time to see the dark figure loping across the far corner of the parking lot.

Flashing lights from two police cruisers swept across the front of the supermarket, accompanied by the whoop of sirens. Since none of the officers had noticed the black-armored demon running out onto the street, they were sure to hold Connor entirely responsible for trashing the store. Connor had no intention of stopping to explain or to answer a hundred questions. Without hesitation, he scrambled up onto the hood of the nearest police car, leaping over the roof lights and across the trunk, avoiding the long, whip-like antennas like a slalom skier weaving his way around course flagpoles.

Connor cleared the parking lot at a sprint while the police cars looped around in tight turns on screeching tires to give chase. *They'll have to shoot me or run me down,* Connor thought. *That's the only way they'll stop me.*

Unlike the demon, though, the police cars were constrained to roads. The demon cut across lawns, backyards, up walls, over houses and buildings, leaping rooftop to rooftop, down alleys, over locked fences. And Connor followed every step of the way. Within a mile, accustomed to pursuing human criminals, the cars had fallen behind. By the time reinforcements arrived, Connor and the demon had slipped well out of their reach.

Past a row of houses, Connor saw the demon bolt across a knoll fronting a construction site and disappear within the skeletal wood framework of an unfinished house. Some of the two-by-four framing was exposed. In other areas, plywood had been nailed in place, creating blind spots.

Connor looped around to the back, expecting the demon to exit there. After long moments of silence, he concluded that the demon was waiting inside the house, hoping to lure Connor into the deep shadows . . . into a trap. But at least he *knew* it was a trap. That was some consolation.

He entered the house through the framed back door and edged toward the interior, his head swiveling back and forth. Plywood covered the floor joists, so his footing was secure. Above, the row of uncovered ceiling trusses looked like the exposed ribs of a slaughtered beast. Some of the trusses were hidden from Connor's view, making an attack from above a definite possibility.

To his right was the framed doorway into the kitchen. He peered into the gloomy room, saw nothing, and turned back as a dark shape rose out of a hole in the ground and charged him with a flash of claws. Instinctively, Connor ducked.

The two-by-four behind his head exploded from the force of a ferocious blow, splitting in half. The demon had been aiming for Connor's face. Connor didn't have the luxury of a helmet. That attack would have pulped his face.

He threw his shoulder into the demon, staggering him sideways, and giving Connor enough time to wrench the split two-by-four from its base. Simple as that, he had a makeshift club. He swung it like an ax, battering the demon's helmet and shoulders repeatedly.

The demon raised a hand, finally intercepting one of the overhead blows, and his claws sliced through the wood, splitting it lengthwise. Then he lashed out with a leg, his heavy boot striking

Connor in the abdomen, forcing him to stumble backward to maintain his balance. The demon charged, and Connor attempted to plant his back foot—*attempted* because the floor wasn't there!

He stepped back into a pit and tumbled down wooden stairs, busting right through a meager wooden railing and falling into darkness, striking cement with a bone-jarring thud. *Basement,* he thought. *He attacked me from the basement. Probably felt right at home down here.*

From above, Connor heard heavy footfalls, then abrupt silence.

He's getting away!

Connor lumbered up the stairs two at a time, then ran down the hall to the front of the building—the direction of the receding footfalls—and the front doorway. He saw something leaning against the sill of an intended front window: a claw hammer. Plucking it from the ledge, he hurried through the framed doorway and out into the night. No cars or pedestrians on the street. Nothing. "No!" Connor whispered angrily. *Not all this for nothing!*

He took a deep breath, tried to calm himself, and the first thought that came to him was—*south!* Although the demon's final destination was unclear, Connor knew he would continue south. *Without anyone following him,* Connor reasoned, *he'll head straight to the Summoner.*

Connor raced south at full speed, figuring he was

only a couple of miles from Inglewood. The demon had had less than a ten-second head start and would probably have to slow down to take telepathic directions to the Summoner's lair, after reporting that he'd slipped free of Connor. *Just as well,* Connor thought. *Maybe I'll catch them all off-guard.*

He almost missed a turn. Running as fast as he could on the pavement, heading south on the east side of the street, he caught a glimpse of a shadowy shape darting around a corner, bearing west. *The demon!*

As Connor had expected, the demon was slowing, listening to the Summoner's mental call, changing course as instructed. The demon was more than a block distant, too far to hear Connor's footfalls, too busy listening to his master's voice to pay attention to much else. Given the distance between them, Connor decided to maintain his stealth advantage. *Avoid the distraction of detours,* he told himself, *keep the demon in sight, and follow him to the Summoner.*

The demon thought he'd won, but Connor refused to give up and would not accept failure. One way or another, he would catch the demon and force the hell-spawn to tell him where Gunn was.

Trapped in darkness, confined to a space with the approximate physical dimensions of a coffin, Gunn lay stunned for a moment. Briefly, he wondered if that was how a new vampire felt upon waking in his grave. Since the thought of drinking blood wasn't appealing at all, he assumed he hadn't joined the ranks of the undead.

Nevertheless, he wasn't sure where he was or how he'd gotten there. His consciousness had blipped out, but for how long, he couldn't say. Had he lost minutes or days? As he probed the edges of his world, pushing first up and then to the sides, he tried to remember his last waking moment. For a while, nothing came to him. Then he remembered he'd been with Connor, walking up Vine to Hollywood Boulevard, and Connor had been goading the doomsday and salvation crowds, providing a distraction.

He remembered examining the demon face of the monolith, feeling the vibration, noticing the visual discrepancy. The police officer! Kicking . . . he'd kicked the monolith out of pure frustration, and then a storm . . . no, winds. Winds pushing him toward the monolith. And light . . . he remembered blinding light . . .

Was he blind? He raised one hand up to his face, pressed it against his nose, but couldn't see his fingers. Complete darkness or blindness. *Either way,* Gunn thought, *doesn't matter in here. Doesn't matter until I get out.*

Falling. That was the last thing he recalled. The

ground had somehow opened up beneath him during the whiteout, and he'd flailed around without touching anything. And now he was trapped . . . in a body-sized stone prison cell. He started to imagine the walls closing in on him, about to squeeze him, crush him to pulp. Deep breaths calmed him, helped stave off the creeping claustrophobia. "It's okay . . . okay . . . just chill. . . ."

With the tips of his fingers, Gunn explored the walls of his cramped cell. The ceiling, cold and solid above him, the walls inches away on either side, and the slab of cool rock beneath him. Searching for a lever, a switch, any kind of release, he discovered many tiny holes beneath his body, bored into the stone. Too small to accommodate his thumb or fingers. He wondered what purpose they served. Ventilation, he guessed. "At least I can breathe in here."

But the holes had another purpose.

Moments later, Gunn felt something warm ooze out of the holes, seeping around his body. He imagined blood—and worse things. "Hey! Hey!" he yelled into the merciless darkness. "Get me outta here! Now!"

The gushing warmth swelled over his body, covering his legs, his abdomen, and chest. He raised his head as high as he could, his forehead pressed against the cool stone above, but the warm tide flooded into his ears and cleared his jaw, creeping toward his mouth, nose, and eyes.

Wherever his flesh was exposed, the warm goo pressed against his skin—*into* his skin—seeping into his pores with the sound of whispering, demented voices. Seconds, or an eternity, later, it began to burrow under his skin like wriggling fire. Gunn convulsed, thrashing helplessly in the stone coffin and, with his last free breath before his mouth became flooded with the malevolent ooze, he screamed.

CHAPTER TWELVE

On the second floor of the condemned office building, Sehjenkhai maintained his vigil in expectant silence. Standing in darkness, he peered out into the night, and sensed the monolith's presence—its interdimensional weight—several miles away on Hollywood Boulevard. With the passing of every hour, the portal had become more substantial to him, and his anticipation had increased. He'd summoned a bridge between worlds, and would soon witness its completion. *And wolves beyond counting will cross over to this vast field of sheep,* Sehjenkhai thought.

Though Sehjenkhai waited in quiet anticipation, his companions were far less patient. Agitated, the demon mastiffs prowled around Sehjenkhai in a protective circle, as if they were aware of some unknown threat to him. The khaipuhr had uncanny instincts and, since they had saved his life on more than one occasion, Sehjenkhai trusted those instincts without question. It was possible the khaipuhr merely sensed the coming war and the slaughter of tens of thousands of humans. Or, since they were attuned to him, perhaps they were simply giving physical expression to his contained excitement. And yet, his ever-cautious nature made him consider the possibility of a threat. He had guarded his true nature, if not his true name, which would be meaningless to present-day humans. Some might connect him to Rebecca Wade, but he couldn't be implicated in the disappearance of the selfish Hollywood actress. By the time the authorities even suspected foul play, it would be too late for anyone to care about one foolish girl. They would be much too busy running for their lives, watching helplessly as their cities burned. Certainly there was no way anyone could connect him to the appearance of the monolith, especially since the humans were unaware of its true purpose. *Unless the early arrivals would be foolish enough to lead a human threat here,* he thought, *I have nothing to fear.*

By occasionally eavesdropping on their squabbling, Sehjenkhai had learned the names of the early arrivals: Krrjn and Jrrg, half-brothers from the same mother. After they'd become bored with the decapitated human head, Krrjn had tossed it to the khaipuhr. The half-brothers laughed as the demon mastiffs fought over the bony morsel. And Sehjenkhai was happy to have the last of the woman's corpse destroyed. Nothing to link her death to the demon warriors, or them to Sehjenkhai.

Without any mayhem to occupy their time, the half-brothers removed their breastplates and began a game of battle taunts and grappling. The game involved attempts to rake the flesh of one's opponent with slashing claws. The first to draw blood scored a point. Then they would square off for another round. Presumably reaching a certain number of points would mean ultimate victory, but the contest never progressed that far. Whenever one made the other bleed, they would spend the next several minutes trying to kill each other before calling a truce and starting over.

Sehjenkhai tolerated their vicious pastime, and wouldn't have been too disappointed if they managed to kill each other. As long as they were bored, they represented a threat of exposure. In the meantime, he encouraged the game ostensibly as a way for them to hone their battle reflexes.

As he watched, a pulse of pressure struck him behind the eyes. As fast as the pain had come, it was gone.

Another early arrival!

One this time, he realized. But regardless of the number of arrivals, the threat was immediate. The new arrival would seek him out, sensing Sehjenkhai's connection to the monolith, a supernatural gravity pulling the demon into the Summoner's psychic orbit.

Sehjenkhai closed his eyes and opened his mind to the other awareness, his consciousness rippling across the miles that separated them. Already Sehjenkhai sensed violence—thwarted violence! Something—someone—had engaged the demon warrior in battle—and that someone was holding his own. *Remarkable,* Sehjenkhai thought. *Perhaps this is the threat that the khaipuhr sense.*

Not wanting to distract the new arrival in the middle of a battle, Sehjenkhai eased out of the demon's mind, continuing to sense his movements, but not attempting communication. The new arrival broke away from the battle and continued south, as the Summoner knew he would. Each time Sehjenkhai was about to speak into the new one's mind, the battle was renewed. He sensed the demon's confusion. His relentless adversary was a young man who seemed ordinary but appeared to be as strong and as fast as the demon himself. Pride wouldn't allow the new one to admit the possibility that his tenacious foe might be stronger or faster.

Sehjenkhai permitted the demon free and destructive rein for a while, but after a multiple-car traffic accident, the Summoner finally spoke, his voice a whisper filtered through Sehjenkhai's mind to the mind of the new one. *"Welcome to a new world, brother, a world ripe for conquest. Yes, it is I who called you to this world. Even now, you follow the path to me unbidden. It is in your nature. Soon, all your warrior brothers will cross over to this world, but for now we few must bide our time. Two of your brothers—Krrjn and Jrrg—wait with me here! Come to me, but come alone. Free yourself from this bothersome pursuer. By any means necessary. Then come, but be sure you curb your appetites! Lead the humans not to my door! They are oblivious to what awaits them, and I would keep them in the dark—until the dark is all they know of us."*

Sehjenkhai waited a moment for the demon to assimilate his message. *Will he listen?* Sehjenkhai wondered.

"I am called Rrjk."

"Welcome, Rrjk!" Sehjenkhai sent back to the demon's mind. *"Join us in stealth, for soon we will have the human world at our mercy. And then the humans will learn we are merciless!"*

Sehjenkhai sensed Rrjk taking a hostage to slow his pursuer, but the demon had no recourse but to kill the hostage and use the corpse as a projectile weapon. He climbed up a wall, crossed a roof, and dropped onto the other side. And the human followed. The demon weaved through traffic, threw obstacles in the path of the human—including a motorcycle—but nothing slowed him.

With his remote mental awareness, Sehjenkhai followed the battle through a supermarket, and nervously witnessed the close brush with law enforcement vehicles. The demon rushed through a housing development, hurdled fences, scaled walls, ducked down alleys, and took random turns in a dizzying course no human should have been able to follow. And yet somehow the young man kept pace with every step, jump, and lunge of the way.

Rrjk slipped into the skeletal shadows of an unfinished house and ducked into an opening in the floor that led to the basement. He waited, and attacked when the human's back was turned.

Sehjenkhai was surprised when the human survived the attack. Rrjk must have misjudged his blow. He winced as the human struck Rrjk with a section of wood, but ultimately the demon got the upper hand. He kicked the human down the basement stairs and fled. Sehjenkhai could only hope the human had broken his neck in the fall. Regardless, Rrjk had escaped his pursuer. He could now join Sehjenkhai, Krrjn, Jrrg, and the khaipuhr as they waited the final hours before the crossing.

"Open your mind, Rrjk, and I will show you the way."

"It's like trying to find the proverbial needle in the haystack," Wesley said from the passenger seat of the GTX.

Angel had the convertible top down to improve visibility, which would have helped if there were anything to see. So far, they'd had no luck. "If the needle knew you were looking for it," Angel added. "And was trying to hide."

"I'm beginning to fear the Summoner won't show his hand until after the megalith phases into our dimension."

"Wonder if Gunn and Connor are this bored?" Angel asked.

"I imagine Gunn is sick of looking at the megalith by now," Wesley said. "But they should endeavor to enjoy the calm before the storm."

"Especially considering the size of the coming storm."

"Precisely," Wes said grimly. A few moments of quiet, fruitless driving passed.

"No reason for him to reveal himself," Angel said. "The Summoner, that is. Let's hope the demons and his guard dogs aren't as careful."

"True," Wesley said. "As a general rule, demons are notoriously impatient."

"This . . . Sehjenkhai has been trying for three thousand years to pull off this bit of summoning," Angel commented. "Counts as patient, in my book. Persistent, anyway."

"Of course, there are exceptions. The most famous being the N'aa'taakn demon, which hibernates nine hundred and seventy-three years between feasting on thirty raw human livers in three days."

"Then what?"

"Another nine hundred seventy-three years of hibernation."

"As demons go," Angel said, "a real under-achiever."

"The N'aa'taakn is the size of a common house cat," Wesley said. "After thirty human livers in three days, it's rather bloated."

"Yeah, but is it really worth almost a millennium of indigestion?"

"From what I hear, the N'aa'taakn are rather fond of human livers," Wesley explained. "But there are other examples of demons exhibiting unusual degrees of patience. The Tokkori are known to hang upside down in caves for years at a time, and the—"

"Wes."

"Sorry, I was simply attempting to pass the—"

"What's that look like to you?"

Wes leaned forward in his seat. "Those two men standing in line at the ATM?"

Angel nodded. "The one in back, the big one in the Panama hat and trench coat, seems a bit over-dressed for the weather. And the young Hispanic gentleman in the black T-shirt and blue jeans, standing at the keypad . . . around his neck, is that some sort of scarf?"

"No!" Angel said, swerving the GTX up the bank's driveway and along the lane leading to the ATM. He shifted the car into park and jumped out, walking toward the pair. He noted a crushed hub-cap leaning against the curb.

If they weren't together, the man in back was definitely invading the other man's personal space. That had been Angel's first clue. The neck bulge had been the second.

"Is this one out of service too?" Angel asked casually. "I really hate when that happens, don't you?"

The man in the trench coat spoke in a smooth yet threatening voice. "Go away."

The younger man shuddered and croaked, "Yeah, man, do like he says." His hands were trembling over the keypad. "This one's out of cash."

"Oh, I don't need much," Angel said. "I could probably take it out of this guy's hide."

"*Muy loco*," the Hispanic man muttered. "Get lost, *amigo!*"

The trench-coated man hissed, "You had your chance," and lifted the younger man three feet off the ground, holding him aloft with a slick black tentacle that extended from the front of the unbuttoned coat. The tentacle constricted around the man's throat, choking him. His face turning red as he lost the fight for air, he clawed ineffectively at the powerful serpentine loops.

"Let him go," Angel said in a dangerous voice. "Now!"

"Not until his head pops off like a champagne cork," the demon said in his deep, silky voice. "Then it's your turn."

Wesley stepped up beside Angel and said, "There are two of us."

"That's okay," the demon said, and shrugged off his trench coat, revealing a writhing nest of oily black tentacles sliding around his torso. "I have sixteen tentacles!"

The Hispanic man's head was lolling to the side. Angel flipped the smashed hubcap into the air with the tip of his foot, caught it in his hand, and hurled it like an oversized shuriken. The spinning disk sliced through the extended tentacle. The Hispanic man fell to the ground as thick yellow fluid spurted from the severed tentacle stump. The demon hissed in pain. "Better double-check," Angel said. "I only count fifteen."

As he scrambled to his feet, the Hispanic man peeled the coils of the severed tentacle away from his throat with a mixed expression of fright and disgust. He threw it as far away from him as possible. "Run!" he shouted to Angel and Wesley. *"El Diablo!"* The man ran from the bank's parking lot without a single glance back.

Wesley nodded in the direction of the fleeing man. "Suppose that was the sensible thing."

"Never was the sensible type myself," Angel said, wary as the demon stalked toward him. His legs seemed to be thicker versions of the tentacles, but not as eel-like and flexible. Same for the arms, which ended in four boneless, finger-like feelers. Beneath the rumpled Panama hat, the demon's head was smooth, matte black, with liquid black eyes. Vaguely human from a distance, but not even remotely human up close.

"You owe me an arm," the demon said. Two tentacles, each with a ten-foot reach, snapped out like bullwhips and wrapped around Angel's arm. "And a leg for good measure." Two more tentacles flashed at Angel, curling around his calf.

The tentacles were extraordinarily powerful, and the demon had no trouble hoisting Angel in the air and slamming his body into the brick wall of the bank. With his free hand, Angel pried at the tentacles securing his arm, but after a moment's effort, a fifth whipping tentacle caught his free wrist and yanked his hand away. The demon smashed Angel into the wall a second time. Wesley rushed forward, but Angel shouted, "Wes—no!"

Wesley halted not a moment too soon. Several tentacles whipped and snapped inches from his face, arms, and legs. The demon stepped toward him.

"Wes, now might be a good time to"—*SLAM!*— "raid the trunk!"

Angel attempted to grab the tentacles in his

hands, hoping to squeeze them hard enough to cause the demon pain, but they were too slick with some sort of natural exudation for him to maintain a firm grip. By the time the demon rammed him into the brick wall a fourth time, Angel's other leg had been ensnared by two tentacles.

"Demon muggers," Angel said, and grunted as his body struck brick a fifth jarring time. "What's the world coming to?"

"In my defense, I only kill those with account balances below daily ATM withdrawal maximums," the demon said. "But you I will kill on principle."

"Or not at all," Wesley said, slicing the blade of a machete through one of the tentacles holding Angel's right arm.

With a roar, the demon lashed out at Wesley with a flurry of tentacles. Wesley, expecting the attack, dodged back out of range, circled around, and lopped off one of the tentacles holding Angel's left leg. Angel stretched his right arm toward Wesley, hand open. After a quick double feint, Wesley stepped in close and slapped the hilt of a hunting knife against Angel's palm.

Though his freedom of movement was too limited to hack through the tentacles gripping his left arm, Angel managed to twist enough to position the short blade against the surface of one of them. Several sawing strokes and he'd cut his way through the tentacle. While Wesley continued to seek an opening, Angel began to cut through the remaining tentacle on his left arm.

Enraged, the demon lifted Angel overhead, then slammed him against the blacktop parking lot. While the tentacles were extended and taut, Wesley darted in from the side and hacked through two more with the machete. Unfortunately, he misjudged the distance and couldn't slip away fast enough to avoid having his own legs entangled in thrashing tentacles. He fell awkwardly and began kicking his feet, attempting to retreat in a crablike fashion.

Sensing victory, the demon focused his attention on Wesley, catching his forearm and slamming it to the ground to dislodge the machete. For the moment, the demon disregarded Angel, who was much closer and had a weapon of his own.

Knowing Wesley probably wouldn't survive one of the demon's patented tentacle smackdowns, Angel flung the knife at the demon's head, striking one of the liquid black eyes. The blade sunk in to the hilt. At once, the uninjured tentacles started thrashing. Angel felt himself lifted and thrown, colliding in midair with one of the drivethrough's support columns before dropping to the ground.

Wesley had flung himself backward, beyond the reach of the writhing tentacles. As a precaution, he scooped the machete off the ground and waited.

The demon staggered sideways a couple steps,

stumpy arms raised to his smooth black face, as he struck and rebounded from the ATM machine. First the mass of tentacles fell limp, then the demon's body flopped over, lifeless. Yellow fluid oozed out of the demon's skin and began to bubble and foam. The slick, black, rubbery flesh deflated and decomposed, leaving nothing behind but the Panama hat in the middle of a hissing yellow puddle.

Angel stared at the demon's liquid remains, while Wesley stood panting at his side. "Don't suppose he was one of the escapees?"

"I should hope not," Wesley said. "This one seemed to have an established routine for shaking down the locals, figuratively and literally. And yet, strangely, he was unconcerned about having the ATM security cameras record his image."

Angel pointed at the dark camera panel above the keypad. "He had it covered," Angel said. "Figuratively and literally."

Wesley peered closer and saw a sticky yellow substance smeared across the panel. "Indeed," Wesley said. "I imagine it evaporates or degrades after several hours."

"Long enough for the demon mugger to remain anonymous."

Wesley glanced back at the dissolving yellow puddle. "Pity, really," he said. "Since he's been operating in this area for a while, he might have seen or heard something about the megalith demons."

"I'll remember that," Angel said with grim sarcasm, "next time a demon is about to scramble your brains across the sidewalk."

"I'm not ungrateful, Angel," Wesley said. "I'm quite fond of my brains staying right where they are." He took a deep breath, adjusted his narrow glasses, and continued in a somber tone. "But the seriousness of the coming threat outweighs the risk of any personal misadventure any of us might suffer. Especially if it means gaining valuable information about stopping the demonic equinox."

"I hear you, Wes," Angel said, knowing the former Watcher was right. Personal sacrifices might be necessary—or unavoidable—if they were to succeed. The stakes were too high to let emotions dictate battle decisions. *Doesn't mean I have to like it*, Angel thought. "If the Inglewood demon population has information on the escapees, let's hope Lorne has better luck rooting it out."

CHAPTER THIRTEEN

Sea breeze in hand, Lorne was beginning to feel a little bit guilty.

He could tell from Cordelia's tensed, slumped body and Fred's frequent cursing that they were running into brick walls as often as crash test dummies. Cordelia's frustration came by way of telephone as she pressed her tattered network of Hollywood acquaintances for information about Mr. Sehjenkhai. Her fingers might be doing the walking, but they were walking in circles. At least Cordelia's fruitless conversations were with human beings. Poor Fred had been having a one-sided conversation with the computer monitor for almost thirty minutes, with similar results.

Lorne shared their frustration and should have been out making his own rounds one more time. But he was running out of friendly—and some not-so-friendly—demon faces to question. Nobody knew anything about monolith demons. Nobody knew anything, period. Maybe it was a bit of the live-and-let-live attitude that had served the demon community so well over the years. As much as the demon party line seemed to be "Don't call us, Lorne, we'll call you," Lorne had to hope that somewhere there was someone who would talk. "Now, procrastination," Lorne said softly to himself. "We can talk about that another day."

Cordelia dropped the telephone receiver in its cradle and heaved a rib-rattling sigh of resignation. "I don't believe it."

"No luck, princess?"

"I found half a dozen people who've maybe seen this guy," Cordelia said. "But that's it. They don't know anything about him. He never talked to any of them. Whenever he was with Rebecca Wade in public, he would whisper into her ear, never speaking loud enough for anyone to hear the sound of his voice. The consensus is that the guy is creepy, but that's not gonna help us find him."

"He's one technophobic demon," Fred said, looking up from the computer monitor she'd been cursing moments ago. "No information online at all. No public or private records. No addresses or phone numbers. No credit reporting. No police record. No utility bills. He must have paid cash for everything with lots of bribes and aliases along the way."

ANGEL

"There must be something," Cordelia said desperately.

"Well, a few gossip columns mention his name, but they don't know anything about him either. He lived with Rebecca Wade. Never caused any trouble—well, nothing to trigger an investigation."

"Surprised the industry rags didn't dig up something on him."

"I'm sure they tried," Fred said. "Nothing's there."

"Let's not forget, gang," Lorne said, "old Sehjenkhai has been running in stealth mode, working behind the scenes for this big day for three millennia, mostly undetected."

"Meaning?" Cordelia asked.

"Practice makes perfect," Fred said. "He's had lots of time to perfect major supernatural mojo to cover his tracks."

"Erasing personal history? Deleting information from public records?" Cordelia asked.

"Wouldn't doubt it," Lorne said. "Now toss in some hexes, spells, or potions to mess with human short-term memory and you have one Mr. Mysterioso."

"Maybe that's one of his aliases," Cordelia said, exasperated.

"Don't you see, sugar plum," Lorne said, "with the right magic whammy, he wouldn't need any aliases."

"And he would remain forever vague," Fred added.

"Ooh," Lorne said, and shuddered. "Now there's a chilling fate."

"From the man—er, demon—who never met a spotlight he didn't like," Cordelia said, "and who once headlined in Vegas."

"Those memories, sweetheart, not all sunshine and joy," Lorne said with a frown. "But you're right, I've never been of the faint of fame. Three thousand years of complete anonymity would definitely qualify as hell on earth for yours truly."

"Obviously Sehjenkhai has a different concept of hell on earth," Fred replied. "And he wants everyone to experience it."

"With those uplifting words of motivation," Lorne said, "it's time for me to head back out there and find us a lead. After all, those demons aren't about to interrogate themselves." Lorne drained his sea breeze and placed the empty glass on the desk, next to the TV set. He turned up the volume as the station switched from a live shot of the milling crowd to a piece recorded earlier showing the daylong gathering of the two tribes of fanatics: the doomsayers and the true believers. Halfway through the reporter's recorded voice-over, the picture went dark, changed to a blue screen, then to a live shot at the monolith.

Agitated, the doom-and-gloom crowd on the

south side of the street was moving en masse toward the north side, where the candlelighters were gathered.

The KTLA news reporter spoke urgently in a live voice-over. "This is Sarah Swanson reporting live from the eerie Hollywood Boulevard monolith, where, until moments ago, it has been peaceful and quiet. That changed when a young man started antagonizing the crowd gathered here—"

In the background, someone shouted, "Out of here! Go home! You're all crazy!"

Lorne looked at Cordelia and Fred as they came to watch the report. "Call me crazy," Lorne said, "but that sounds like the Boy Wonder."

The camera operator panned left and right, attempting to find the source of the booming voice, zooming in for brief glimpses before losing him again.

"Not only sounds like, but is," Cordelia said.

Fred frowned. "Shouldn't he be—?"

"A little more inconspicuous?" Lorne finished. "Kid doesn't know the meaning of the word."

"No," Cordelia said. "He's being too conspicuous. Look—!"

The camera had zoomed out and panned toward the north side of the street, providing a fleeting glimpse of Gunn.

"Charles," Fred said, concerned. "Behind the megalith."

"Correct me if I'm wrong, peanut," Lorne said, "but that wasn't part of the grand plan, was it?"

Fred shook her head. "No," she said. "What's he trying to do?"

"Maybe something happened and he needed a closer look," Cordelia suggested.

"Wouldn't the reporter tell us if something had happened?"

"Maybe she didn't notice."

Through the TV set's small speakers, they heard Connor yell at the miracle bunch, "Blow out your candles! No miracles today! Salvation is cancelled!"

Sarah Swanson spoke again in hushed urgency. "As far as we know, there was no provocation for these verbal attacks. The youth is antagonizing both groups while the police are attempting to restore order."

When the camera operator pulled back for a wide shot, they glimpsed Gunn again, hiding from the police on the other side of the monolith. For a few moments his hands brushed the surface of the demonic face, but then he began to pound the stone, as if frustrated by something.

When Cordelia and Fred looked at Lorne, as if for an explanation, he shrugged and said, "Can't find the doorbell?"

The camera left Gunn and zoomed in on one of the policemen as he came around the monolith and shone a flashlight at Gunn. In the background, they could hear Connor shouting at somebody to get their hands off him.

"Doesn't look good, gang," Lorne said. "How much bail money do we keep in petty cash?"

"Not enough," Cordelia said softly, without looking away from the televised scene.

"C'mon, Charles," Fred said anxiously. "Listen to the nice policeman and step away from the megalith."

The camera jerked, catching a shot of Connor eluding the grasp of the other policeman and running to Gunn's side of the statue.

Sarah Swanson spoke again in voice-over. "We can't be certain, of course, but it appears these two men may be working together. It is, however, unclear what they are trying to accomplish—"

"You're telling me," Cordelia scoffed.

The camera swung back to Gunn, his hands now raised in apparent surrender.

"—unless this is simply an elaborate attempt at vandalism."

In another sign of frustration, Gunn lashed out at the base of the monolith with his foot.

The KTLA reporter appeared in the camera frame with the monolith visible over her shoulder. "That's been the extent of the excitement here at—" A howling sound overwhelmed the television microphone the same moment the anchor stumbled. For a moment, static filled the small screen. "—not sure what—can you—"

"Something's happening," Cordelia said.

"Something weird," Lorne said.

"Do you think . . . ?" Fred said. "Are we too late? Is the portal opening?"

The camera danced wildly as the operator fought for control against the buffeting wind. In and out of the frame, Sarah Swanson struggled to keep her balance and make sense out of what was happening. "—sudden, freak storm coming—don't know what—"

Blinding white light burst from the demon-faced side of the monolith, enveloping everyone in its path, including Gunn and Connor and the two police officers. After that first moment, the camera image blacked out, was replaced by a blue screen, then flickered several times before showing the street scene again, minus the flare of light.

"Wow," Lorne said. "Talk about your Cecil B. De Millean fireworks!"

People at the scene were yelling and screaming, fleeing in all directions. The reporter seemed stunned and spoke softly, hesitantly. "Did you see that? Did you see . . . ?" The cameraman made a halfhearted attempt to track the mass of dispersing crowd members before returning his attention, and the camera lens, to the monolith.

"I saw it all right," Lorne said. "Let's hear it for the faithlessly departed."

"Okay," Cordelia said nervously. "So what was that?"

"Oh, God," Fred said, stumbling as she backed up and plopped down in the nearest chair. "Oh, no . . . no."

"Fred?" Cordelia said. "Fred, what is it? What's wrong?"

Fred trembled. "It's Charles. He's . . . he's gone."

She stared at the screen, hoping she was wrong, but only Connor and the two police officers stood next to the megalith, blinking and shaking their head in confusion. Charles was nowhere in the shot.

"Fred, no, he just backed away, after the light flashed. We don't know—"

"I know," Fred said. "He's gone. Just like the Bakers. The megalith . . . it . . . it has him now."

Cordelia and Lorne scrutinized the television image, hoping to spot Gunn somewhere to prove to Fred that she was wrong. Fred watched the image as well, but without hope. Gunn had triggered something in the megalith and it had snatched him right out of their dimension. *And what if he's—*

"Look!" Cordelia said, interrupting Fred's dire thoughts. "Something's happening!"

Part of the television image seemed to die, to go completely dark. The camera operator must have noticed as well, judging by the shift of focus. Sarah Swanson's stunned voice whispered, "It's not there. The other side of the street—it's gone!"

But the darkness receded as suddenly as it had appeared. A moment later, a gleaming black shape flipped across the frame. The camera operator tried to follow the movement, but it was too fast. Connor darted through the frame, sprinting in the same direction, then he, too, was gone.

"On me, on me," Sarah Swanson urgently instructed her camera operator, who complied by swinging the lens to her as she attempted to finger-brush her windswept hair.

"Folks, I'm not sure what we just witnessed," she said. "I can only guess it was some sort of elaborate stunt."

"What!?" Cordelia said with a major frown. "Did she see what we saw?"

"If you'll recall," Sarah Swanson said to her audience, "we first witnessed the diversion created by the young man who taunted the crowds, distracting police attention from the other side of the monolith, where the young man's accomplice was apparently placing some sort of incendiary device, perhaps a magnesium flare."

"Is she insane?" Cordelia asked, looking to Fred and Lorne for support.

"As you can see," Sarah Swanson continued, stepping out of the shot so the camera operator could zoom in on the megalith, "there is no damage to the structure." She stepped back into the shot. "This is Hollywood, after all, land of special effects. I think those two gentlemen were attempting to pull off a hoax right under the watchful eyes of L.A.'s finest. Unfortunately, I think they underestimated the gullibility of their intended audience. . . ." The camera operator panned from the south side to the north side of Hollywood Boulevard, revealing abandoned doomsday signs and a scattering of extinguished white candles before returning to a close-up of Sarah Swanson, who displayed a knowing grin and winked. "Nobody stuck around for the miracle. This is Sarah Swanson, KTLA News. Back to you, Dan."

A studio anchor appeared, shaking his head in amusement before wondering aloud what some people wouldn't do for their fifteen minutes of fame. "This has been a special report from—"

Lorne muted the sound.

"Deluded much?" Cordelia commented.

"Forgive them, princess," Lorne said. "They know not what they see."

"You saw it, though—right?" Fred asked. "After the darkness? That thing . . . ?"

"Another escapee," Cordelia said, nodding.

"With Junior in hot pursuit," Lorne added.

Fred placed her elbows on the desk and rested her forehead in her hands. First, the Bakers; and now Charles. Gone. *Sucked into that thing,* she thought angrily, *which, technically, isn't even here yet.* "This doesn't make any sense."

"What doesn't make any sense?" Cordelia asked.

"Charles," Fred said, looking up. "Why Charles? Angel and Wesley were there, right? They stood right where Charles was! And there were two of them. Same as the Bakers. And it took them—but not . . . I mean, why?"

They looked at her, unable to offer answers or comfort.

Fred dropped her head in her hands again. *Why Charles?* She thought about how she'd been avoiding him, telling him to wait, to wait for her, that she wasn't . . . that it wasn't right. She needed time after everything that had happened. Space . . . and time.

She sobbed softly, but it turned abruptly into a bitter chuckle.

"Fred, what?" Cordelia asked, placing a hand on her shoulder.

"Space and time," Fred said.

"What about space and time?"

"He sure gave me that, right?" Again, the chuckle escaped her lips, and she thought she might be losing it. "Space and time. Get it? The space-time continuum." She grabbed a tissue from a box on the desk and dabbed at her eyes and nose. "I mean, let's face it, he's probably in a whole different space-time continuum now! Another dimension!" She blew her nose. "Assuming he's not already . . . because, you know, there's no guarantee he's still—still . . ."

"Hey, let's not go there, sweet pea," Lorne said. He patted her other shoulder comfortingly. "That's one resourceful young man."

But Fred wasn't so sure. Gunn had been unarmed, and it was possible—no, probable—that he had crossed over to the place that was about to bring an apocalypse to earth. *Careful what you wish for, Fred,* she thought bitterly. *I asked Charles to give me some time, and now I'll probably never see him again.*

"We should call Angel," Cordelia said gently. "To tell him about . . . about the monolith. And about Connor and the new escapee."

Another escapee, Fred thought. *Instead of Charles, we get another escapee!* She looked up with a faraway gaze. *It makes sense. The Bakers and two escapees. Charles and one more.* "That's why . . ." Her voice trailed off.

"What was that, kiwi?" Lorne asked. "Couldn't hear what you said."

"Newton's Third Law of Motion," Fred said.

"Is this about a snack-food craving? Because I'm—"

"For every action there is an equal but opposite reaction," Fred said. "Newton's Third Law of Motion."

"Like burritos and indigestion," Lorne said. "Anyone else getting hungry?"

"Gunn and the escapee, right?" Cordelia asked, realization dawning.

"It's like an early warning system," Fred said. "A response to aggression. First the Durango slammed into it, with two occupants in the car, which it saw as a weapon and an attack. Then when Charles struck . . ."

"So whenever mega-rock is attacked, it's able to . . . suck in the attacker or attackers and spit out an equal number of armored demon-y things."

"A supernatural 'tit for tat,'" Lorne said, nodding as he picked up the reception desk telephone. "We'd better get Angel into this loop."

CHAPTER FOURTEEN

Angel spotted the late-model white Ford Windstar parked in the far corner of the Grocery King parking lot. The interior rear cargo light attracted his attention. When he parked the GTX beside the white minivan, he caught the distinctive scent.

"What is it?" Wesley asked as he climbed out of the passenger side of the GTX and joined Angel.

"Blood," Angel said. "Human blood."

"Are you—?" Catching Angel's look, Wesley aborted his own question and cleared his throat. "Yes, of course. How could I forget?"

Angel began an examination of the exterior of the minivan. The hatchback door was down but not latched securely, which had caused the interior light to stay illuminated. He noticed several fresh scratches on the rear bumper.

Performing his own inspection, Wes called from the front of the minivan, "Driver's side door is unlocked. Keys on the front seat. Can't imagine it's been sitting here long with such a blatant invitation to theft."

"Not long enough for blood to dry." Angel crouched behind the Windstar, examining the paint from one side to the other. Dust clung to some sections. Other spots seemed too clean. *There should be a uniform coating of dust,* Angel thought. *Unless somebody wiped it clean to hide evidence of blood or fingerprints.*

Under the smell of blood, a heavy musk lingered, something neither human nor animal. *Demonic,* he surmised. But as the ATM encounter had reminded him, there were demons running loose in L.A. with no connection to the monolith.

Finding no blood on the rear panels, Angel examined the ground beneath the minivan. Old blacktop, pitted and crumbling. Damp, but not with blood. Angel turned his attention to the undercarriage and found more evidence of random wiping but, again, no blood. Since his eyes weren't helping him, he let his nose lead him toward the scent. After a moment, he picked up the direction of the scent's origin and turned his head to the left, then down and lower. He leaned under the minivan and saw it as a slick spot on the axle side of the left rear tire, the red hidden against the black in the night shadows.

Angel dabbed his right index finger against the

slick spot and felt the stickiness. He looked at the red smear on the pad of his finger and called to Wesley, "Found the blood." He inhaled. "Definitely human."

Wes joined him, and Angel pointed to the spot on the tire where he'd found the blood. "Somebody went to a lot of trouble to hide evidence of foul play," Wesley said.

"Something else is there," Angel said, leaning forward again. Something was stuck to the slick spot—a strand of hair. Angel plucked the hair away from the tire and held it up to the parking lot lights. "And this definitely isn't."

"Isn't what?"

"Human," Angel said. The hair was black, thicker and coarser than human hair. "What do you think? Monolith demon? Or—?"

"Khaipuhr," Wesley decided. "We know that they clean up after the Summoner's sacrifices."

"Odd place for a sacrifice."

"Indeed," Wesley said, surveying the parking lot on the chance he might find an altar among the scattered shopping carts. "Most likely a random act of evil, which presents three possibilities: the khaipuhr were cleaning up after themselves, the Summoner, or the new demons."

"The Summoner has been too careful to kill somebody out in the open like this."

"Good point," Wesley said. "And logically he

wouldn't allow his demonic guardians to commit such a public act of violence, since it could also lead to him. Which leaves the monolith demons as the likely culprits."

"But they're working for him too."

"They may not see it that way," Wesley said. "I'm sure he would want to keep them on a short leash until the megalith has phased into our dimension, but he may not exert total control over their violent impulses."

"They were here," Angel said. "And not that long ago. But we're still no closer to finding their hideout." Angel's gaze swept back and forth down the street. He shook his head in indecision. "We were lucky to find this minivan. If I hadn't noticed the interior lights, I never would have stopped to investigate." He sighed, and at the same moment, his cell phone rang. He answered and said, "Hi, Lorne," upon hearing the demon's voice. "What's up?" Angel listened to Lorne's account of what had happened at the monolith, facts filtered secondhand from the jumbled live news broadcast. "They'll be coming this way," Angel said. "We'll try to intercept them."

After Angel hung up, Wesley asked, "What's happened?"

"Another escapee."

"Connor is in pursuit?"

Angel nodded. "That's not the worst part," he said. "Gunn's missing."

"Missing how?"

"The monolith," Angel said. As they climbed back into the GTX, he explained what Lorne and the others had seen during the broadcast, and Fred's assessment of what had happened. "A bizarre exchange program," Angel said. "Human sucked in, demon spat out." Angel drove off the lot and headed north, toward Hollywood.

"But the monolith isn't in phase yet," Wesley said. "There must be some sort of mystical . . . loophole."

"Apparently triggered by human aggression."

"Humans mirroring demonic traits," Wesley said thoughtfully. "Aggression, anger, hate—literally bridging the gap between the species. Prematurely."

"Live by the sword," Angel said, "get sent to the sword makers."

"Angel, I . . . ," Wesley began awkwardly. "That is, it's unlikely that a demonic race poised for global conquest would take hostages."

"I know," Angel said grimly.

"We must face the possibility that Gunn is—"

"I know," Angel interrupted before Wesley could finish the morbid thought. "It's a . . . thing, all right? We've been through things before. Gunn has . . . Gunn can take care of himself."

"Of course."

Gunn's resourceful, Angel thought. *No question.*

Regardless of whether he's unarmed and alone against uncounted legions of warmongering demons. Just don't dwell on the negative. "He'll be fine." Wesley was quiet. "I mean, 'cheating death' is in our job description, right? We've all done it. I've done it. You've done it, haven't you?"

"Oh, yes," Wesley said supportively. "On several occasions."

"Exactly," Angel said. He snapped his fingers. "Justine cutting your throat!"

"Something I'd rather forget," Wesley said, touching his hand gingerly to his throat, as if the wound were still raw. "But, yes, that would certainly qualify."

"Gunn, too," Angel said, nodding. "Close to the fire."

"We'll get him out of there," Wesley said with hope.

"But first we have to find Connor and the demon he's chasing."

"Right," Wesley said, striking the dashboard affirmatively with the side of a fist. "Our first course of action."

Angel nodded. *Keep the faith, Gunn. Don't give up on us.*

Apparently, I suck at stealth, Connor realized. *Tracking, hunting, fighting? Not a problem. But can I tail a demon for several blocks without giving away my position? As Cordy would say, that's a big fat no.*

If Connor were capable of such a simple assignment, he obviously wouldn't be sprinting a block behind the fleeing demon. Connor had followed the demon into Inglewood before something had given him away. One moment, the demon was loping along at a brisk but leisurely pace; the next moment, he stopped, spun around as Connor popped out of the shadows, then fled at top speed.

He didn't know what had gone wrong. Connor had been unerringly quiet and patient, waiting until the demon had turned a corner before closing the gap between them. Always staying back far enough so that if the demon happened to look over his shoulder, he would have no idea Connor was following him. That had been the plan, and Connor had stuck to it—until something had given his position away. Scent, maybe. Or the Summoner, noticing something amiss through his third eye. He'd given instruction to the demon. Why not a warning?

Again, Connor worried that he'd lose sight of the demon, or that he'd lose the scent, and his failure would doom Gunn. He wasn't thinking about L.A. or California or the world. He had his hands full worrying about one man, which was all the responsibility he could handle at the moment.

The demon ran down a long driveway in an industrial park, with Connor thirty feet behind him. Ahead, Connor saw a dark guard station and a gated lot, closed and chained for the night. Concertina coils of razor wire topped the ten-foot-high fence. Connor wasn't surprised when the demon leaped up onto the fence and tried to scramble over the top.

Connor jumped and caught the demon around the throat with his left forearm, pulling him backward as the demon clung to the galvanized steel links. In his right hand Connor held the claw hammer he'd swiped from the construction site. He took aim and swung the flat head of the hammer against the demon's helmet, where he thought the demon's ear would be, assuming the demon had an ear. The impact of metal on metal was booming and must have been deafening inside the confines of the helmet.

The demon shook his head, his grip on the fence slipping.

Connor pounded the hammer against the helmet again.

The third time was the charm. With a frustrated roar, the demon's clawed hands slipped free of the fence and he fell backward with Connor riding him to the ground. Connor rolled away from the impact, but couldn't dodge the demon's enraged charge. They staggered back, snapping the lowered wooden arm of the parking gate, and slamming into the locked guard station. A wild swing of the demon's claws smashed the window of the guard booth.

"You're not the only one with claws anymore," Connor said. He spun the hammer in his hand and struck the double-clawed end into the meat of the demon's arm.

The demon snarled and lashed out with a boot, striking the inside of Connor's right knee. As Connor fell back in pain, he stuck his left leg in front of the demon before he could flee. The demon dropped to hands and knees, but pushed himself up and ran toward the side of the factory.

Connor scrambled to his feet and lunged forward, several loping, stumbling strides, stretching out as he collapsed to hook the demon's ankle with the clawed end of the hammer. The demon rolled onto his back and, as Connor tried to pin him down, kicked his heavy boot out, hitting Connor on the chin.

Stunned, Connor stared up into the night sky and, for a moment, thought he was alone. Until the stench washed over him. The demon's stink. He turned his head, and the demon was standing there, beside him. "What . . . ?" Connor croaked.

"Had enough of you!" the demon shouted, kicking Connor in the ribs, doubling him over. Another kick, to the stomach. A third, to the head. Connor was reeling a bit, fighting waves of nausea that tugged on his awareness. The demon clutched his shirt collar, then struck him in the face with a curled fist. Speckles of darkness joined the nausea, inkblots of darkness spreading across his field of vision, slowly overwhelming him. The demon opened his handful of claws and held them above Connor's exposed throat.

Connor didn't think about dying. He thought about failing—and that was enough to fight off the darkness and despair that had been overwhelming his consciousness.

The demon crouched above him. Connor could see the demon's mottled chin, in shadows, between the edge of the protective helmet and the edge of the breastplate.

The points of claws settled around Connor's throat, in position to slash through his jugular, carotid, and esophagus.

Connor's fingers fumbled around on the black-top, found something hard and smooth, cool to the touch. The head of the hammer. *Wrong end,* he thought. But there was no time to make an adjustment. His fingers curled around the metal, and he drove the handle up hard, the flat base striking the demon's exposed chin with enough force to snap his head back.

Connor rolled over, the hammer still clutched in his hand. With his free hand he yanked the helmet off the stunned demon's head. For the first time, he had an unobstructed view of the demon's mottled red-and-black flesh, the deep-set smoldering red eyes, the flattened ears and nose, and the horrible mouth filled with snarled, pointed teeth, and it sickened him. The demon was an evil, murderous abomination intent on the destruction of mankind, and it disgusted him. It had tried to kill him, and he had every right to execute it.

Nearby, there was a sudden squeal of tires.

Connor wouldn't allow himself to be distracted. He'd almost let the abomination escape. Almost let it kill him.

The demon staggered to its feet.

Connor stalked forward full of murderous rage, hammer clenched in his hand. He'd switched his grip to the handle and was ready to pound the demon's head with it again. This time, the helmet wouldn't get in the way. Connor hissed, "Die, you son of a bitch!"

He raised the hammer high, then swung with all his might at the demon's skull, but something blocked his wrist mid-stroke, jarring his arm and dislodging the hammer.

Hand clamped around Connor's wrist, Angel whispered fiercely, "Connor, no!"

"Why?" Connor asked, outraged. *Why did everything always have to be Angel's way?* "This . . . thing tried to kill me."

Angel continued in his forceful whisper. "Kill the demon, and we lose any chance of finding Gunn!"

"How do you know about—?"

"The miracle of live television," Angel said. "You made the evening news. Lorne called us."

"You want to interrogate it, fine," Connor said, wrenching his arm free of Angel's grasp. *Let him do it his way,* he thought. *But without my help.*

The demon had backed away from them and, while Connor and Angel spoke, retrieved and donned his helmet. While crouching to reclaim the helmet, the demon had picked up something else. As Connor pulled free of Angel's restraining grasp, the demon cocked his arm back over his head.

Angel was looking at Connor.

"Look out!" Connor yelled at the same moment an approaching Wesley cried, "Duck!"

Connor dove, driving his shoulder into Angel's midsection and taking them both down as the claw hammer hurtled past the spot where Angel's face had been.

Angel and Connor scrambled to their feet.

The demon raced toward the side of the factory, where it jumped to and scuttled up the cement wall in a flurry of gouging claws.

Wesley veered past father and son toward the factory, wielding a loaded crossbow. He fired the bolt a moment before the demon scrambled over the roof. The quarrel struck the side of the wall and ricocheted, splitting in two. "Missed," Wesley said in bitter frustration.

"We're close to the Summoner," Angel said. "We'll follow the demon."

"Just as well, I suppose," Wesley said as they raced back to the lot entrance, where Angel had haphazardly parked the GTX. "These warrior demons would most likely resist our interrogation methods."

Connor asked, "How'd you find me?"

"Super hearing, remember," Angel said, tapping his ear for emphasis as he climbed into the driver's seat. "All that breaking and smashing, I figured it was either you or a turf war."

"Wait," Connor said abruptly, one hand poised on the car door. "I should follow on foot. Gives us two chances of locating the hideout."

"You're right," Angel agreed. "But if you find it first, come get us. Don't go in alone. Understood?"

Connor nodded, then sprinted back toward the factory. Behind him, the GTX engine roared to life. A moment later, headlight beams swept past him. With Angel and Wesley covering street level, Connor decided he should take the high ground. A ten-foot-high overhang shielded the factory's front entrance. Connor jumped, easily grasped the lip of the overhang, and swung himself on top of it. From there it was another leap to the roof.

Several bulky air-conditioning units dotted the sprawling rooftop, and Connor wondered if the demon was hiding behind one of them, ready to spring an ambush. He looped around them, giving each a wide berth, but it was a needless precaution. The demon was gone.

Connor raced to the south side of the factory rooftop and paused for a visual sweep. Evenly spaced streetlights and the occasional flagpole lights diluted the darkness blanketing the industrial park. Looking to the south, Connor detected movement, turned his head, and spied a flash of deeper darkness skirting the pools of light. Loping along, more than a hundred yards away, the demon hurried but was no longer fleeing at top speed.

Connor dropped to the ground, absorbed the impact by flexing his knees, and raced after the demon. This time, if the demon spotted him, Connor would try to steer him toward the street, toward Angel and Wesley. Once they made visual contact, Connor could drop back to give the demon a false sense of security. *Assuming I still suck at stealth,* he thought.

Angel drove along the north-bound road that serviced the industrial park at what he hoped was a casual speed. If he drove too slow or too fast, he risked drawing attention to the car. He scanned the left side of the street, while Wesley focused on the right. As they sat exposed in the convertible, Angel wished that they'd put the top up. Although the demon might have had a fleeting glance at Wesley, he'd seen Angel's face up close, and long enough to try to embed a claw hammer in the center of it. *Too late to worry about that*, Angel thought. *If we see the demon, we'll have to hang back, give him enough rope to hang the Summoner—right after we have a little heat-to-heart chat about the monolith.*

"Connor's merely trying to prove himself to you," Wesley said.

"You got it wrong, Wes," Angel said. "He's not trying to prove he's good enough for me. He's trying to prove he's better than me."

"Be that as it may—"

"Look!" Angel interrupted, pointing past a row of beech trees bordering the front lawn of a factory. The demon raced up a side street, cutting through the lawn.

"The demon," Wesley whispered.

The demon glanced over his shoulder.

"And is that . . . ?"

"Connor," Angel confirmed.

"But the demon knows he's . . ."

Fifty feet in front of the GTX, the demon darted across the street and angled toward the next intersection, heading east. Connor looked at them, gave a slight nod, and slowed his pace.

Angel guessed what Connor had in mind. "He herded the demon toward us." Angel turned left at the intersection and saw the demon almost a block ahead of them.

"He's passed the baton to us," Wesley said.

"Right," Angel said. "So let's try not to drop it."

CHAPTER FIFTEEN

The demon doubled back a few times, verifying he'd given Connor the slip, before turning south again. Angel had to be careful not to get too close, and one time he spotted Connor paralleling their path, one block to the north.

After a half mile, the demon turned east, south, then east again, into a rundown business district. Abandoned, condemned, and vacant buildings lined the street. Scattered throughout the district were several businesses on life support, including a corner bodega, a video-rental store, a pizza parlor, a used-car lot, and a secondhand furniture store. Half a dozen men stood outside the bodega, chatting and laughing intermittently.

The demon hurried toward a condemned office building, looking up and down the street before ducking into a recessed doorway. Street traffic was light.

Angel parked the GTX next to the used-car lot, two blocks from the building the demon had entered. After hours, the car dealership's office lights were dark, but the lot remained quietly festive with strings of multicolored pennants crisscrossing overhead from one lamppost to another. The cars facing the street had Day-Glo advertisements painted on their windshields touting LOW MILEAGE! and FULLY LOADED! and A/C!

"Car shopping?" Wesley asked drolly to cut the tension.

"Connor's birthday's coming up," Angel said dryly. "Boy needs his own set of wheels."

"Shouldn't he learn to drive first?"

"Details."

Connor stepped up behind the GTX and rapped his knuckles on the trunk.

Angel made eye contact with him in the rearview mirror. "I saw you coming."

"So open the traveling arsenal already," Connor said. "I have a few demons to kill."

"Remember," Angel said as he walked to the rear of the car and unlocked the trunk. "We need the Summoner alive to tell us how to send the monolith back where it came from."

"Then can I kill him, Dad?" Connor said sarcastically.

"Let's not get ahead of ourselves, son." Angel

indicated the weapons and said, "Help yourselves."

Without hesitation, Connor grabbed a long sword and a double-headed battle-ax. Wesley, knowing his best chance at survival was battling from a distance, again equipped himself with a crossbow, a dozen quarrels and, for backup, a short sword tucked into his belt. Angel took a long, double-edged sword and a flat-handled knife balanced for throwing.

After Angel closed the trunk with a soft *clunk*, the trio strode toward the condemned office building. While they were half a block away, Wesley said, "Somebody should guard the rear, in case the Summoner tries to escape."

"Good point," Angel said.

"I'll do it," Connor said.

"Okay," Angel said. "Wes, you're with me."

Angel knew Connor could defend himself, and that his—and Wesley's—chances were better without the potential for distraction. Angel was accustomed to fighting with his team. Connor, for the most part, remained a loner.

"Before you come through the back door," Angel said, "wait for us to make our move."

"Should I yell 'surprise'?" Connor asked sarcastically.

"That's funny," Angel said, forcing a smile.

But Connor had a point. Angel hoped to catch the Summoner completely off-guard. Unsettled and unprepared, the demon was more likely to tell Angel what he needed to know.

"You lost him, Rrjk?" Sehjenkhai asked the newest arrival. "That's what you're telling me?"

"Lost him," Rrjk said, his voice muffled by the helmet. He pounded his chest. "Boy couldn't keep up with me."

"Is that what you think?"

Rrjk nodded, but with a slight hesitation.

"Did you happen to notice the car?" Sehjenkhai asked.

"Car?"

"The automated human vehicle?"

Rrjk nodded emphatically. "Yes. Many cars."

"Did you happen to notice the car that was following you?"

"Boy not in car," Rrjk said. "On foot. Like Rrjk."

"What about the other two?" Sehjenkhai asked. "Or have you forgotten your recent skirmish at the factory?"

"No . . ."

"Well, they're here," Sehjenkhai said. "All of them. They followed you."

"Why Summoner not warn Rrjk of car?"

"Because I've had enough of them," Sehjenkhai said. "And I thought the three of you might enjoy some . . . sparring before the main event."

All three warrior demons laughed heartily.

The khaipuhr climbed to their feet and licked their chops in anticipation.

Angel and Wesley stayed away from the curb and close to the row of broken-down buildings as they approached the condemned two-story office building. While the view through the cracked and broken windows revealed nothing but darkness, the ambient light outside, unfortunately, would make Angel and Wesley plainly visible to someone inside peering out.

A sheet of plywood riddled with graffiti covered the bottom panel of the front door. The plate glass in the top panel was spider-webbed with cracks, the result of some frivolous vandalism. Angel tugged on the door handle and discovered it was unlocked, that the deadbolt mechanism had been torn out.

He eased the door open and slipped inside, with Wesley following close behind. They stood in a tiled hallway with a closed door leading to the first-floor office space on the left, and a stairway leading up to the second floor on their right. Straight ahead, the hallway continued to the steel rear door, which had a push-bar handle and a small square window inlaid with security mesh. Connor peered through the small window, saw them standing inside, and pulled the door open to join them.

Angel positioned Wesley at the foot of the stairs

while he and Connor went through the first-floor office door. Two rows of cheap, battered desks filled the space, with irregular gaps between some. Angel guessed the office had once been home to a stable of telemarketers or travel agents. *Long gone,* he thought.

Along the far wall was a large closet for file storage or office supplies, but it was empty now, aside from a few scattered paper clips. Connor returned from a back room and mouthed the word "Restroom."

They left the ground-floor office and rejoined Wesley at the stairwell. Angel whispered, "Nothing down here."

Wesley looked up the stairs and tightened his grip on the crossbow.

Angel led the way up the stairs, placing his feet at the edges of each step, where they would be least likely to creak under his weight. If at all possible he wanted to retain the element of surprise, but something was bothering him. It wasn't until they reached the second-story office door that he understood the cause for his concern. Unless the demon they'd followed had entered the building and immediately slipped out the back door, then he, the Summoner, two other escapee demons, and the khaipuhr were waiting on the other side of the office door. And that was the problem. *If they're all in there, why is it so quiet?*

Angel reached for the doorknob and turned it far enough to discover that this door, too, was unlocked. He looked back at Connor and Wesley and nodded toward the door, silently asking if they were ready. They nodded and edged closer. Angel flung the door open and rushed inside, the others fanning out behind him, Wesley to his left, Connor to the right.

Remarkably, Lorne found a demon underground bar where the entire clientele didn't moan when they saw him enter, although business there wasn't exactly booming. Lorne called amicable greetings to everyone, mixing in personalized exchanges with those he recognized. "Hey, Groktel, how's the wife and hell-spawn? Ki'iku, long time, no molt! Looking good, Ocilis! That sixth eye-sprout is a real keeper!"

Most of the demons had bellied—or thoraxed—up to the bar, preferring the three-legged stools that kept them in close proximity to the four-armed bartender. Three grunting, green-scaled demons with shoulder horns sat at a far table playing five-card stud, using desiccated human ears as poker chips. Lorne's gaze, however, settled on one of the few demons sitting alone at a round table—and not just because he was melting. The mourdrigahen demon, whose pale flesh had the consistency of tallow, was melting faster than normal. And he seemed in a hurry to down his frosted mug of sour milk and crickets.

As the demon started to rise, Lorne caught his malleable forearm and motioned him down into his chair again. Lorne sat opposite him. "Turgahlee, what's the rush?"

"No, no, no rush," Turgahlee said, looking around nervously. His left eye slid down his face, creating a moist runnel in his soft cheek. Absently, Turgahlee pushed the eye up into the socket again, but the facial reconstruction seemed like a losing battle. His right ear was a lumpy mess, and his bottom lip drooped away from his flat teeth and gray gums, revealing unpleasant deposits of milk and cricket legs. "Who—who said anything about, about a rush?"

"From where I'm sitting," Lorne said, "it looks like you're burning at both ends."

Turgahlee chuckled nervously. "Good seeing, seeing you, Lorne. But I should, should go."

"Where are you headed? Maybe I could catch a ride."

"Oh, no, no, Lorne. Far away. Outta town, yes, way out. Long, long trip."

"Correct me if I'm wrong, Turgahlee, but aren't mourdrigahens a little bit prescient?"

Turgahlee scoffed, picked up his empty glass, and tried to take another swallow. Mourdrigahens were also notoriously timid. "Whoever told, told you that, Lorne?"

Lorne leaned forward so that only Turgahlee would hear what he said next. "Turgahlee, I'm not looking to cramp your style here, but if you know something, I'd like to know something, too, if you know what I mean. Just between us."

Turgahlee sighed. "Ah, Lorne, what I wouldn't give, give for a bag of cow eyes."

Lorne patted the demon's warm hand, noting that two of the fingers had fused together. "Next bag's on me, champ."

"Lorne, I'm not a violent, violent demon. Live and let, let live, right?"

"Sure."

"Mind my own, own business. I'm a lover, not, not a fighter."

Lorne tried to avoid forming any mental images and simply nodded.

"If I stick around, around here," Turgahlee held up his arms palms out, "I'll be a puddle of goo, goo or worse, you know. This prolonged stress is no, no good for my constitution. Last night I found one of my teeth in my, my ear canal!"

"So what can you tell me, Turgahlee?"

"Hours," Turgahlee said grimly. "Hours, Lorne. Feeling hit me soon as I ordered, ordered my drink. Hours. That's all, all there is."

"Until what?"

"What do, do you think? Hours until they, they come. I was you, Lorne, I'd run, run like hell.

'Cause that's what's coming. Legions of hell. And if it's true what they say about, about the infernal fire, then a soft mourdrigahen's got no business waiting around for hell." Turgahlee stood and made a token effort to fix his right ear, then shrugged. "No time, time to pack," he muttered to himself as he stepped away from the table. "Just hop, hop in my Beetle and go. You go, too, Lorne."

"Thanks, Turgahlee," Lorne said sourly. "So glad we had this little talk."

Angel scanned the dark second-floor office, which was cloaked in shadows, about three quarters the size of the first-floor bullpen of desks. He noted an open closet opposite the door, and two closed doors to the right. One probably led to a restroom, the other to an office or a bigger storage room. Facing the windows looking out on the street was a tattered lawn chair.

"I smell them," Connor said softly.

Angel noticed white residue on the floor, and his gaze traveled upward. Movement—"The ceiling!" he shouted at the same moment that three demons released their claw-holds and dropped to the floor behind them.

The demons had probably expected Angel and the others to make a cautious entrance and, as they stepped slowly into the office, the demons would have fallen on top of them, sharp claws and teeth making quick work of the group.

In the first few moments of the ambush, Connor lost his sword but retained his battle-ax, while Wesley fired a quarrel harmlessly at the breastplate of one of the escapee demons. Before Wesley could reload, the demon was slashing at his face with its claws. Wesley dropped the quarrel and held up the stock of the crossbow to block the blow. By the third swipe, Wesley lost his grip on the crossbow and grabbed his sword.

Angel pressed the attack against the demon closest to him, hoping to end the battle quickly and help Wesley. He swept the double-edged sword against the demon's breastplate and helmet with little effect. When Angel swung low, the demon leaped into the air and avoided the sword stroke.

Connor had a similar problem with the long-handled battle-ax. His demon was nimble, and with each swing, Connor opened his side and back to the raking punishment of claws.

Wesley backed up, fending off blows with his short sword and, when he saw an opening, striking at the demon. His blows clanged off the armored head and torso of the demon as well. Unfortunately, the demon was pressing him toward the front of the office and the cracked and broken panes of glass. Wesley might not survive a fall through the glass to the street below.

"Under the chin!" Connor yelled. "Gap in the armor."

Angel saw instantly what he meant: the gap between the demon's helmet and breastplate.

Flipping his sword around in his double-grip, Angel drove the butt of the hilt into the demon's helmet, rocking his head back. In a blur of motion, he spun the sword around again and shoved the point under the demon's chin with so much force that the tip broke through the top of his skull and popped the helmet off his head. The demon fell over, twitched once, then lay still. Angel had killed the demon, but the sword was lodged in his skull.

"Little help here!" Wesley called. As he absorbed yet another blow with his short sword, his right elbow was forced back, shattering what had been one of the few unbroken panes of glass. Before Wesley could adjust his grip, the other set of claws slashed downward, shredding the front of his shirt. Buttons clattered on the floor. Four shallow, parallel wounds on Wesley's chest oozed blood.

The demon flashed an anticipatory grin—then howled in pain, falling sidewise and clutching the hilt of the throwing knife protruding from the back of his right knee. As the demon twisted around to pull the knife free and examine the injury, Wesley had noticed a flash of mottled red-and-black skin. He gripped his short sword in both hands and drove the point under the lip of the helmet. The demon's back arched, his entire body taut and thrumming with agony for a second or two, then he collapsed in a limp heap.

That left one escapee demon.

Angel turned around to locate Connor in the dark office.

"Sword!" Connor yelled.

Though Connor had pointed out the vulnerability of the demon's armor, he'd been unable to take advantage of that knowledge. The broad double-blades of the battle-ax weren't suited to jabbing into a tight spot.

"Heads up!" Angel called.

As Angel tossed Connor the sword he'd dropped, Connor shoved the demon back with the tip of the battle-ax, then let the long-handled weapon fall, freeing both hands to snag the sword hilt out of the air.

Aware of Connor's strategy, the remaining escapee demon kept his head low, tucking his chin against his chest as he advanced. "Rrjk almost kill boy before," the demon taunted, his sunken red eyes smoldering with hate. "Finish job now."

He's the one I've been chasing all over L.A. tonight! Connor realized, turning his attention to the T-shaped gap. The horizontal slit was wider than the vertical one, but maybe not wide enough.

It gave Connor an idea, though. He turned his sword blade flat and thrust it toward the helmet gap in front of the demon's left eye.

Maybe the narrow gap would have been wide enough to accommodate the point of the sword. Connor didn't know, but it didn't matter, because the thrust had been a feint, intended solely for the reaction it would cause: a flinch. When the demon saw the sword point darting toward his left eye, his protective reflexes took over. The demon jerked his head back.

Before the demon could recover, Connor changed the angle of the attack and drove the blade straight into the demon's throat and out through its spine. He raised a foot against the breastplate and tugged the blade free. The demon's body toppled over with an impressive crash of armor.

Moments after the last demon died, the three armored bodies began to shimmer and fade, becoming no more substantial than shadows, and finally disappearing altogether, leaving no evidence of their murderous existence behind.

"Clean up after themselves," Connor said, grinning. "Kinda like that."

Angel shook his head, ignoring Connor's comment, and looked at Wesley. "No chance we imagined all that, right?"

Wesley shook his head. "I believe their death somehow returned their bodies to their own dimension. They failed in their mission."

"Maybe we failed in ours," Angel said. "We still don't know—"

"Their failure is insignificant!" proclaimed a deep, smooth voice from the back of the office. One of the rear doors had opened, and in front of that doorway stood a cadaverously thin, bald man dressed completely in black. "But your failure was in not minding your own business."

No, Angel realized, *not a man. A three-thousand-year-old demon.* "You're Sehjenkhai. The Summoner."

"The fact that you even know that much annoys me to no end."

"Then you know why we're here."

"Yes," Sehjenkhai said. "To die."

CHAPTER SIXTEEN

"I've waited three millennia for this night," Sehjenkhai said angrily, "and I have no patience for interlopers."

"For someone outnumbered three to one," Angel said, smiling, "you're very confident."

With a devilish smile of his own, Sehjenkhai replied, "Oh, but I'm not outnumbered."

As if on cue, Angel heard the deep, rumbling sound of dangerous animals growling with unbridled menace. From the shadows behind Sehjenkhai, two darker, four-legged shapes emerged and took positions on either side of him.

"The khaipuhr," Wesley said softly, almost in awe. "Impressive."

"Not so much with the fan-boy comments, Wes," Angel said wryly, but he agreed with the assessment . . . that is, until it became apparent they had only seen the doglike dimensions of the guardian demons.

In the next few moments, the khaipuhr underwent a demonic metamorphosis, their shoulders rising beyond the level of the Summoner's waist even as their chests expanded to the size of wine barrels. Teeth and claws that were already dangerous extended to three times their original length. When the transformation was complete, the khaipuhr looked more powerful than bulls, more dangerous than tigers.

Wesley cleared his throat. "Not a word."

"Stay behind us," Angel advised.

Wesley eased behind father and son, but continued to sidle along, finally crouching to retrieve his crossbow. Keeping one eye on the four-legged demons, he slipped back behind Angel and Connor before attempting to load a quarrel.

"Connor and I will handle Rover and Spot," Angel said to Wesley. "Grab the Summoner and convince him to make them heel. But remember, we need him—"

"Alive, yes. I know," Wesley said tightly.

"And when you threaten their master," Connor said, "try not to think about those big demon dogs eating human beings whole."

"Won't give it a thought," Wesley replied dryly.

Sehjenkhai motioned the khaipuhr forward with a single, unequivocal command. "Kill!"

The four-legged demons lunged forward, claws tearing divots from the tile floor with each bounding stride. Angel and Connor rushed forward to meet their charge.

Connor swung his sword in a chopping motion as the khaipuhr struck, but never completed the stroke. The weight of the beast drove him back and down, knocking the sword from his grip. Connor's hands clamped against the muscle-bound neck and held off the powerful, snapping jaws.

Taking a different approach, Angel held his sword like a spear, hoping the weight of the pouncing khaipuhr would impale it on the blade. But the lesser demon aborted its leap and circled Angel, snapping at his legs and arms. Angel backed away cautiously, but a momentary glance of concern toward Connor provided sufficient time for the khaipuhr to lunge for Angel's throat.

Angel staved off the attack by shoving his sword crosswise into the khaipuhr's snapping jaws. He'd been forced to brace the end of the blade with his left hand and could feel the steel cutting into the flesh of his palm as he struggled to keep the demon dog at bay.

Connor wrestled his way out from under his attacker, but before he regained his balance, the khaipuhr rushed forward, carrying Connor over its left shoulder and ramming him into the wall.

Wesley looked from a dazed Connor, fighting close to the body of one khaipuhr, to Angel, who winced as blood dripped from his left hand in his struggle to stay upright. With both battles precariously balanced, all it would take was one small mistake by either Angel or Connor and their demon attackers would rip out their throats in a trice. Even before he confronted Sehjenkhai, Wesley needed to tip the odds in the favor of his companions. Connor's battle was too tight, so Wesley directed his crossbow at Angel's foe, aimed for the throat, and fired.

The khaipuhr lunged the same moment the quarrel shot from the crossbow. Instead of hitting the demon's throat, the bolt struck it in the left shoulder, under the slashing left paw. The khaipuhr yelped in pain, but continued to press its attack against Angel.

Wesley hurried to reload and aim a second shot. As he squeezed the trigger, he noticed a rushed movement out of the corner of his eye—the Summoner bearing down on him, the bejeweled dagger raised high. Wesley's shot missed, thudding into the far wall. He had a moment to pivot on his heel and block the plunging dagger with the front of the crossbow.

Sehjenkhai attacked ferociously, jabbing and slicing with the ceremonial knife to keep Wesley on the defensive. The blade of the dagger struck the stock and bow, gouging the wood frame and striking sparks off the metal plating. Wesley angled his retreat to his former position, shoved the crossbow high, then dropped into a crouch to scoop up his abandoned short sword.

Whereas Wesley was mindful of the need to keep the Summoner alive and thus fought hesitantly, Sehjenkhai had no such worries about his opponent's welfare. He battled with murderous intensity. Wesley's sword deflected the dagger, fending off the frenzied rain of blows, but he was unable to gain any advantage with the longer weapon. He fought on, hoping that he'd eventually manage to disarm the three-thousand-year-old demon. If he could, he'd be able to threaten the Summoner and command him to call off the hounds.

Angel's left hand became too slick with blood to hold on to the sword. With a one-handed grip and bearing the full weight of the khaipuhr, he let the sword fall, settling for hand-to-paw combat. His fingers pressed into the matted fur as he clutched the dog-demon's thick neck and managed to keep the snapping jaws inches from his face. The razor-sharp claws, however, continued to dig into his sides and chest as the khaipuhr lashed at him.

Working in Angel's favor was the crossbow bolt stuck under the dog-demon's left shoulder. Wesley had given him an advantage, and given the khaipuhr a disadvantage. Black blood streamed from the puncture wound, and the dog-demon's left side began to grow noticeably weaker than the right. Angel bided his time—counted in extended, agonizing seconds—until he thought the left side deficit was significant enough. Then he shifted his hand from the left side of the demon's throat, down under the foreleg, wrapping his fingers around the embedded quarrel. Twisting his head away from the lunging head of the beast, Angel thrust his curled fist against the demon's hide, driving the quarrel deeper into its muscular body, a savage attempt to puncture a vital organ or two.

At last the khaipuhr convulsed in pain, staggered, and lost its momentum. Using the shaft of the quarrel for leverage, Angel swung the khaipuhr around and shoved it into the wall with crushing force, smashing plaster and lath. As the demon dropped to all fours, winded and pained, Angel changed his grip again, switching his right hand to the right side of the demon's canine jaw and his left hand to the back of its skull. Angel felt his own features transform into his demonic vampire visage, furrowed brow and fangs. He wrenched the dog's skull against the powerful base of the neck, exerting his vampiric strength until he heard the loud snap of the demon's spine surrendering. Dropping the limp body, Angel's face reverted to its human appearance as he turned his attention to Connor's battle.

Once again, the powerful four-legged demon had pinned Connor to the floor. The boy's hands clenched both sides of the demon's thick neck while he held his head away from the viciously snapping jaws. The demon growled with ferocious effect, spraying Connor's face with thick saliva as it strained to sink its rows of sharp teeth into his flesh. While the demon tried to rip into Connor's throat with its lethal mouth, its fore-claws swiped at his shoulders and outer arms, and its rear legs made every effort to disembowel him.

Forced to fend off the tooth-lined maw and four sets of claws, Connor had no choice but to allow the fore-claws to rake his flesh in glancing, but painful blows, because his bigger concern was the back claws. He kicked at the demon's back legs to keep it continually off-balance and unable to unleash a fatal swipe. For the moment, Connor was holding on, but he was gradually losing the battle. His foe outweighed him at least two to one, and Connor was unarmed against a demon with the equivalent of five lethal weapons at its disposal. With each ravenous lunge, the khaipuhr's snapping and gnashing teeth inched closer to Connor's throat.

Angel picked up the first weapon he found, Connor's double-headed battle-ax. With a powerful overhead swing, he cracked the khaipuhr's skull down the middle, but the demon continued to struggle. Wrenching the curved blade free of the wounded skull, Angel swung a second time and nearly split the skull in two.

For several moments, the demon's jaws continued to strain at Connor's throat, but the effort waned and the demon finally succumbed to the mortal wound. Emitting what sounded like a long, disgruntled sigh, the khaipuhr sagged on top of Connor, lifeless.

Bellowing in anger, Connor flung the heavy canine body to the side, then climbed wearily to his feet. As he brushed futilely at the gobs of saliva on his bloodstained clothes, he said calmly to Angel, "I had that under control."

"Never doubted you."

"Didn't ask for your help."

"And I didn't ask for Wesley's," Angel said with a shrug. "So we're even."

Perhaps noticing the death of his demon guardians for the first time, Sehjenkhai shrieked in rage and desperation. The Summoner raised the ceremonial dagger over his head, clutching its ornate hilt in white-knuckled hands, before thrusting it downward at Wesley's face.

Reacting to the threat without considering the apocalypse at hand, Wesley thrust his sword forward to meet the charge. The tip of the blade pierced Sehjenkhai's torso below the ribs, and the surge of his own attack drove it deeper.

Hunched over the sword, the Summoner gasped. The ceremonial dagger slipped from his numb fingers and clattered to the floor. He staggered backward, two halting, agonized steps, then collapsed sideways, curled around the sword, which Wesley had released in horrified silence the moment he realized his critical mistake: They needed the Summoner alive to ward off the apocalypse.

Wesley looked at Angel, eyes wide with the potential ramifications, "I couldn't . . . he . . ." Wesley shook his head, unwilling to excuse his actions, even if they had saved his life. If his lethal reaction caused the mission to fail, then he'd succeeded in buying himself nothing more than a few more hours of life, and at what cost!

Angel strode toward the Summoner, fearful that all their efforts had been wasted. If the Summoner was dead, they were no closer to averting the apocalypse than they had been the moment the monolith appeared. Worse, they had no time to devise or execute a backup plan. Their next and last move would be to wait at the monolith, to fight until the hordes of demons overwhelmed them and swept across the city and, eventually, the world.

Angel crouched at the fallen Summoner's side. The ancient demon was breathing, though weakly. "He's not dead!"

Wesley sighed in relief.

Angel propped Sehjenkhai up, lifting his head. At the slight movement, the Summoner winced in pain, blood frothing at his lips. Angel feared that removing the sword would cause the demon to bleed out in moments. As it was, they had maybe a minute or two with him before he died or lost consciousness. Angel needed answers fast. "It's over," Angel said. "Tell me how to stop the monolith."

Sehjenkhai chuckled, but the bit of mirth caused him to gasp in pain. He rasped, "My only regret is that I won't live to witness the end of your world."

"Dying, but you have time to gloat?"

The Summoner started to shrug, but thought better of it. "If that's the last thing I do . . ." He smiled at the thought. "It will do nicely."

"Nasty wound," Angel said, gripping the hilt of the sword. "Hurts like hell, doesn't it?" Sehjenkhai stared at him, an appraising look, and nodded slowly. "Considering what you've done and what's about to happen because of you, I think the last thing you do should be, I don't know—scream in agony, maybe!" Angel twisted the sword, driving the tip of the blade into fresh internal territory.

Sehjenkhai became paler, if that was possible, and moaned through clenched teeth as he writhed in Angel's grasp.

"Angel," Wesley said.

"Don't try to stop me, Wes, I—"

"Wouldn't think of it, but . . . ," Wesley said. Angel looked at him and saw the throwing knife the former Watcher held in his hand. "I was about to suggest you use this instead."

"That's the spirit," Angel said, taking the knife and

reacting broadly for Sehjenkhai's benefit. "Okay, Sehj, old buddy. You should know I've had years of practice in the inflicting-lingering-deaths department. What do you say? Ready for some pain?"

"It"—Sehjenkhai coughed, spraying red blood over his hand—"doesn't matter."

"Of course it does," Angel said, positioning the point of the blade over Sehjenkhai's right thigh.

"No!" the Summoner said, waving away the threatened assault. "It's too late. Too late to do . . . anything. From the moment it appeared . . . you were doomed."

"That's not gonna cut it, Sehj," Angel said menacingly. "But this will!"

Sehjenkhai howled in agony as the knife sank two inches into his leg. "Don't you see . . . ?" he moaned. "If you attack the portal before alignment, you doom yourself to become a host for that which you fear and despise. Your friend . . . the one who released Rrjk . . ."

Moving forward, Connor said, "What about Gunn?"

Sehjenkhai nodded. "Your foolish friend will soon number among your enemies." Sehjenkhai laughed weakly, but without joy—with merely wicked satisfaction. "The ritual is complete. The portal will open. There is nothing you can do to stop it."

"Unacceptable," Angel said, tightening his grip on the knife.

"Wait! Listen to me," Sehjenkhai said. "The portal may only be stopped from aligning . . . by entering it *before* it aligns!"

"Don't give me that paradox crap," Angel said, prepared to thrust the knife deeper and twist it for good measure. "There's something you're not telling us."

"Only . . . safe way to enter the portal before alignment is by the hands of *two* Summoners, in accord. You see? Even if I wished to . . . stop the crossing now, I could not! Your kind murdered my brother, making me the last Summoner. And you are doomed because of it. . . ." He coughed weakly and with that effort he seemed to exhaust the remaining strength in his body. A weak grin spread across his face. "Ironic, don't you think?"

"How much time do we have?"

Sehjenkhai's eyes had lost focus, but the maddening grin remained in place. Angel jerked the knife upward, restoring a pained moment of clarity to the Summoner's face.

"How long?"

With his deep-set dark eyes brimming with hate, the Summoner stared at Angel, and the last trace of his pleased smirk had vanished. "At midnight," Sehjenkhai said, "your world will bleed." Then his eyes grew dim, unblinking, and his head lolled to the side.

Angel shoved the lifeless body aside and climbed to his feet. The sense of desperation was like a living thing, growing inside him. All their plans had worked but, in the end, were pointless. If Sehjenkhai had been telling the truth, they needed two Summoners to abort the demonic equinox. And the last one had just died in Angel's arms.

"Look!" Connor said, pointing at the khaipuhr.

Even if their own deaths had been insufficient to release them from the Summoner's service, his death apparently was enough. Now that he'd breathed his last, the doglike demon guardians faded just as the escapee demons had faded before them, leaving not a trace of their bodies.

Someone else was missing. "Where's Wes?"

"Right here," Wesley called as he stepped out of the back room where Sehjenkhai had waited with the khaipuhr before attacking. Wesley carried an ancient tome bound in branded, leathery flesh—*probably human flesh,* Angel realized—and he was shaking his head as he flipped through brittle yellow pages. "This book was among the Summoner's few, meager belongings."

"And?"

Wesley stopped turning pages, stared down at his place in the book, then looked up at Angel, his face grim. "Angel, I fear he was telling the truth."

"Meaning?"

"We won't be able to stop the megalith from aligning."

"Said it before, Wes, and I'll say it again. Unacceptable."

"But it's true," Wesley said, coming forward to show Angel the damning page. "Look at this illustration."

Angel frowned as he examined the crude illustration of two black-robed men standing on either side of a two-faced monolith, drawn in dotted lines to indicate its state of pre-alignment. Each man held a palm pressed against the smooth, carved recesses of each giant stone mouth. Wavy lines representing light or energy radiated outward from both faces.

"This clearly shows two Summoners accessing the power of the megalith prior to alignment," Wesley said, confirming Angel's own fearful interpretation. "I'm just beginning to make sense of the accompanying text, but it confirms what the Summoner told us."

Angel walked across the room and picked up the ceremonial dagger. The hilt depicted tiny demonic faces and was inlaid with gems that glittered in the ambient light of the abandoned office. The Summoner had waited three thousand years for the right time to find someone like Rebecca Wade to willingly carry out his sacrifices and advance his ancient plans. After what must have seemed an eternity to the Summoner, everything had come together for this one night, to change the face of the world. And all their efforts to stop the demonic equinox had ended in failure. The events of the Summoner's life, leading up to the appearance of the monolith on Hollywood Boulevard, had the undeniable weight of predestination behind them. *It would be easy to give up now,* Angel thought. But he reminded himself that appearances can be deceiving. *Things aren't always what they seem.* He knew that from personal experience. *Not always what we want them to be or wish that they were.*

In light of Angel's apparent indecision, Wesley proposed a course of action. "The last escapee's crossing was televised," Wesley reminded them. "Perhaps it's not too late to notify the authorities, the governor, to explain what's about to occur and have him mobilize the National Guard, cordon off the megalith. They can't attack the megalith until it aligns, but—"

"No," Angel said. He looked at the Summoner's corpse and hoped the ancient demon had deluded himself into believing in the inevitability of his obsession.

"No?" Wesley frowned, not following. Connor looked intrigued.

"Never say never, Wes," Angel said with a wry smile.

"I'm afraid I don't—"

"You figure out how we stop the crossover on the other side," Angel said, nodding toward the flesh-bound book in Wesley's hands. "I'll take care of opening the portal before alignment. Deal?"

CHAPTER SEVENTEEN

Dismayed by Turgahlee's premonition of doom in mere hours, also known as T-minus-get-out-of-town-now, Lorne returned to the Hyperion to report the dire news. Since he believed the waxy demon's prediction would indeed happen, he had to ask himself, why bother returning to the hotel at all? Why not phone it in and head for the hills, or keep running to try to stay one step ahead of the apocalypse? But the answer wasn't a revelation. The gang at Angel Investigations had become Lorne's surrogate family, and there was, truth be told, no place he'd rather be than with them, even if the time left would be spent grasping at straws. "Which probably sums up my dilemma," Lorne said to himself as he entered the lobby of the Hyperion. "Be it ever so humble . . ."

Cordelia and Fred were arguing. While Cordelia was waving a ballpoint around for emphasis, Fred was gripping an enormous battle-ax in both hands.

Hope Cordy realizes nobody ever said anything about the pen being mightier than a battle-ax, Lorne thought. "What's this, pumpkins?" he asked. "Family squabble?"

"What?" they both snapped at him simultaneously.

"Sorry, kittens," Lorne said with a placating smile. "Seems I ran a bit too far with an interior monologue metaphor. Like running with scissors, I guess."

"Fred's crazy," Cordelia said. "Go ahead, tell him."

"I have to do something!"

"Whoa, slow down, sweet pea," Lorne said. "Wouldn't want to accidentally lop off any heads with that thing."

"I'm taking this to him," Fred said, almost frantic. "He's unarmed in there."

"Who?"

"Gunn," Cordelia said. "She wants to give the battle-ax to Gunn."

"That interdimensional ship has sailed, sugar plum," Lorne said. "Gunn's crossed over."

"Precisely!" Fred exclaimed, as if that explained everything.

"What? I missed something?"

"Gunn crossed over without a weapon," Fred said. "He's helpless!"

"Gunn is anything but helpless," Lorne said. "But how do you propose to get that to him, peanut?"

"Isn't it obvious?" Fred said. "By attacking the megalith with it."

"But that means you'll cross—"

"Exactly," Cordelia said. "Crazy!"

Fred shook her head. "I'm sick of waiting! We're sitting here reading books, looking up Web pages, and Charles is—he's probably fighting for his life! I can't continue to sit here and do nothing."

"We're all doing our part, cupcake," Lorne said. "It's a team effort."

"But it's not! It's—Charles is over there alone with the evil team," Fred said, her voice strained as she wiped a tear from her cheek with the back of her hand. "We're safe here, but he's over there alone."

"We may not be safe for long," Lorne said softly, reminded of the reason why he had returned to the Hyperion. "Not long at all."

"I'm—done here," Fred said. "I can't wait around, wondering if he—if he's . . . don't you understand? I have to do something!"

Fred strode across the lobby, carrying the oversized battle-ax with grim determination. As Cordelia ran from behind the reception desk to stop her, Lorne caught her arm. "She's made up her mind, darlin'," he said. "Just . . . let her go."

"But it's—it's suicide."

"And staying around here isn't?"

"Lorne, what is your affliction?"

"Terminal case of doomsday drearies," Lorne said. He released her arm and sat on a banquette, head hanging. "I have it on very good authority—a certain waxy demon with a touch of prescience and a roaming eyeball—that the clock's ticking."

"What clock?"

"Doomsday clock," Lorne said. "In less than two hours, hell breaks loose, literally, in Hollywood."

Cordelia sat beside him, looking as forlorn as he felt. "Oh . . ."

"Have you heard from Angel? Wesley? Junior?"

Cordelia shook her head. "They should know— if . . . you know, it's that soon."

"Right," Lorne said. He heaved a sigh and pushed himself out of the comfortable seat. "Don't get up, lamb chop. I'll make the call."

"Sucks to be the messenger."

"Unfortunately," Lorne said, "my misery will have plenty of company."

Once again, Angel drove the GTX toward the intersection of Hollywood and Vine. Wesley was engrossed in the Summoner's flesh-bound tome, his three-thousand-year-old legacy of plotting to dethrone humanity from Earth. He cross-referenced the crude illustrations with the explanatory text, seeking clues to the mystery of the monolith. Sitting in the backseat, Connor was quiet, a faraway look in his eyes.

Angel wondered if the boy ever allowed himself to doubt. Connor had been raised in a hell dimension, where losing confidence in one's abilities could prove instantly fatal, where triumph was far from guaranteed, but failure was not an option. Connor had supreme confidence in his superhuman powers and in his fighting abilities, and that confidence had served him well. But if they failed to stop the monolith's alignment, if they allowed the demon crossing to happen, even Connor would have trouble believing he would live through the night.

His cell phone chirped, startling him. He fished it out of his pocket on the second ring and answered before the third. It was Lorne.

"Got news, boss, and it ain't good."

"Lot of that going around," Angel said.

"Finally got a tidbit from the demon underground," Lorne said, and related Turgahlee's prediction.

"Word from the Summoner himself is that we have till midnight."

"Ah, new day, and all that," Lorne said. "Top marks in the department of 'how appropriate.' But I have some more bad news, about Little Miss Firecracker."

"Cordy?"

"The other firecracker," Lorne said. "Fred. She walked out of here with a battle-ax that weighs more than she does. She plans to deliver it to Gunn personally, by way of attacking mondo-rock."

"That's crazy."

"Cordelia agrees."

"It won't work," Angel said. "She won't be able to give it to him. If she attacks the monolith, she joins the demon club. Stop her, Lorne. Catch her. Tie her down, if you have to. We're on our way to the site now."

"Angel-face, please tell me you found a way to turn back the clock on this demon equinox."

"We're, uh, working on it, Lorne. Keep the faith."

"Angel, wait a sec," Lorne said. "Cordelia has something."

"More bad news?" Angel asked wryly.

"On special tonight," Lorne said before passing the phone to Cordelia.

"Angel, hi," Cordelia said briskly. "I'm watching the broadcast, and there are more of them. A lot more."

"Escapee demons?"

"No," Cordelia said. "Monoliths. They're popping up all over L.A. Smaller, but same two-faced design. In Glendale and Burbank, North Hollywood and Rancho Park, Culver City and—anyway, I started marking the locations on a map, and the baby monoliths form a circle around the big mamma. If Fred were here, I'm sure she'd probably call that one a 'focal point' or 'ground zero' or something."

"You're right," Angel said. "Not good." He relayed the information to Wesley and Connor.

"The original megalith is the key," Wesley said. "If we stop that, I believe we will stop the others."

"The mission remains the same," Angel said for Cordelia's benefit.

"Okay. But Angel, there's something else," Cordelia said, her voice betraying her nervousness. "I'm looking at a live shot of momma monolith and it's getting all glowy."

Angel turned to Wesley. "She says the monolith is beginning to glow."

Wesley nodded. "The last stage of alignment," he said. "Perhaps some sort of cosmic friction created by the mystical overlapping of dimensions."

Angel thanked Cordelia and ended the call.

He began to hit traffic snarls, which worsened as he neared Hollywood Boulevard. People hurried by on the sidewalk carrying boxes and suitcases stuffed with their belongings, many of them trying to hail the overtaxed fleet of taxicabs. Most of those fleeing in cars lay on their horns to encourage less reckless drivers to either accelerate or move out of the way. Double-parked cars created problems for northbound and southbound traffic.

The asphalt arteries of the city were clogging fast with panic and fear.

"Here's something about averting the crossover," Wesley said, tapping a page in the Summoner's journal. "It seems the two Summoners must act as one . . . 'turn the eyes away and none shall pass.' Then there's an illustration. Odd . . . ?"

"What?" Angel asked, trying to keep his eyes on the unpredictable traffic patterns, but sparing a glance at the open page of the book. "Is that a drawing of . . . ?"

"The DNA double helix," Wesley finished. He raised his eyebrows in a mixture of surprise and puzzlement. "The Summoner said that humans who crossed over would become the enemy—that is, demons. Perhaps this is a symbolic representation of the melding of human and demon forms, echoed again in the dual faces of the megalith. And yet, DNA is a fairly recent discovery, predated hundreds, perhaps even thousands of years by the information in this journal. Of course, it's possible that . . ."

"What?"

"It's certainly possible that this is a literal representation of what lies on the other side of the megalith," Wesley said. "The text refers to a passageway leading down. This says, 'The two in opposition must agree at each step.' Ah . . . steps! This is a depiction of a spiral staircase carved in stone.

Two of them, actually, their spirals always in opposition."

Connor, leaning over the front seat, looked up at Angel. "Two in opposition? Sounds like you and me."

Angel asked, "You up for it?"

Connor flashed a wry grin. "Can't think of two better opposites."

Soon, driving became an exercise in frustration. When Angel spotted a minivan pulling away from the curb on the opposite side of the street, he swerved around a double-parked pickup truck, its bed overloaded with roped furniture, and swung into the vacated parking space. "We'll make better time on foot."

As they stepped out of the GTX, Angel said, "Feel that?"

Wesley nodded. "Ground's vibrating."

Angel crouched, placing his palm against the cement. "Rhythmic pulsing," he said. "And it's accelerating."

"The lathe of evil," Wesley commented. "Shaping one dimension to fit the parameters of another."

Connor scoffed, "Where do you come up with this stuff?"

"We'll have time to wax poetic after we throw a wrench in the works," Angel said. He opened the trunk and handed Connor a duffel bag, keeping another for himself, along with two stained canvas bags with long drawstrings.

Wesley kept the journal, but took no weapons. Clutching the oversized book against the bloodied tatters of his ruined shirt, he looked like a haunted doomsday preacher who'd witnessed whereof he spoke.

Slipping the duffel bag's strap over his shoulder, Angel said to Connor, "We should blend in."

"Except we're heading the wrong way."

Angel shrugged. "In all the panic, nobody will notice."

As they reached the intersection, the monolith came into view. A pulsing white-violet aura surrounded the dark lifeless rock faces, some sort of mystical energy that rippled in time to the vibrations shaking the ground, which had become much more noticeable. The power of the vibrations had created hundreds of stress fractures in the street, zigzag patterns that continued to spread outward.

Around the monolith, mass confusion reigned. Cars avoided driving past the menacing tower by turning north or south on side streets or by making reckless U-turns. Panicked pedestrians raced along the sidewalk and darted across the street, pushing and shoving, tripping and falling, or kicking and trampling anyone who got in their way. Screams of fear, pain, and indignation punctuated frantic shouting, with wailing car alarms and breaking windows providing a strident doomsday chorus. Two blocks away, an abandoned car had struck a fire hydrant, which now sprayed a thick geyser of frothy water into the air, creating a miniature lake on Hollywood Boulevard.

A few dozen police officers in riot gear should have replaced the several cops assigned to the traffic detail. The situation had spiraled out of control too fast for the civil authorities to respond appropriately. The inert statue had lulled the city into a dangerous sense of complacency. For now, the cops all but ignored the vehicular traffic as they attempted to maintain order among the pedestrians and restrain them from assaulting one another.

The trio hurried along the sidewalk, closer to the monolith. The unnatural quality of the rumbling tremor began to make Angel's bones ache. Wesley looked a little green around the gills. "Wes, you okay?"

"A little interdimensional nausea to season the pervasive dread emanating from the megalith."

"This is the last place anyone should be," Angel said.

Connor grinned. "Naturally."

"Fred," Angel said.

Wesley looked confused. "What? Where?"

Angel pointed along the sidewalk to where Fred, carrying what Angel assumed was the long battle-ax wrapped in black cloth, was about to step off the curb to assault the monolith. "Stop her, Wes," Angel said. "Connor and I will take it from here."

Wesley nodded and sprinted toward Fred.

"Ready?" Angel said to Connor.

Connor nodded. "All my life."

Angel couldn't help thinking, *Wish I'd been there for it, Connor.*

Wesley's overriding concern about the impending apocalypse had narrowed into a pinpoint of fear for the one person who meant more to him than anyone else. His anxiety rendered him breathless by the time he intercepted Fred, catching her upper arm as she stepped off the curb. Her head whipped around, and she glared defiantly at him for that one moment before recognition dawned. The look of determination, however, never left her face.

Wesley glanced at the concealed battle-ax and shouted above the horns, sirens, and alarms, "That won't work!"

Fred was desperate, almost hysterical, "How do you know?"

Wesley showed her the flesh-bound journal. "The Summoner's journal," he said. "If you assault the megalith, you won't help Gunn. You'll join him."

"But—Charles—he won't be alone."

"As demons," Wesley admitted, "you'll become the enemy."

"But, Charles . . . ? No!"

"There is another way," Wesley said, offering her the thread of hope she needed to survive the crisis. "As long as Angel and Connor abort the inter-dimensional alignment in time, there's a chance—"

"What if they can't stop it?" Fred demanded.

Wesley had lost Fred's affection to Gunn, if there had ever been a competition between the two men in the first place. In his optimistic moments, Wesley liked to think there might be a place for him in her heart. If not before, then maybe someday. He still cared for her more than words could convey, and because of that, he took no satisfaction in the recent turn of events. Under other circumstances, Gunn's disappearance might have given him a chance to find a place at her side. But Fred's concern for Gunn's life was palpable. She was in pain, and that pained him. Setting aside his own feelings, what he wished for Fred, ultimately, was happiness. And no matter what they fought about, Wesley would never wish harm on Gunn.

"This is our best chance, Fred."

But she was persistent. She repeated her question, but a gnawing fear had begun to seep into her voice. "What if they fail, Wesley?"

A swirling wind kicked up, blowing newspapers, empty cans, and plastic bottles down the street in jittery spirals. People rushed by, shouting in anger and fear. Car headlights swept back and forth as drivers seemed to loop in confusion. And through it all, the rise and fall of sirens and alarms shattered the night, like a reckoning of banshees proclaiming uncounted deaths to come.

Wesley shrugged in resignation. "If they fail, then one way or another, it's over for all of us."

•

CHAPTER EIGHTEEN

Angel and Connor approached the side of the glowing monolith, all but ignored by everyone in the mass confusion. Anyone who noticed their purposeful walk toward the towering statue probably assumed they had a death wish. Angel would have had a hard time arguing against that assumption.

They stopped beside the statue as the continuing tremors, at their strongest here, rolled beneath them in shuddering waves, and the air seemed to buzz with some weird electricity that sparked feelings of growing dread.

"Now or never," Angel said. "Literally."

Angel gave Connor one of the two stained canvas bags he'd brought from the trunk of the car. Each bag had drawstrings, which they fastened to a belt loop on their pants. Angel then gave Connor a nod to proceed. In unison, they reached into the bags and withdrew identical but opposite items:

the severed left and right hands of the Summoner.

"If this doesn't work, we're gonna look real foolish," Connor said.

"If it doesn't work," Angel said, "we'll have bigger problems."

"Good to know there's an upside."

"Let's go," Angel said, and unzipped his duffel bag. Connor followed suit. Together they removed the sword each bag had concealed. Angel had warned Connor that once they exposed their swords, they would need to make the crossover attempt quickly or risk interference from the police. "Positions."

They separated, losing sight of each other as Angel walked around to the monolith's demonic face and Connor approached the agonized human face.

Angel noted that the visual discrepancy was almost gone. The stone looked solid and impenetrable, as if it had already aligned with their dimension. Logically, he knew the time hadn't arrived, but it was perilously close.

"On three!" Angel called. "One . . ." Concerned that they might face immediate opposition after crossing over, he gripped his sword firmly in his right hand, blade upright. "Two . . ." He adjusted his grip on the pale, severed hand so that the palm faced the carved recess of the demonic mouth. "Three!" He slapped the Summoner's palm against the surface of the stone, hoping that Connor had mirrored his action with the opposing hand at that precise moment.

He needn't have worried. Within two seconds, the recessed section of stone that comprised the gaping demonic mouth became a shadowy substance, a mere veil over reality hinting at its former solidity.

It was possible they were about to step into a trap. Not that it mattered. With alignment imminent, they were out of options. Holding the severed hand before him like a talisman, Angel stepped between the upper and lower rows of pointed stone teeth into darkness and silence, and the symbolism wasn't lost on him. *Into the belly of the beast*, he thought.

As he dropped the severed hand into the canvas bag, Angel noticed a subtle shift in the air currents. That sensory clue prompted him to reach back and confirm his sudden suspicion that the stone wall had reformed behind him. *No turning back . . . yet*, he thought as he waited for his eyes to adjust.

He stood on a broad rectangular stone platform, suspended like an island in space, beneath a vaulted ceiling that extended into utter darkness. Behind him was the resealed entrance, and to his left and right the platform looked out over an abyss, but in front of him was the first step of a vertiginous spiral staircase, descending as far as his vampiric eyes could see.

"Dad!" Connor called from his left, standing on a platform identical to Angel's, but twenty feet away and nearly swallowed by the oppressive darkness. Connor also stood atop a dizzying spiral staircase made of stone, but each turn was exactly opposite Angel's, in the double-helix pattern illustrated in the Summoner's journal.

The intertwined stairways had no visible support, but were somehow magically suspended in the darkness. *Construction in progress in a dimension where the laws of physics don't apply,* Angel thought. *Are these the interdimensional versions of siege towers?*

He walked toward the first step of the stairway and peered down twenty feet at a flickering light source. On a small landing, next to a short obelisk, a fire burned in a freestanding stone torch stand. Forty feet down, another torch burned, and again at sixty feet, and so on, repeating in the type of infinity illusion created by facing funhouse mirrors. The most distant fires, mere pinpoints, resembled flickering stars in the winter sky on a cloudless night.

Angel looked over at Connor on the opposing platform. "Ready?"

Connor nodded, and they began the long descent.

As Connor continued past the first landing, Angel called a halt. He examined the four-foot-tall obelisk beside the torch stand. A column of strange, engraved symbols decorated each of the four sides of the stone obelisk, but what caught Angel's attention was the sphere mounted on top of it. At first he mistook the sphere for a globe—some kind of world symbol. But closer inspection of the artwork engraved on the surface revealed that the orb actually represented an eye. The eye was *looking* at Connor's landing, where an identical obelisk had an eye sculpture that was probably looking back at Angel's platform. Angel recalled something Wesley had gleaned from the Summoner's journal. He pointed at the front of the stone eye and yelled to Connor, "'Turn the eyes away and none shall pass!'"

Angel laid his sword down, then gripped the basketball-sized stone sphere and rotated it 180 degrees. The sound of stone grinding against stone echoed back and forth across the vast chamber as Connor also turned the eye of his obelisk. When they finished, the eyes looked away from each other.

They picked up their swords and descended to the next set of opposing landings, each of which held another obelisk with a stone eye facing inward. By the fourth landing, Connor had sprinted ahead but soon discovered he could not turn his eye unless Angel turned the opposing eye simultaneously. This restriction forced them to work together, and neither of them could have performed the alignment-cancellation ritual alone.

After a dozen landings and a dozen pairs of eyes, Angel and Connor became better at synchronizing their descents and eye-turning motions, performing like true mirror images of each other. At some point, when the first landing was no longer visible and the bottom landing was nowhere in sight, Angel's mind began to play tricks on his perception. He was no longer safe in the assumption that up was over his head and down was beneath his feet. What if the spiral stairways descended on an angle, and what if they began to curve upward again? With no walls to anchor the stairs and darkness closing in from every side, Angel felt adrift in space, like a man trapped in an Escher perspective illusion, climbing upward and descending in the same mind-bending tableau. If the laws of physics were compromised here, what about gravity itself? At that very moment, Angel might have been running upside down and not have realized it.

Ultimately, whether gravity pulled up or down in this interdimensional limbo didn't matter. Angel had weight here. Gravity pressed him to the stone stairs, and if he toppled off the edge of the rail-less staircase he would fall in the direction he perceived as down, maybe to a crushing impact below or above, or maybe he would fall for eternity without ever reaching bottom or top, trapped in an endless freefall of failure. Turning the stone eyes away from each other might be the first part of the challenge, but the more difficult test might be to maintain one's balance in the midst of pinwheeled perception.

Angel had been keeping a running count of the number of obelisk eye platforms they modified. When he reached one hundred—a descent, he estimated, of two thousand feet—he could make out a roofless, circular chamber below. The two spiral stairways dropped into that exposed chamber, where they apparently ended. From their present height, the chamber appeared unoccupied. Without any spoken agreement, Angel and Connor slowed their descent. They worked their way down through the several obelisk landings that remained, but kept a watchful eye of their own on the chamber that awaited them.

Angel noticed dark archways spaced at even intervals along the interior perimeter of the chamber. From his bird's-eye vantage point, Angel looked at the darkness beyond the chamber, outward from one of the archways, and he made out the silhouette of a covered passageway that vanished in deeper darkness as it receded into the far reaches of the abyss. Soon after locating one spoke-like covered tunnel in the darkness, he saw the others, one branching away from each archway. The chamber was a hub with multiple access points.

When he and Connor rotated the next-to-last obelisk eye, approximately forty feet up from the floor of the chamber, their luck ran out. Twenty armored demon guards filed into the chamber, one from each archway, to surround a large obelisk in the center of the round chamber, like an honor guard.

Angel motioned for Connor to proceed quietly and, despite the distance that separated them, he thought he saw the boy roll his eyes. Nevertheless, Angel had to be sure he was on the same tactical page as Connor, who might have thought nothing of screaming a battle cry and charging into the mass of demons, counting on the element of surprise to carry him to victory.

Staying low, they crept down the stairs leading to the final platform, twenty feet above the chamber. Angel nodded to Connor that he was ready to turn the last obelisk eye, but made a hand gesture to indicate a slow turn to minimize the stone-grinding noise. As they turned the eyes away from each other, Angel watched the demons, who continued to stand at attention in the center of the chamber.

They had turned the obelisk eyes less than ninety degrees when the demons began to look around, alarmed. A moment later, twenty pairs of deep-set, smoldering red eyes looked upward. As many saw Angel as Connor. With a collective roar, the demons split into two groups of ten and

mounted the twin stairways. Angel and Connor
hurriedly finished the eye rotation, then picked up
their swords, ready to make a stand on their opposing platforms.

Connor nodded toward his obelisk. "Are we finished?" he asked.

"No," Angel called, pointing his sword toward
the large obelisk in the middle of the chamber
below. If they had been resetting pins in a mystical
lock, Angel would bet good money that the final
obelisk was the most important pin of all. "One
left."

"Figures," Connor replied.

"Don't get yourself killed," Angel yelled.

"Right!"

Fortunately, the stairs weren't wide enough to
accommodate two bulky demons abreast, forcing
them to attack single file. These guard demons
wore the familiar helmets and breastplates but,
unlike the escapees, they were armed with swords
or spears in addition to their fearsome claws.

Angel stayed on the last landing, which gave him
better footing and more space to maneuver. The
first demon in the charge had a sword, which he
wielded as if it were a club. Angel parried several
powerful stokes before he saw an opening and
thrust his sword point between breastplate and
helmet. He yanked the blade free, then kicked the
demon in the chest, knocking him into the demon

behind him. Both fell over the unprotected edge of the staircase. They missed the chamber and kept falling into the black abyss below. The demon who had the misfortune to be second in line continued to scream until the sound of his voice was too far to carry.

The third demon lunged forward with a barbed spear in a double-handled grip aimed at Angel's chest. Angel grabbed the spear in his free hand and yanked the demon forward, past his center of gravity, causing him to stumble. Before the demon could recover, Angel hooked his arm around the shaft of the spear and shoved the demon's helmeted face into the torch fire. The demon shrieked, jerked backward, and toppled off the platform without his spear.

The fourth demon rushed at Angel with a sword gripped in both hands. Angel flipped the spear around and hurled it. The demon ducked, and grunted with satisfaction when the spear missed.

But Angel hadn't missed. He'd been aiming for the left thigh of the fifth demon, who dropped to his knees, moaning in pain as he clutched the shaft of the spear protruding from his leg.

Angel fought the fourth demon sword to sword, waiting for an opening. But the demon had learned a lesson from the first one killed and kept his head low. When a double-handed swing missed Angel's head by an inch, the force of the blow turned the demon sideways. Angel chopped down at the demon's left hamstring and almost severed his leg at the knee. As he collapsed on his side, the demon lost his sword over the edge. Angel planted a foot on his rear and shoved hard enough for the demon to join his weapon.

The fifth demon continued to wail about the spear lodged in the meat of his thigh, so much so that the sixth demon grabbed his shoulders and threw him aside, out of the way, and off the stairway. The fifth demon shrieked indignantly on his way down.

Angel said to the sixth demon, "With friends like you, who needs enemies."

The demon hurled his spear at Angel, who swatted it out of the air with his left forearm, and said, "Is that all you got?" The demon cackled, reached down, and pulled out two daggers from scabbards buckled to his boots. With the knives held in overhand grips, he lumbered up the stairs toward Angel with a ferocious roar.

Connor cried out in pain.

Angel looked his way. "Connor?"

"I'm fine!"

One dagger flashed past Angel's face, slicing a thin line down his cheek, while the other blade bit into his shoulder. Angel drove his knee into the armored abdomen of the knife-wielding demon. Neither he nor Connor could afford distractions.

We have to trust each other's abilities or we're both doomed!

Angel snap-kicked the demon's right knee with enough force and follow-through to hyperextend the brawny leg. The demon lashed out wildly with the dagger in his left hand. Angel's sword swept inside the arc and severed the demon's forearm halfway to the elbow. The hand, still clutching the dagger, fluttered end over end across the landing before arcing down into the darkness. Angel leaped into a 360 spin kick, striking the demon squarely on the helmet with a sound like a cannon shot, wickedly snapping the demon's neck. Dead or unconscious, the demon toppled over, struck the corner of the stairs, and vanished into the depths.

The seventh demon decided he didn't like one-to-one odds. He tried a different approach. Sprinting up the steps to build momentum, he launched himself high into the air, spear held out to the side. At first, Angel was confused, but then he realized the attack wasn't an attack at all; it was an attempt to reach the high ground. As he came down on the steps above and behind Angel, the eighth demon was already rushing forward, sword in hand.

Angel parried the first sword blow and the second. When he smelled the demon behind him lunging forward with his spear, Angel dropped low, but not soon enough. He winced as the demon's spearhead sliced his right bicep.

At that moment, Angel was facing Connor's platform, so when his son cried out in pain, Angel saw what happened next. Connor staggered from a blow to his head, took a step backward into nothingness, and dropped like a stone—

"No!" Angel roared.

—before his left hand lashed out and caught the edge of the stone platform.

Connor dangled over the abyss, the four fingers of his left hand all that stood between him and oblivion. Dislodged from his grasp, Connor's sword flipped end over end into the bottomless pit, almost as if to foreshadow his imminent fate.

The demon with the sword that had managed to knock Connor from his perch walked to the edge of the landing and laughed malevolently. Placing the sole of his boot on top of Connor's straining knuckles, he began to grind them against the stone.

Thrown into action by Connor's crisis, Angel shoved his sword straight up into the throat of the demon that was leaning over him with the spear. Yanking the shaft of the spear from the demon's slack grasp, Angel drove the spearhead into the leg of the eighth demon, nearly ripping off his kneecap. As that demon doubled over in pain, Angel caught the inert body behind him toppling forward, flipped it over his shoulder, and tossed it against the wounded eighth demon. Both of them rolled down the steps into numbers nine and ten, who had to scrabble for purchase. Meanwhile, Angel scooped up the dropped spear and yelled, "Connor! Catch!"

Grimacing in agony as his crushed fingers lost their grip on the platform, Connor glanced toward Angel in time to see the spear tossed his way lengthwise. Snatching the spear out of the air in his right hand, Connor then looked up at the demon towering over him and smiled at the perfect angle. The patch of mottled-red-and-black skin seemed as large as an island. He hurled the spear straight up with so much force that the booted foot grinding his fingers into the stone rose from the platform, and the demon's helmet popped off his head. His sword slipped from numb fingers and clanked against the landing. Displaced by the shaft of the spear, the demon's deep-set eyes bulged in their sockets. And the spearhead protruded two inches from the top of his breached skull.

Connor reached up with his right hand and tugged on the shaft of the spear, which caused the demon's lifeless body to jackknife and plummet over Connor into the hungry darkness. With both hands, Connor boosted himself onto the obelisk platform again. Before he could pick up finger-crusher's sword, the next demon in line—his ninth—charged with his spear lowered at Connor's midsection.

Connor spun to the side, avoiding the spearhead with the grace of a bullfighter but without the benefit of a red cape. He caught the shaft of the spear and pulled hard, using the demon's momentum against him. As the demon continued to lunge forward, Connor stuck out his foot and tripped him. The demon cartwheeled down into darkness.

Snatching up the sword, Connor stared down at his tenth and final demon. He had one bitter and determined thought: *This one's gonna pay!*

CHAPTER NINETEEN

With Connor past his immediate crisis, Angel had to battle two last demons to gain entry to the round chamber and the final obelisk. The ninth and tenth demons shoved the lifeless body of the seventh and the screaming body of the eighth off either side of the spiral staircase, which granted Angel a short respite.

Unsure how much time had passed since he and Connor had entered the interdimensional space, and without even knowing if time passed differently there, Angel wondered if midnight might have come and gone. Had the ring of monoliths surrounding Hollywood Boulevard already opened to invading forces? Without returning to witness the devastation, he might never know. And yet his gut told him that the alignment would not occur—could not occur—unless the eyes in this space were facing each other. Further, he understood that the last obelisk, waiting below, was the primary key. A pair of willing demons could reverse everything he and Connor had done so far to avert the demonic equinox. Switch the platform eyes back and the equinox would happen as planned. But not the obelisk in the chamber below, the one that had merited an honor guard, the one at the center of everything here, the hub of all that they could distinguish in the darkness. *Reset that one,* Angel knew somehow, *and Earth is safe.*

Maybe it buys us another three thousand years.

He intended to test that theory.

The ninth demon charged with a leveled spear. Angel wrapped his left arm around the shaft and pulled the demon into a clinch before plunging his sword into the neck gap. He hurled the demon off the platform and motioned the tenth forward with a little bravado. After dispatching nine of the demon's comrades, Angel felt entitled to a bit of cockiness—and immediately wondered if that was a trait Connor had inherited from him.

After several sword parries, Angel backed up toward the obelisk and the torch stand, appearing to tire. Angel blocked an overhand strike, and the sword hilts slammed together. The demon thought he could overpower Angel and pressed against his upraised arm. Angel smiled, and the demon cocked his head, confused.

With his free hand, Angel plucked the torch out of the stand and laid the fire against the demon's coarse trousers, which burst into flames. "Definitely not flame-retardant," Angel said.

The demon spun in a circle, howling as he slapped at the flames engulfing him. A moment later, he stepped off the landing and hurtled into darkness. Though the freefall might extinguish the flames, the fall itself might never end.

Angel looked across to the opposing staircase and saw that Connor had defeated his last demon in brutal fashion and was already racing down the last steps into the round chamber. Descending his last set of stairs into the chamber, Angel first peered into the archways. Although the flickering light from the chamber's four wall-mounted torches did little to dispel the darkness of the tunnels, it seemed to Angel that they were—for the moment, at least—alone.

He turned his gaze to the large obelisk, but found his thoughts drifting to Gunn. A grim notion entered his mind, an idea that might have paralyzed him in battle had it occurred earlier. *What if one of the demons I killed on the stairs was Gunn? Has he already become one of them . . . or is there still hope?*

Connor circled the main obelisk. "This one's different."

Mounted on a round dais of smooth stone, the chamber's obelisk was, at eight feet, double the height of the stairway obelisks. Each of its four sides had two columns of engraved runes or symbols. More importantly, there was no single eye orb on the primary obelisk. Instead, two stone eyes larger than the others flanked the obelisk on freestanding stone towers ten feet high and sunk into large round pedestals. Bisecting each stone tower at mid-height was a polished wooden turning handle as thick around as a utility pole.

"The eyes face each other," Angel commented. "Turn them and we cancel the equinox party."

"So what are we waiting for?"

"Nothing," Angel said. The bisecting handles had been designed to accommodate two demons on each tower pedestal. Angel hoped he and Connor would be able to turn each tower alone. *Not likely any demons will help us out,* Angel thought. He stood on the closest pedestal and wrapped his forearm around the thick handle. "Ready when you are."

"Go!"

Pulling was marginally easier than pushing the wooden handles. For better traction, Angel dug his heels into the grooves between the square stones of the pedestal and tugged the handle a few inches before releasing his grip, repositioning his heels, and tugging again. Tug, release, reposition—tug, release, reposition—over and over again, for every protesting couple of inches of stone grinding against stone. Fifteen minutes to rotate the eyes

90 degrees. "Halfway!" Angel called to Connor.

"A walk—in the park!" Connor grunted with the effort of another few inches.

"Do you even know what that means?" Angel asked, a smile momentarily erasing his grimace of effort.

"No," Connor said, "but it—sounds nice!"

"Depends"—Angel tugged again—"on the park!" After a few more pulls, Angel thought he heard another sound under the scraping and grinding of stone against stone. "Stop!"

"Tired?" Connor asked, amused.

"Listen," Angel said. The white-noise rush of sound he'd first noticed between pulls increased in volume. "Rumbling . . . ?"

"Marching."

"Demon troops," Angel guessed. "Lots of demon troops."

"Coming down each of the tunnels," Connor said. "Must be close to midnight. Sounds like thousands of them."

"Tens of thousands," Angel said. "Break's over!"

With redoubled effort, they tugged on the stone tower handles again. In between pulls, Angel tried to gauge the distance of the invading army, but the sound came from every direction and seemed to echo endlessly. He looked up as he repositioned, and saw that he'd turned his eye almost all the way around. Encouraged, he gritted his teeth and hurried through the last three pulls needed to reach 180 degrees. Connor finished a few seconds after Angel.

Without the grinding of stone to mask it, the sound of advancing troops seemed dangerously close. As they stepped down from the tower pedestals, the entire chamber began to tremble violently. Cracks and fissures spread along the high walls, dislodging chunks of stone that fell to the floor and broke apart, creating clouds of dust.

"The troops?" Connor asked.

"No," Angel said. "We're responsible for this destruction. The alignment created this chamber and the spiral stairways. These structures connect the dimensions. They might even be metaphysical in nature. But we've cancelled the alignment, so . . . this can no longer exist."

"Fine," Connor said. "Let's go!"

"In a minute," Angel said, examining the walls of the chamber.

"Do I need to remind you that we have about half a mile of stairs to climb to get out of here, Dad?"

"Haven't forgotten, son."

"Then what—?"

"Gunn," Angel said softly as he moved to the wall opposite the stairways, where he noticed rows of recessed slots reminiscent of morgue drawers. Most of the slots were empty, but a group of three in one row housed stone containers. *Three is definitely the right number,* he thought. *And Gunn will be in either end unit. If we're not too late!* "Help me."

Angel directed Connor to one end unit, while he took the other.

Connor laid his sword down to tug out his receptacle. Without hesitation, he pried the lid up and slid it aside, revealing a sleeping demon with red-and-black-mottled flesh lying in tangled shreds of human clothes. Exposed to fresh air, the demon woke, its deep-set, smoldering red eyes opening wide. A moment later it reared up, its claws slashing at Connor's face.

Leaning away from the lethal claws, Connor snatched up his sword and drove the point under the demon's chin and up through its brain, killing it instantly. It flopped back into the receptacle, arms dangling over the edges, claws clicking together briefly from a few misfiring nerve impulses.

Belatedly stunned, Connor looked at Angel and said, "Tell me that wasn't Gunn."

"It wasn't," Angel said, pointing down at the receptacle he had already opened.

Trembling, his clothes a shredded mess, Gunn sat up in the coffin-sized stone container, panting in fear or relief. Though he was bloody and bruised seemingly from head to toe, he was still human. The first thing he said was, "'Bout damn time!" But there was only relief, not anger, in his tone. He'd come terrifyingly close to losing his humanity, and he knew it.

Gunn examined his arms, which were riddled with tiny cuts and speckled with drops of blood. Hundreds of crease-shaped bruises covered his skin as if he'd been struck repeatedly with a wooden ax blade. His fingers traced one of the longer, narrow bruises. "These squirmy things were crawlin' all over me, digging under my skin. . . ." Gunn shuddered at the visceral memory. "Whispering in my head, about to drive me crazy. For a while, I thought maybe I was crazy. Then, all of a sudden, everything started shakin', and those things—those damn, freaky, squirmy things—were gone." Gunn snapped his fingers. "Like that."

"It wasn't complete," Angel guessed. "When we turned the last set of eyes away, to stop the alignment, the transformation reversed itself."

"Works for me," Gunn said. "But . . . what's that loud scary sound?"

"Which one?" Connor asked. "The chamber tearing itself apart? Or the hordes of bloodthirsty demons marching this way from every one of those tunnels?"

Gunn shook his head. "Forget I asked."

"Right," Angel said. "Let's move."

"What about the demon in the middle?" Connor said, nodding toward the remaining receptacle.

"The other Baker," Angel said, indicating, for Gunn's benefit, the transformed demon Connor had killed. "They were taken out together. Odds are it's . . ."

"Better make sure," Gunn said. "Could have been me."

Connor removed the last container and, as Angel stood ready with a sword, lifted the lid. "Too late!" Connor said as the newly formed demon's eyes flashed open. Angel dispatched it a moment later.

Gunn looked around the quaking chamber, then toward the twin stairways that spiraled into impenetrable darkness above but that had already begun to crumble as well. "Guys," Gunn said worriedly, "looks like our train's about to leave the station."

One of the stone-eye towers began to list away from the obelisk. A fissure snaked across the floor, causing the tower to dip and lean even further. A moment later, the tower split in half, the top crashing to the floor with a thunderous sound, like an explosion, and the large stone eye broke in two. From the dark tunnels, a rallying cry sounded, echoed by thousands, and the rumbling cadence of marching feet became a battle charge.

"Gentlemen," Angel said. "Let's get out of here. Fast."

In their haste, they ran to the nearest staircase, but as they mounted the stairs, a section of ten steps above them crumbled away, disconnecting the stairs from the chamber. The resulting gap was too wide and steep to attempt to cross, especially for Gunn, who was still recovering from his physical ordeal. Since the other staircase was in much better shape at the moment, they sprinted to it and ascended to the first landing, twenty feet above the chamber, without incident.

A deafening roar erupted from below.

Angel stopped by the torch stand and looked down. A mass of armored and armed demons had crammed into the disintegrating chamber, which seemed to wobble on an invisible axis. As some of the demons pointed up to Angel's group, the other eye tower toppled over, crushing several of them beneath the shower of stone. Fractures split the primary obelisk and chunks of stone broke free, leaving the previously smooth stone pockmarked. It almost seemed as if the runes engraved on the sides of the obelisk were erasing themselves, relinquishing their power.

With a shouting surge of anger, the demons rushed up the staircase, pressing together so close that some fell back into the chamber, while others toppled into the bottomless dark beyond. Once the demons mounted the stairs, hundreds more poured into the ravaged chamber via the arched tunnels.

"Anyone got a plan?"

"Run," Angel said, leading the way up to the next landing and the one above it, with Connor and Gunn right behind him.

Packed together, the demons scrambled up the stairs after them, but their combined weight began to hasten the destruction of the stairway. Chunks of rock and whole stairs dropped away, causing some of the demons to stumble and others to lose their footing altogether. Intermittently, falling demons would yell in fear and anger as they spun down into the darkness.

A vast grinding, groaning sound filled the darkness and sent a frightening tremor up the length of the spiral staircase.

Angel stopped and glanced down at the distant chamber. He stood in awe as, one by one, the connecting tunnels, the spokes connected to the chamber hub, broke away from that central room. Long, dark sections of stone tunnel *whooshed* down into the darkness like derailed train cars plunging off a lofty trestle. Spilling out of the crumbled ends were all the demons who had been unable to reach the chamber or retreat to safe ground. Seconds later, the chamber itself broke free of the last few supporting tunnels and spun end over end down into the abyss—accompanied by the fading screams of a hundred trapped demons—shrinking to what seemed like the size of a poker chip before vanishing in the deep.

Gunn looked up into the darkness and asked, "Do I even want to know what's holding up this impossibly high staircase?"

Connor said, "Probably not."

"Very little," Angel added, "and nothing at all if we wait around much longer."

"Good point," Gunn said.

They resumed their hurried ascent. At the next landing, Angel glanced at the demon contingent below. They no longer had to worry about tens of thousands of warrior demons chasing them. Only a hundred or so had made it onto the stairway before the chamber broke free. And those hundred had a hard time staying one step ahead of the entropic forces. Beneath the crowded mass of demons, stairs crumbled away one after another. Now and then a trailing demon would place his foot down and find nothing to support it. Some who felt themselves falling clutched at the demon in front of them, and then two would plummet into the unforgiving darkness.

For its own survival, the demon column thinned to single file. Bunched up, they climbed inefficiently and had jostling accidents that would knock one of them off the trembling stairway every few seconds. Once they ascended in an organized single file, the threat they represented became too serious to ignore.

Gunn showed signs of fatigue. "How much . . . farther?" he asked.

"Another sixteen hundred feet, maybe," Connor supplied with brutal honesty.

Angel might have said, "a little farther," or "not too far," or "we'll be there before you know it," but any of those half-truths would have given Gunn false hope. *Probably better that he knows what lies ahead*, Angel thought. "One step at a time, Gunn," Angel said. "Don't worry. We won't leave you behind."

A glance back revealed the lead demon less than twenty feet below, and gaining. At that rate, the demons would overtake them long before the stairway disintegrated. Across the darkness, the empty stairway also crumbled from the bottom up but, without the added weight of eighty-some demons on it, at a much slower pace. That gave Angel an idea. "Connor," he said. "Stay with Gunn. Keep moving. I'll buy us some time."

"Don't think that's possible," Connor said, but he continued to climb, rather than stop and debate the point.

"You never know."

Gunn looked back at Angel. "You sure about this?"

"Yes," Angel said. "Now go!"

"All right," Gunn said. "Too damn tired to argue."

Angel spun around on the landing, sword raised, to face the column of advancing demons. *Operation Logjam*, he thought nervously. *If this is a mistake, it will certainly be my last one!*

CHAPTER TWENTY

The lead demon reached the first step beneath the landing but could advance no farther because his path was blocked by Angel, who met his sword strokes blow for blow. Angel had a positional and tactical advantage because the demons could not advance without defeating him, and because he wasn't trying to win the battle. Nor was he trying to lose. For the next minute or two, Angel was fighting for the stalemate.

As the one-to-one battle raged on without hope of a clear victor emerging, the demons farther down the stairs first became angry, then terrified. Those in the rear began to scream as, one by one, they lost their footing as the stairs fell out from under them and they hurtled into the darkness.

Angel matched the lead demon thrust to parry, parry for thrust, without losing or seeking an advantage—until the inevitable occurred. The demons in the rear began to turn on one another, with those farthest back trying to wrestle those in front out of their way so they could advance a precious few life-preserving steps higher on the stairway.

When the lead demon grew weary, Angel chose not to seize the advantage. Meanwhile, the force of eighty-odd demons fought a desperate battle amongst themselves that continued to deplete their ranks. By the time only about fifty demons remained, the lead demon had trouble lifting his sword. He stared in resignation at Angel with his burning red eyes, seemingly waiting for the vampire to deliver the coup de grâce. But Angel was not forthcoming. The deadly stroke came—but it was from behind.

The second demon in line grabbed the first's helmet, pulled his head to the side, and plunged a dagger into his throat before shoving him off the staircase. A thunderous cheer arose from the crowd of demons on the stairs.

"Not very sporting," Angel said to the new lead demon as he placed the toe of his shoe on the center of his breastplate and shoved him back into the mass of bodies.

Several demons shrieked as the falling demon dislodged them from the stairs. More dropped from the bottom of the crumbling stairs. The vibrations traveling up the disintegrating staircase became more pronounced. Angel stumbled. When he recovered, there were twenty-some demons left. Every few seconds another one plummeted from view. The landing below Angel's crumbled and disappeared, taking another three demons with it. The freed torch spun away into darkness like a falling star charting a weird elliptical course.

Halfway down the remaining stairs, a riser buckled and gave way, allowing a demon's foot to break through an otherwise solid step. His leg sank to the knee, and as he frantically tried to free himself, his panicked effort accelerated the rate of decay. The stairs beneath him broke away in one big section, taking ten surprised demons with it, including the demon whose leg was finally unrestrained. A dozen nervous demons remained.

Angel noticed fissures forming beneath his feet, spiderweb lines of decay as the formerly impressive stone construction assumed the structural integrity of a drying sand castle. There were only seconds left. Suddenly white-hot pain blossomed in his side.

A spear hurled in desperation had caught him unaware, impaling the right side of his abdomen. Another exultant cheer arose from the ten remaining demons, who rushed up the stairs in unison.

Angel couldn't afford to hesitate, couldn't allow more than one demon to reach the landing. The barbed spearhead had gone all the way through and would cause worse damage if he tried to pull it out. Instead, Angel dropped his sword, gripped the spear shaft in both hands, and shoved the spear the rest of the way through his body.

He lunged forward to grapple with the first demon to reach the landing, using his momentum to push that one back as far as he could. But he wasn't fast enough. Two more demons stepped onto the fractured landing, which was one demon too many. Stone scraped against stone, and the lip of the landing broke free, taking the steps below with it, along with the last demon to reach the landing and the seven behind him.

Two demons remained on the compromised landing with Angel. He grappled with the first demon, holding dagger and claws at bay, keeping that demon between him and the other one, who was itching to use his sword. The first demon freed his empty hand and slashed his claws against Angel's chest. The torch stand teetered for a moment, then dropped away, momentarily distracting the demon. Angel heaved him back into the restless second demon, bumping him back one step too far and over the edge.

"Just the two of us," Angel said as he caught the last demon's free hand by the wrist.

Beneath them the landing quaked, beginning to crumble.

The demon nodded. "We die together, I think."

Angel head-butted the helmeted demon, which caused more damage to Angel's forehead than to the demon's helmet, but the move succeeded in startling the demon. Following up with a knee to the groin, Angel pushed off the demon, hurling himself onto the stairs above, and lying awkwardly on his back as the rest of the landing dropped out of site. Angel yelled down at the plummeting demon, "You think too much."

He had a second or two to savor the hard-fought victory, but then fissures and cracks spread beneath his sprawled body, releasing tiny, then larger chunks of stone as the stairs continued to crumble. Angel rolled over and climbed to his hands and knees. As he stood, the lowermost step fell away, causing him to lose his balance and fall facedown. The stairway swayed, and the stress threatened to break off large sections of it.

Angel scrambled up several steps on his hands and knees, racing far enough ahead of the disintegration to climb to his feet without fearing the stone beneath him would be gone before he could complete the motion. He scanned the spirals above, visually tracking the turns until they disappeared into the vault of darkness, but saw no sign of Connor and Gunn. His goal had been to buy them some time, but also to slow the rate of decay. Without the weight of the demons, their stairway should decay at the slower rate of its twin. Or so he had supposed. Entropy had other plans, namely an accelerated rate of decay.

Whatever grace period we had to exit this interdimensional plane, Angel realized, *it's running out fast!*

Despite the agonizing pain in his pierced side, Angel took the stairs two at a time, then three at a time, sacrificing balance and safety for speed. Below him, the steps fell away like a row of toppling dominoes. Next, sections of five or ten stairs broke free, dropping silently into darkness. Then the sections became larger, until they stretched from landing to landing.

It seemed eerie that so much destruction should be so nearly soundless. Other than the cracking groans and pops of pieces breaking away, the quiet fall of the spiraling debris was almost hypnotic. Angel wondered if somewhere, miles down, the demons continued to fall and scream in rage and fear. *And what happens to this place when the destruction is complete? Will it vanish as if it had never existed? Or will it reappear in a few thousand years, and be home—and hell—again to countless demons who will resume an eternal fall through endless darkness?*

At some point in his headlong ascent, Angel spotted Connor and Gunn several complete spiral turns above him. While he was gaining on them, entropy was gaining on him. Connor had his arm looped around Gunn's back, and Angel could tell by the pair's reduced speed that Connor was supporting most of Gunn's weight.

After climbing another several hundred feet, Angel caught up to them. Connor, showing strain on his face, said, "Welcome back."

Panting, Gunn simply nodded at Angel.

"You need to go faster," Angel warned them.

"Not possible," Gunn said.

"Straight down is a lot faster."

"Good point."

"Connor, let me help Gunn for a while."

Connor appraised the large bloodstain on Angel's side. "You're wounded."

"Who isn't?" Angel said, downplaying the seriousness of his injury. Yes, it hurt like hell, but it was pain. Not exhaustion. He could help Gunn long enough to give Connor a breather. "You'll know when I'm struggling."

"Fine," Connor said as he released Gunn.

Gunn shook his head. "Compared to this place, goin' up the Statue of Liberty must feel like climbin' a stepladder."

Angel wrapped an arm around Gunn. "We get out of here," he said, "we'll take a trip and find out."

"No thanks," Gunn said.

Angel was tired, but he dipped into his reserves and, together, the three of them climbed faster than Connor and Gunn had as a pair.

Freed of his burden, Connor looked over to the other stairway and had a suggestion. "If we jump down, across the gap, we might be able to land on the other stairway."

"Without a railing to stop our momentum, it would be too risky," Angel said, having thought about and dismissed just such a desperate stunt early in their climb. "Besides, the entropy has speeded up on both sides. The time it would take to stop and make the jump, assuming we were successful, would be no more than the time gained by switching tracks. And that's assuming the force of our landing didn't break the staircase at the point of impact." Angel shook his head. "Risky and pointless."

"Just a thought," Connor said defensively.

"I know," Angel said diplomatically. "One I considered as well."

They continued the arduous climb in silence. At each landing, Angel chanced a look down. For a while, it seemed that they put more distance between themselves and the crumbling entropy effect, increasing the gap to eighty feet. But they continued to tire while the rate of decay accelerated. The gap narrowed to seventy feet, then sixty, then fifty.

Angel stumbled.

"My turn," Connor said, reaching for Gunn's arm.

Gunn shook his head. "'Bout time I sucked it up, don't you think?"

"You're injured," Angel said.

"Who isn't?" Gunn reminded him pointedly. "Besides, I got some grit left in these regular human bones of mine."

Before they could argue with him, Gunn took the lead.

Connor shrugged and followed.

Angel brought up the rear, after a quick glance below. The second-to-last landing below them disintegrated and toppled away. *Less than forty feet,* Angel thought. As he followed the other two up the winding steps, he looked ahead to the spirals above. Several turns ascending into a cloak of darkness, but how many were beyond that? *Too many,* Angel thought grimly. He'd lost count and was afraid to guess. *Don't think we're gonna make it.*

"They're not gonna make it . . . ," Fred said as she stared at the glowing megalith. A gusting wind continued to swirl, forcing Styrofoam cups, newspaper pages, aluminum cans, and plastic bottles to cavort around the stone structure as if they'd been possessed by woodland spirits. Fred leaned against her battle-ax, which was draped in black cloth, with the head resting on the ground and the base of the shaft gripped between her palms. "Are they?"

"We don't know that," Wesley said, trying to sound reassuring. He held the Summoner's flesh-bound journal under his arm. Several times since Angel and Connor had disappeared, Wesley had paged through the arcane book, hoping to find some way to help them, contact them, or bring them back. But if information existed to accomplish any of that, the Summoner hadn't seen fit to record it for posterity.

The fate of Angel and Connor—and Gunn—was in their own hands. If Wesley could have joined them, he would have, without hesitation. If there were some spell or incantation or mystical charm that would have allowed him to cross the dimensional barrier, he would have done so in a heartbeat. *Because this is worse,* he thought. *Left behind to wait and hope, not knowing what's happening, and feeling ever so helpless.* "Definitely worse," he murmured.

"What?" Fred asked, glancing at him.

Avoiding eye contact, Wesley said softly, "Nothing."

Lorne and Cordelia had found them on the sidewalk, which hadn't been difficult, considering the street was practically deserted. The pedestrians were long gone, and Hollywood Boulevard was devoid of vehicular traffic. A few blocks away, additional sawhorses and numerous police cars—with their roof lights flashing a continual visual warning—blocked access to the street. In the distance, the sirens of fire trucks and ambulances sounded intermittent wails. Fortunately, the whooping and shrieking of car alarms had finally ceased.

Smoke from distant gas line fires and other accidents was drawn to the megalith or to the atmospheric disturbance it produced, worsening the nighttime haze. On the ground, fissures radiated from the megalith as the street and sidewalk continued to tremble, buckling in places from extreme stress.

"Something's happening to the megalith!" Fred exclaimed.

All eyes turned to the fifteen-foot stone tower as the smooth, carved surface began to show signs of wear and damage. Cracks formed at the base and raced upward, opening crevices in the sculpted faces. Tiny bits of stone fell from the steep sides of the megalith and bounced on the ground. Then, larger chunks came loose and shattered on the street.

"Those chunks—!" Cordelia said, pointing at some of the falling debris. "They're vanishing!"

Wesley nodded. The loose pieces, separated from the interdimensional portal, could not maintain an independent existence in the human dimension. "Angel and the others," Wesley said uneasily. "They've done something."

"Averted the apocalypse, maybe?" Lorne asked with a shaky attempt at bubbly optimism.

"Too soon to tell," Wesley said, but he sounded almost hopeful.

"Will they make it?" Fred asked Wesley. "Will they all make it back to us?"

Without thinking, Wesley repeated his assessment in the same noncommittal monotone. "Too soon to tell," he said, and wondered if he had failed her after all. Had he offered hope—or dashed it? He cleared his throat and said, "If there's a way back, Angel will find it."

CHAPTER TWENTY-ONE

"I only see two loops above us!" Connor yelled down excitedly.

He had taken the lead, with Gunn in the middle and Angel bringing up the rear. Despite the puncture wound in his side, Angel could have passed Gunn, but that wasn't about to happen. If Gunn's energy flagged, Angel would prop him up and support him the rest of the way. Abandoning Gunn was not an option.

"Always darkest before it goes completely black," Gunn said grimly.

"No," Connor said. "We're near the top."

"Better not be teasin' a man with spaghetti legs."

Connor was right. Angel could see the underside of the main platform seventy feet above them. As Angel stepped off the third-from-last landing, he felt the weight of it break away beneath him. "Hurry," he yelled to the others.

At the next landing, Gunn stumbled, but Angel didn't miss a beat catching his arm and helping him regain his balance. Gunn nodded his thanks. Although soaked with perspiration and trembling with exhaustion, he had a look of renewed determination as he took the remaining steps two at a time. As a vampire, Angel possessed superhuman strength and accelerated healing, which made Gunn's thoroughly human effort that much more impressive.

Angel saw Connor reach the top platform and look down at their progress. The boy shook his head nervously. "The decay's about half a second behind you!"

Doubled over with effort, Gunn raced past the final small landing and stumbled up the last section of stairs, reaching forward with his hands to pull and push himself the rest of the way. Connor leaned down, grabbed one of his hands, and tugged him into the air and onto the platform.

Without Gunn's weight on the stairs, the entropic force might have slowed a millisecond or two, but it had already passed Angel. He saw the cracks forming ahead of him. Each time he planted his foot, he felt the step under him break into hundreds of pieces. In desperation, he jumped up several steps at once, but the weight of his landing caused a fissure to break wide open. Somehow he knew that the rest of the steps would all fall at once. He pushed off one last time, leaping almost ten feet in the air to catch the edge of the platform. He swung by his fingers, glimpsing the last of the stairs tumbling away into unfathomable darkness.

As he pulled himself up onto the platform, Connor offered a hand, and Angel was glad to accept it. Connor grinned. "Not as spry as you used to be, huh?"

"I manage."

"Hate to spoil the reunion, folks," Gunn said. "But this platform ain't exactly terra firma."

The platform was larger than the obelisk landings, but it was succumbing to entropy just as everything else had. Fissures raced along the stone, widened into cracks, and the edges of the platform began to crumble away.

"We got a plan?"

Angel looked at Connor and said, "Slight complication with the plan."

"Don't have time for no complication," Gunn said. "Seriously?"

"Let's try the hands here," Angel said. He and Connor removed the severed Summoner hands from their canvas bags and pressed them to the black wall behind the platform. Nothing happened.

"Wrong key?" Gunn asked.

"Wrong combination," Angel replied as they

returned the severed hands to their bags. He pointed to the opposing platform, which had just lost the rest of its stairs. "Connor and I entered on separate platforms. One of us has to be over there to open the portal."

"That's a twenty-foot jump," Gunn said, alarmed.

"I can make it," Connor said. But Angel realized the extended battles and the climb had taken their toll on his son. Connor was tired and winded, but would never admit weakness—especially in front of his father. And in his present condition, Angel doubted he could make the jump himself.

"If you fall," Angel said carefully, "we all die."

"Suppose you think *you* should make the jump," Connor said.

Angel shook his head. "Not sure I'd make it either."

"No way in hell I make that jump," Gunn said emphatically. "You tellin' me after all we been through we're gonna stand around and wait for the bottom to drop out?"

"No," Angel said, looking at Connor.

Connor flashed an obligatory frown. "Teamwork, right?"

"Something like that," Angel said. "A boost."

"Could work," Connor said with a grudging nod.

"What could work?" Gunn asked.

"I think a running start would be best, son," Angel said.

"Agreed, Dad."

As Connor backed to the far edge of the disintegrating platform, Angel positioned himself on the other side, closest to the opposing platform. Crouching, he interlaced his fingers to form a cradle. Mindful of the crumbling edge of the platform, Gunn stepped out of the way.

"Ready?" Connor called.

"GO!" Angel exclaimed.

Connor sprinted across the platform, then took a small leap that set his left foot in Angel's hands. He leaned forward as Angel heaved himself from a crouch, pulled Connor's weight up with both arms, and hurled him toward the other platform. Connor's speed and momentum, combined with Angel's strength, carried him across the wide gap. He landed hard on the landing, almost flat on his stomach, legs dangling over the brittle edge. The sudden impact accelerated the unnatural decay of the stones, which crumbled and fell away as Connor scrambled to his feet.

"On three!" Angel called to Connor.

He held the Summoner's hand up before the black wall, waiting as Connor fished the other hand out of his bag. "One . . . two—"

"Three!" they shouted simultaneously, and slapped their hands against the dark, solid wall.

At first, nothing happened.

Gunn crowded against Angel as the platform

crumbled and tilted away from them. On impulse, Angel grabbed Gunn's hand and pressed it against the cold flesh of the Summoner's hand as well. Gunn stared at him questioningly. Angel explained, "You might need to be touching this to pass through!"

"Now you tell—!"

They would never be certain if it had been necessary.

The solid wall seemed to vanish, and they toppled through into a deeper darkness and stumbled back into their world.

Angel and Gunn turned around to look at the monolith. At first, Angel was surprised to see it riddled with cracks and crumbling before his eyes, but then he realized it mirrored the decay within. By averting the alignment, they were destroying the monolith, which was nothing more than a representation of the other dimension's encroachment on theirs. The pieces that had broken free vanished almost before they struck the highway. All around L.A., he imagined the secondary monoliths had suffered a similar fate, and the early morning news reports would confirm that guess.

Before their eyes, the entire monolith faded away, and Angel saw Connor standing on what had been the other side, looking back at him with satisfaction and pride. Where the monolith had stood, the highway was undamaged. As abruptly as the monolith had vanished, the rumbling of the tremors ceased, leaving behind an eerie but welcome stillness.

Cordy shouted, "Thank God, you made it!"

"We were so worried!" Fred cried.

Clapping his hands, Lorne exclaimed, "Never doubted you for a microsecond!"

"Good show!" Wesley called, smiling with relief. And with that, everyone rushed forward to welcome and congratulate the three of them.

Lorne surveyed the damage, debris, and assorted litter and said to Cordelia, "This town has seen much better days, princess, but I wouldn't trade this moment, right here, right now, for anything. Crazy, huh?"

Cordelia flashed him her dazzling smile, took his arm as if they were strolling down a red carpet together, and said, "Put me in the loony bin right beside you, Lorne."

Despite his exhaustion and shaky legs, Gunn was thrilled to be back on familiar ground, even if that ground, like him, had taken quite a beating. He'd made it home in one piece, with his humanity intact, and was back among the living—well, mostly living, since Angel was technically undead. He marveled at the familiar world around him and thought it had never looked better, despite the mess. He inhaled air that had never tasted better, in spite of the lingering dust and smoke. Feeling it was a night to rejoice, he smiled broadly and looked around at his surroundings and at his friends, until his gaze settled on Fred. Before his smile could falter under the weight of the uncertainties between them, he saw that she was smiling without reservation, tears of happiness brimming in her eyes. He decided then that her smile was the most wonderful thing he would ever see.

Releasing something wrapped in black cloth, which struck the ground with an ominous clang, Fred rushed into Gunn's arms, hugging him tight. "Thank God you're all right, Charles!" she whispered fiercely. "I never want anything to happen to you."

Though her words were not quite what he had wanted to hear, Gunn felt their warmth, if not as a welcome back into her heart, definitely as an invitation back into her life. Or maybe it was just the recognition that, where it counted most, he had never left.

Could be a new beginning, he thought. *And that's not a bad way to end the day. Not bad at all! Whatever comes tomorrow or the next day, we'll deal with it.*

Wesley hung back a bit, letting the others welcome back Angel, Connor, and Gunn first. He was no less grateful for their return and, obviously, no less pleased with the success of their mission. Angel and Connor had, after all, averted an apocalypse and saved Gunn. The fact remained that Wesley— because of his well-intentioned but ill-advised abduction of the infant Connor—remained a half step out of sync with the group's camaraderie . . . or, one might say, a wee bit out of alignment. Though Angel had forgiven him, Wesley had much to forgive of himself. But he was earning his way back, a step at a time, regaining the trust he had lost.

He approached Angel to congratulate him but paused when he noticed Fred embracing Gunn. Thinking of what might have been or what yet might be was a mental game best reserved for another day. Tonight, he was surprised to find himself smiling at them, genuinely happy for the reunited couple. Then he realized it was no surprise at all. He was happy because Fred was happy. At that moment, nothing else mattered.

Angel crossed the unbroken ground where the monolith had stood between him and Connor. The obstruction was gone but, in its place, was the knowledge of what they had accomplished together by cooperating and respecting each other's ideas and abilities. Unlike the monolith, those memories would endure. Before Angel could speak, he noticed Wesley approaching.

"Congratulations to both of you," Wesley said. "One apocalypse safely averted."

Angel smiled. "Let's hope we get a few days' rest before the next one."

"I'd be interested in hearing all about this one."

"And I'd be happy to tell you about it," Angel said. "Tomorrow."

"Fair enough," Wesley said. He turned to Connor and nodded. "Welcome back, Connor. Good job!"

Connor returned the nod, pleased with the reception but more so the tone of respect with which Wesley addressed him. After clapping Connor and Angel on the shoulder, Wesley joined Gunn and the others.

While they had a quiet moment, Angel looked at Connor and felt anew that surge of father's pride. Angel could never replace the idealized version of Holtz that Connor had clung to after those stolen years together in Quor-Toth. Angel and Connor had lost those years and, with them, so many opportunities. Sometimes the fragility of their relationship disheartened Angel, but he would never give up—on Connor or himself. Some things were too important to abandon, no matter how difficult the struggle.

What mattered was that, today and every day that followed, Angel had the opportunity to be a father, a guiding hand, a person Connor could come to for help or advice. It was ironic that, in destroying the bridge between dimensions, they had begun to rebuild the bridge between themselves, as father and son. And each new day was full of opportunity.

Angel gripped Connor's shoulders. "Great work in there, son," he said. "Couldn't have done it without you."

"Got that right," Connor said with false sarcasm.

"A simple 'thanks' would have sufficed."

Connor smiled. "Thanks, Dad." Then, with a mischievous glint in his eyes, he added, "But you have to admit. You and stone face? The resemblance was kind of spooky."

ABOUT THE AUTHOR

JOHN PASSARELLA is coauthor of the Bram Stoker Award–winning First Novel, *Wither,* of which the *San Francisco Chronicle* said, "hits the groove that makes TV's *Buffy the Vampire Slayer* such a kick." John's other novels include *Wither's Rain,* Buffy the Vampire Slayer: *Ghoul Trouble* (a *Locus* best-seller), and Angel: *Avatar.* Angel: *Monolith* is his fifth novel. John maintains his official author Web site at www. passarella.com, where he encourages readers to send him e-mail at author@passarella.com, and to subscribe to his free author newsletter for the latest information on his books and movie projects. A member of the Authors Guild, the Horror Writers Association, the Science Fiction and Fantasy Writers of America, and the Garden State Horror Writers, John resides in Logan Township, New Jersey, with his wife, three young children, and assorted pets. Look for *Wither's Legacy: A Wendy Ward Novel* in late October 2004.

As many as 1 in 3 Americans
who have HIV...don't know it.

**TAKE CONTROL.
KNOW YOUR STATUS.
GET TESTED.**

To learn more about HIV testing,
or get a free guide to HIV and
other sexually transmitted diseases:

**www.knowhivaids.org
1-866-344-KNOW**

Everyone's got his demons....

ANGEL™

If it takes an eternity, he will make amends.

Original stories based
on the TV show
Created by Joss Whedon
& David Greenwalt

Published by Simon & Schuster

2311-01

BUFFY THE VAMPIRE SLAYER can toss a one-liner more lethal than her right hook—without breaking a sweat. Now fans of BUFFY's wicked wordplay won't want to miss this exhaustive collection of the funniest, most telling, and often poignant quotes from the Emmy-nominated television show.

"'Her abuse of the English language is such that I understand only every other sentence. . . .'" —Wesley Wyndham-Pryce (quoting Giles) on Buffy, "Bad Girls"

CATEGORIZED and complete with a color-photo insert, this notable quote compendium will have you eagerly enhancing your BUFFY-speak.

"If I had the Slayer's power, I'd be punning right about now."
—Buffy Summers, "Helpless"

Buffy the vampire slayer™

THE QUOTABLE SLAYER
THE LAST WORD ON LIFE, LOVE,
AND LINGO IN THE BUFFY-VERSE!

Compiled by Micol Ostow and Steven Brezenoff

AVAILABLE DECEMBER 2003 FROM SIMON PULSE